PRINCE OF TWILIGHT

PRINCE OF TWILIGHT

MAGGIE SHAYNE

THORNDIKE
CHIVERS

This Large Print edition is published by Thorndike Press, Waterville, Maine, USA and by BBC Audiobooks Ltd, Bath, England.

Thorndike Press is an imprint of Thomson Gale, a part of The Thomson Corporation.

Thorndike is a trademark and used herein under license.

The text of this Large Print edition is unabridged.

Other aspects of the book may vary from the original edition.

Set in 16 pt. Plantin.

LIBRARY OF CONGRESS CATALOGING-IN-PUBLICATION DATA

Shayne, Maggie.
   Prince of twilight / by Margaret Shayne. — Large print ed.
     p. cm. — (Thorndike Press large print romance)
   ISBN-13 978-0-7862-9464-0
   ISBN-10: 0-7862-9464-7 (hardcover : alk. paper)
   1. Vampires — Fiction. 2. Large type books. I. Title.
PS3619.H399P75 2007
813'.6—dc22

2006102628

BRITISH LIBRARY CATALOGUING-IN-PUBLICATION DATA AVAILABLE

Published in 2007 in the U.S. by arrangement with Harlequin Books S.A.
Published in 2007 in the U.K. by arrangement with Harlequin Enterprises II B.V.

U.K. Hardcover: 978 1 405 64080 0 (Chivers Large Print)
U.K. Softcover: 978 1 405 64081 7 (Camden Large Print)

Printed in the United States of America on permanent paper
10 9 8 7 6 5 4 3 2 1

PRINCE OF TWILIGHT

PROLOGUE

Fifteenth Century
Romania

"We have to bury her, my son."

Vlad stood in the small stone chapel beside his beloved new bride. Elisabeta's skin was as cold as the stone bier on which she lay. She wore the pale green wedding gown the servants had found for her on the day their hasty vows had been exchanged. The skirt draped on either side of her, swathing the stone slab in beauty. Her hair, pale as spun silver and endlessly long, spread around her head, as if pillowing her in a cloud.

"My son —" This time the old priest's words were accompanied by his hand, clasping Vlad's shoulder.

Vlad whirled on the man. "No! She is not to be put in the ground. Not yet. I won't allow it."

A little fear joined the pity in the old

man's eyes. Not enough, not yet. "I know this is difficult — I do. But she deserves to be laid to rest."

"I said no," Vlad repeated, his tone tired, his heart dead. Then he turned from the priest and focused again where he needed to focus: upon her, upon his bride. Their time together had been too short. One night and then part of a second before he'd been called into battle. It wasn't right.

The priest still hovered.

"Get out, before I draw my blade and send you out in pieces." Vlad's words were barely more than a hoarse whisper, yet filled with enough menace to elicit a clipped gasp from the cleric.

"I'll send in your father. Perhaps he can —"

Vlad turned to send a warning glare over his shoulder. Brief, but powerful enough to reduce most mortals to tears.

"I'm going, my liege." The priest bowed a little as he backed through the chapel doors.

Vlad sighed in relief when the doors closed once again, leaving him alone with his grief. He leaned over Elisabeta's body, lowered his head to her chest, and let his tears soak the gown. "Why, my love? Why did you do this? Was our love not worthy of a single day's grieving? I told you I would come back. Why couldn't you have believed in me?"

A soft creaking sound accompanied by a stiff night breeze and the gentle clearing of an aging throat told him that his respite was over. Vlad forced himself to straighten, to turn and face his father — for truly, the man had become as much a father to him as any had been, since Utnapishtim.

The old king was pale and unsteady. He'd lost a daughter-in-law he'd been close, already, to loving — and for three days he had believed that he had lost his son, as well.

He crossed the small room, his gait uneven and slow, then wrapped his frail arms around Vlad's shoulders and hugged him hard, as hard as his strength would allow. "Alive," he muttered. "By the gods, my son, you're alive after all."

Vlad closed his eyes as he returned his father's embrace. "Alive, Father, but none too glad to be, just now." As he said it, he looked back at his bride.

His father did, as well, releasing his hold on Vlad to move closer to the bier. "I cannot tell you how it grieves me to see you in such pain, much less to witness the loss of such a precious young woman as Elisabeta."

"I know."

"Your friend, the foreign woman — she

told you what transpired?"

Vlad nodded. "Rhiannon is . . . an old friend. And a dear one. She said she arrived here for a visit just after I was called to defend our borders."

"So she did. We put her up. Fussy one, she is, and I don't believe she thought highly of your chosen bride. Were the two of you . . . ?"

"As close as any two people can be," Vlad told him. "But we had no claims on each other. She would not have been jealous."

"She called the princess a — now what was the word she used . . . ? Ah yes, a *whiner,*" the king said softly. "To her face, no less."

Vlad nodded, not doubting it.

"When word came that you'd been killed on the field of battle, poor Elisabeta took to the tower room and bolted the door. I had men trying to break it down right up until —"

"I know, Father. I know you did all you could."

The king lowered his head, perhaps to hide the rush of tears into his clouded blue eyes. "Tell me what I can do to ease your grief."

Vlad thought about that, thought about it hard. Rhiannon was no ordinary woman but a former priestess of Isis and daughter of Pharoah. She was skilled in the occult arts, and she had told Vlad that he would find Elisabeta again — she had foreseen it — in five hundred years' time, if he could live that long. What she hadn't promised was that Beta would be the same woman he had loved and lost, or that she would remember him and love him again.

"There is something I can do for you," the king said softly. "I can see it in your eyes. Speak it, my son, and it shall be done, whatever it is."

Vlad met his father's eyes and felt love for the man. True love, though the king was not his true father. "I cannot let them bury her. Not yet. I need you to send our finest riders upon our fastest mounts, Father. Send them out into the countryside to gather the most skilled sorcerers, diviners, wizards and witches in the land. I don't care what it takes. I must have them here before my beloved is put into the cold ground."

The king looked worriedly into his eyes. "My son, you must know that even the most skilled magician won't be able to bring her back. Buried or not, she resides among the dead now."

He nodded once, closed his eyes against that probing, caring stare. "I know that,

11

Father. I only need to be sure she's at peace."

"But the priest —"

"His prayers are not enough. I want to be sure. Please, Father, you said you would do anything to ease my pain. This shall ease it, if anything can."

The king nodded firmly. "Then it shall be done."

"And Father — until they come, keep everyone from here. And even then, let them in only by night."

The old man was used to Vlad's nocturnal nature by now. He nodded, and Vlad knew the promise would be kept.

The king left, and Vlad drew his blood-stained sword, then stood between the bier and the chapel door. When the sun rose, he barred the door, drew a tapestry from the wall and wrapped himself in it. When the sun set again, he was forced to lay the fabric over Elisabeta's body or witness it begin to change with the ravages of death. And before the third night was through, the scent of death and decay hung heavy on the air.

But finally, at midnight of the third night, the chapel doors opened again, and several men entered. No women were among them. They entered in a rush of wind, dressed in dull white traveling robes of wool, for the most part, though one wore a finer fabric in rich, russet tones, its edges embroidered with a pattern of twisting green vines.

They all dropped to one knee, bowing low before him. The one in the brown said, "My prince, we came as rapidly as we could manage. Our hearts are heavy with grief at the loss of the princess."

"Yes," he said. "Rise. I need your help."

The men looked at one another nervously. There were five, he saw now. Locals, mostly, though one appeared to be from the East, and another was Moorish in appearance.

"We are honored if we can be of service," the apparent spokesman said. "But I know not what we can do. Against death, even we are powerless."

He nodded and thought of Gilgamesh, the legendary king of Sumer. His own desperate search for the key of life had resulted in the creation of an entire race — the Undead. Vampires. Like Vlad, and Rhiannon, and so many others. But it had never resulted in the great king's dear friend Enkidu returning from death.

Maybe, Vlad thought, his own quest was just as mad. But he had to try.

"I do not ask you to conquer death. Only to ensure that when I find her again, I will know her — and that she will know me. And remember. And love me again."

The magicians and sorcerers frowned, seeking understanding in each other's faces.

"A powerful seer has told me that the princess will return to me in another lifetime. But it will be in the distant future."

"But, my liege, you would be aged and she but an infant."

"That's not your concern, sorcerer. I want only to ensure that when she does return — and reaches a decent age — she will remember all that came before, that she will be the woman she was in this lifetime. Can you or can you not fulfill this request?"

One man began to whisper to another, and Vlad caught the words "unnatural" and "immoral," but the man in brown held up a hand to silence them. Then he approached Vlad slowly, cautiously, and at last he nodded. "We can and we shall, my liege. Go, get sustenance, rest. She'll be safe in our care, I promise you."

Vlad gazed at the shape beneath the tapestry. No longer his Elisabeta, but a shell that had formerly held her essence. He looked at the men again. "Do not fear to try. It is a lot I ask of you. I give my word, I will not exact punishment should you fail, so long as you do the very best you can. On her memory, I vow it to you."

The men bowed deeply, and he glimpsed relief on their faces. Truly, Vlad was not known for his mercy or understanding. He left them to their work. But he didn't rest, and he didn't feed. He couldn't — not until he knew.

It was four a.m. when a servant boy came to fetch him back to the chapel, and as he hurried there, he saw that the door was open and the priest was coming out, wafting a censer before him. Behind him, men came bearing the corpse, buried in flowers, upon a litter.

And behind *them* came the wizards and sorcerers, who met Vlad's eyes and nodded to tell him that they had been successful. The man in russet came to him, while the others kept the slow pace behind the funeral procession. The priest's servant rang a bell, and the gruff-voiced cleric intoned his prayers loudly, so that others from the castle and the village joined in as they passed, many carrying candles or lamps. No one in the village had slept this night, awaiting the princess's burial, and so the procession grew larger and longer as it wound onward, a writhing serpent dotted with lights.

"My prince," said the man in brown. "We have done it. Take this."

He handed Vlad a scroll, rolled tightly and

held by a ruby ring — the ring he'd given to Elisabeta. It had been on her finger. Seeing it caused pain to stab deeply, and he sucked in a breath.

"I don't understand," he said. "You removed her wedding ring. Why?"

"We performed a powerful ritual, commanding a part of her essence to remain earthbound. The ring is the key that holds her and will one day release her. When a future incarnation of Elisabeta returns to you, all you will need to do is put this ring upon her finger and perform the rite contained on this scroll, and she will be restored to the very Elisabeta she was before. She will remember everything. And she will love you again."

"Are you sure?" Vlad asked, afraid to believe, to hope.

"On my life, my prince, I swear to you it is true. There is only one caveat. And this could not be helped, for we risk our very souls by tampering with matters of life and death and the afterlife. The gods must be allowed their say."

"The gods. It was they who saw fit to take her from me this way. To hell with the gods."

"My prince!" The sorcerer looked around as if fearing Vlad's blasphemy might have been overheard by the deities themselves.

16

"Tell me of this caveat, then," Vlad snapped. "But be quick. I must attend to my wife's burial."

The man boldly took hold of Vlad's arm and began walking beside him, catching them up to the procession, while keeping enough distance for privacy. "If the rite has not been performed by the time the Red Star of Destiny eclipses Venus, then the gods have not willed it, and the magick will expire."

"And what will happen to Elisabeta then?"

"Her soul will be set free. All parts of her soul, the part we've held earthbound, and any other parts that may have been reborn into the physical realm. All will be free."

"And by free, you mean . . . dead," Vlad whispered. He gripped the man by the front of his russet robes and lifted him off his feet. "You've done nothing!"

"Death is but an illusion, my liege! Life is endless. And you'll have time — vast amounts of time — in which to find her again, I swear."

He narrowed his eyes on the sorcerer, tempted to draw his blade and slide it between the man's ribs. But instead, he lowered him to the ground again. "How much time? When, exactly, does this red star of yours next eclipse Venus?"

"Not for slightly more than five hundred and twenty years, my liege, as nearly as I can calculate."

Vlad swallowed his pain and his raging grief. Rhiannon had predicted he would find his Elisabeta again in five hundred years. His chief concern at the time had been wondering how the hell he could manage to survive so long without her; how he could bear the pain.

Now he had an added worry. When he did find her, would it be in time to enact the spell, perform the rite, and restore her memory and her soul?

By the gods, it had to be. He was determined. He must not fail.

He *would not.*

He was no ordinary man, nor even an ordinary vampire, after all.

He was Dracula.

1

Present day

"Melina Roscova," the slender blond woman said, extending a hand. "You must be Maxine Stuart?"

"It's Maxine Malone, and no, I'm not her." Stormy took the woman's hand. It was cool and her grip very strong. "Stormy Jones," she said. "Max and Lou are busy with another case, and we didn't think it would take all three of us to conduct the initial interview."

"I see." Melina released her grip and dug in her pocket for a business card. "I guess this must be out of date."

Stormy took the card, looked it over. The SIS logo superimposed itself over the words Supernatural Investigations Services. In smaller letters were their names, Maxine Stuart, Lou Malone, Tempest Jones and beneath that, in a fancy script, Experienced, professional, discreet and a toll-free number.

She handed the card back. "Yeah, that's pretty old. Maxie and Lou got hitched sixteen years ago now. Of course, we didn't get new cards made up until we'd used all the old ones. You have to be practical, you know."

"Naturally."

"So why all the mystery?" Stormy asked. "And why did you want to meet here?"

As she spoke, they moved through the entrance and into the vaulted corridors of the Canadian National Museum. Their steps echoed as they walked. Melina paid the entry fee in cash, and led the way deeper into the building.

"No mystery. I want you to handle a sensitive case for me. Discretion —" she tapped the old business card against her knuckle "— is imperative."

"You can trust us on that," Stormy said. "We wouldn't still be in business after all this time if we didn't know how to keep our mouths shut." She looked at a threadbare tapestry on display inside a glass case. Its colors had faded to gray, and it looked as if a stiff breeze would reduce it to a pile of lint. "So why this place?"

"This is where it is," Melina said, eyeing several tarnished silver pieces in another case. Bowls, urns, pendants.

"Where what is?"

"What you need to see. But it won't be here for long. It's part of a traveling exhibit. Artifacts uncovered on a recent archaeological dig in the northern part of Turkey."

Stormy eyed her, waiting for her to say more, but Melina fell silent and moved farther along the hall, among line drawings and diagrams of dig sites, framed like pieces of art. Then she turned to go through two open doors into a large room. There were items lining the walls, all of them safely behind glass barriers. Brass trinkets, steel blades with elaborately carved handles of bone and ivory. Stormy glanced at the items on display, then rubbed her arms, suddenly cold to the bone. "You'd think they'd turn on the heat in here. It's freezing," she muttered. Then, to distract herself from the rush of discomfort, she snatched up a flyer from a stack in a nearby rack and read from it. According to it, the items found didn't match the culture of the area in which they'd been located, and many were thought to be the spoils of war, brought home by soldiers who looted them from faraway lands and conquered enemies. The dig site was believed to have been a monastery of sorts — a place where men went to study magic and the occult.

"Here it is," Melina said.

Stormy dragged her gaze from the flyer to where the other woman stood a few yards away, in front of a small glass cube that sat atop a pedestal. Inside the cube, resting on a clear acrylic base, was a ring. It was big, its wide band more elaborately engraved than the gaudiest high school class ring she'd ever seen. Its gleaming red stone was as big as one of those, too, only she was pretty sure this stone was real.

"It's a ruby," Melina said, confirming Stormy's unspoken suspicion. "It's priceless. Isn't it incredible?"

Stormy didn't reply. She couldn't take her eyes off the ring. For a moment it was as if she were seeing it through a long, dark tunnel. Everything around her went black, her vision riveted to the ring, her eyes unable to see anything else. And then she heard a voice.

"Inelul else al meu!"

The voice — it came from her own throat. Her lips were moving, but she wasn't moving them. The sensation was as if she had become a puppet, or a dummy in some ventriloquist act. Her body was moving all on its own, her hands reaching for the glass case, palms pressing to either side of it, lifting it from its base.

A hand closed hard on her arm and jerked her away. "Ms. Jones, what the hell are you doing?"

Stormy blinked rapidly as her body snapped back on line. She saw Melina holding her upper arm while looking around the room as if waiting for the Canadian version of a SWAT team to swarm in.

Stormy cleared her throat. "Did I set off any alarms?"

"I don't think so," Melina said. "There are sensors on the pedestal. They kick in only if the ring is removed."

Frowning as her head cleared, Stormy stared at her. "Why do you know that?"

"It's my job to know. Are you all right?"

Nodding, Stormy avoided the other woman's eyes. "Yeah. Fine. I . . . zoned out for a minute, that's all."

But it wasn't all. And she wasn't fine. Far from it. She hadn't had an episode like that in sixteen years, but she knew the sensations that had swamped her just now. Knew them well. She would never forget. Never. She hadn't felt that way in sixteen years, not since the last time she'd been with him. With Dracula. The one and only. And though her memory of the specifics of that time with him was a dark void, her memories of . . . being possessed remained. And memories of Dracula or not, she'd heard his voice just a moment ago, whispering close to her.

Without the ring and the scroll, I'm afraid there is no hope.

What did it mean? Was he here? Nearby? And why, when she remembered so little about their time together, had that phrase come floating in to her memory now?

No. He wouldn't come back to her when he knew what it did to her mind and body. He'd let her go in order to spare her going through that madness anymore. Or so she liked to believe. She'd awakened in Rhiannon's private jet, on her way back home. And, like all of Vlad's victims before her, her memory of her time with him had been erased.

But not her feelings for him. Inexplicable or not, she had felt a deep sense of loss, and she'd been dying inside a little more with every single day that had passed since.

He wasn't here. He wouldn't put her through that again. Unless . . .

She looked again at the ring. God, could this be the ring he'd been talking about? And what had he meant by that cryptic phrase? It was hell not remembering. Sheer hell. She should hate him for playing with her mind the way he had. Over and over

24

she'd struggled and fought to recall the time she'd spent with him, after he'd abducted her in the dead of night so long ago. She'd even tried hypnosis, but it hadn't worked. Nothing had. He'd robbed her of memories she sensed might be some of the best of her life. Damn him for that.

"Ms. Jones? Stormy?"

Turning slowly, she met Melina's far too curious brown eyes. "The ring is the reason you want to hire us?"

"Yes. What's your connection to it?"

Stormy frowned. "I don't know what you mean. I have no connection to it."

"You certainly had a strong reaction to it."

She shook her head. "I had a head injury a long time ago. Occasional blackouts are a side effect."

"Speaking in tongues is a side effect, as well?"

"It's gibberish. It doesn't mean anything. Look, the condition of my skull is really not the issue here. Are you going to tell me what this job entails or not?"

Melina looked at her, pursed her lips and lowered her voice. "I want you to steal it," she whispered.

Stormy wasn't sure what she had said as

she had made a hasty exit from the museum. She thought she had told Melina Roscova to do something anatomically impossible, and then she'd left. She hadn't stopped until she'd pulled up in front of the Royal Arms Hotel, where she handed her car keys and a ten-spot to a valet.

"Be careful with her," she told him. "She's special."

He promised he would be, and she watched him as he drove her shiny black Nissan, with the customized plates that read Bella-Donna into the parking garage across the street. As he moved into the darkness, she heard tires squeal and winced. "One scratch, pal. You bring Belladonna back with one scratch . . ."

"Madam?"

She turned to see a doorman with a question in his eyes. "You're going inside?" he asked.

"You tell that moron when he gets back that if he scratched my car, I'll take it out of his hide. And it's *mademoiselle*. Not every thirtysomething female is married, you know."

"Of course, *mademoiselle*." He opened the door, his face betraying no hint of emotion. It would have been much more satisfying if he'd been defensive or hostile or even apologetic. But . . . nothing.

She headed straight for her room and started a bath running, intending to phone Max and fill her in from the tub. She was upset. She was shaken. She was damned scared of what the sight of that ring had done to her.

She'd spoken in Romanian. And she knew exactly what she'd said, even though she didn't speak a word of the language and never had.

The ring belongs to me.

Elisabeta. It had to have been *her* voice.

Sixteen years ago, she'd begun having these symptoms. Blacking out, speaking in a strange language, becoming violent, attacking even her best friends and, usually, remembering nothing. It was as if she were possessed by an alien soul, as if her body were a marionette with some stranger pulling the strings.

Max said her eyes changed color, turned from their normal baby blue to a dark, fathomless ebony, during those episodes.

Through hypnosis, she'd learned the intruder's name. Elisabeta. And she knew, in her gut, that the woman had some connection to Vlad. An intimate one.

Vlad had been under attack, had taken her hostage to aid in his escape. Even then, she'd been drawn to him. His muscled, powerful body. His long, raven's wing hair. His eyes — the intensity in them when he looked at her. She remembered kissing him as if there were no tomorrow. Or maybe that had never happened; maybe that was fantasy. A delicious erotic fantasy that left her with a deep ache in her loins and her soul. She remembered hoping he could help her solve the mystery of who Elisabeta was and why she was haunting Stormy. Trying to take over. And maybe he had. But though, upon her return, Max had told her that she had been Vlad's captive for than a week, Stormy remembered nothing.

She only knew that since her return, she'd felt almost no sign of that intruding soul's presence. And she'd determined that it was Vlad's nearness that stirred the *other* to life. As it would stir any woman.

She was still there, though. Stormy had never doubted it. Hoped she was wrong, but never truly doubted. Elisabeta, whoever she was, still lurked inside her, waiting . . . for something.

Stormy stopped pacing and held her head in her hands as she stared into the mirror that was mounted on one of the lush hotel room's antique replica dressers. "Dammit to hell, I hoped you were gone," she whispered. "I honest to goodness was beginning to let myself believe you were never coming back. Not a peep out of you in sixteen years. And now you're back? Why? Will I ever be rid of you, Elisabeta?"

A tapping on her door startled her and brought her head around, and she swore under her breath. She had things to work through, and there was a nice hot bath — and maybe a few tiny bottles from the mini-bar — in her immediate future.

"Please, Ms. Jones," Melina Roscova called from the hallway. "Just give me ten minutes to explain. Ten minutes. It's all I need."

Stormy sighed, rolled her eyes and stomped into the bathroom to turn off the faucets. She pulled the plug on the steamy water with a sigh of regret, then went to yank the door open. She didn't wait for Melina to come inside, just turned and paced to the small table at the room's far end, yanked out a chair and nodded toward it.

"We are *investigators*," she told her unwelcome guest, her tone clipped as she bent to the mini-bar and yanked out a can of ginger ale and a tiny bottle of Black Velvet. She popped the tops on both and poured them into a tall glass that sat beside an empty ice bucket. "Not thieves for hire. We don't break the law, Ms. Roscova. Not for any price."

"Call me Melina," the woman said as she sat down. "And all I want you to do is listen to what I have to say. That ring . . . it has powers."

"Powers." Stormy said it deadpan, dryly, without a hint of inflection. Then she took a big slug of the BV-and-ginger.

"Yes. Powers that could, in the wrong hands, upset the supernatural order — perhaps irrevocably."

"The *super*natural order?"

"Yes. Look, this is very simple. Just . . . just let me make my pitch, promise me it will remain confidential, and then, if you still refuse, I won't bother you again."

Stormy downed half the drink and sat down. "And my word that this will remain confidential is going to be enough for you?"

"Yes."

"Why?"

Melina blinked, and it seemed to Stormy she chose to answer honestly and directly. "Because my organization has been observing yours for years. We know you never break your word. And we know you've kept far bigger secrets than ours."

Another big sip. The glass was getting low,

and she was going to need a refill. Seven Canadian bucks a pop for the BV. And worth it, right about now. "Your . . . organization?"

"The Sisterhood of Athena has existed for centuries," Melina said. She spoke slowly, carefully, and seemed to be giving each sentence a great deal of thought before uttering it. "We are a group of women devoted to observing and preserving the supernatural order." She licked her lips. "Actually, it's the natural order, but our focus is the part of it that most people refer to as supernatural. Things are supposed to be the way they are supposed to be. Humans tend to want to interfere. We don't, unless it's to prevent that interference."

Stormy lifted her brows. "Humans, huh?" She eyed the woman. "You say that as if there are non-humans running around, as well."

"We both know there are."

They both fell silent, staring at each other as Stormy tried to size Melina up. Could she truly know about the existence of the Undead?

Finally, Stormy cleared her throat. "This is sounding awfully familiar, Melina. And not in a good way. You ever hear of a little government agency known as DPI?"

"We're nothing like the Division of Paranormal Investigations, Stormy. I promise you that. And we're privately funded, not a government agency." She licked her lips. "We protect the supernatural world. We don't seek to destroy it or experiment on it the way the DPI did. We are guardians of the unknown."

Stormy nodded. "And why do you want the ring?"

"Strictly to keep it from falling into the wrong hands and being used for evil."

"And I'm supposed to take your word for this? And then, based on nothing more than that, break into a museum and steal a priceless piece of jewelry?"

"Yes." Melina lowered her head. "I'm sorry I can't tell you more, but the more people who know of this ring's powers, the more dangerous it becomes."

Stormy sighed. "I'm sorry. Look, I just can't do this. And even if I wanted to, Max and Lou would never go along with it."

Melina nodded sadly. "All right. I guess . . . we'll just have to find another way."

"You do that. Good night, then, Melina. And . . . good luck. I guess."

"Good night, Stormy." She got up and saw herself out of the hotel room. Stormy followed just long enough to lock the door.

Then she restarted the bath and refilled her glass.

Vlad reread the piece in the *Easton Press* four times before he could believe it wasn't only a figment of his imagination. It was a tiny piece, a two-inch column tossed in to fill space, about a new exhibit of artifacts found in Turkey, currently on display at a museum in Canada. *The most exceptional of the artifacts is a large ruby ring with rearing stallions engraved on either side of the flawless, 20 karat gemstone.*

That was the line that had caught his attention. The one he kept reading, over and over again, until his eyes watered.

"It can't be. . . ." he whispered.

But it could. Surely it could. There was no reason to doubt that this might be the ring he'd placed on his bride's finger centuries ago. And yet, he didn't *want to* believe it. Belief led to hope, and hope led to grief and loss. He wasn't certain he could stand any more of those.

He didn't suppose he'd done a very good job of avoiding them, all these years, though. He'd tried, but dammit, he couldn't let her go. It wasn't in him. She had a hold on him as powerful as any thrall he'd ever cast over a mortal.

Vampires didn't dream; their sleep was like death.

But Dracula dreamed. Of *her.* Tempest . . . or Elisabeta or . . . hell, the two were so entwined and confused in his mind, he didn't know how to distinguish his feelings for one from his feelings for the other. He didn't know how to distinguish them.

He'd purchased a tiny peninsula on the coast of Maine, used his powers to disguise the place. A passer-by would see only mist and fog and forest. Not a towering mansion built to his specifications. It was twenty miles from Easton, where Tempest, who insisted on calling herself "Stormy," lived with her friends, Maxine and Lou, in a mansion of their own.

He'd kept track of her, all these years. He'd watched her, but from a distance. Never getting too close. Never touching her or letting his presence be known. But he knew. He knew everything she did. He knew about the vampires who shared the mansion with the mortals and helped them in their investigations — Morgan de Silva and Dante, who'd been sired by Sarafina, who'd been sired by Bartrone. The vampiress Morgan was the mortal Maxine's twin sister, and though the two hadn't been raised together, they were close now.

He knew about Tempest's family — her parents, retired now and living in a condominium in Florida. She visited twice a year, no matter what. He knew about her relationships with men — though it killed him to know. She saw men sometimes. Dated. And every time it filled him with a rage that he found nearly impossible to contain.

He was dangerous at those times. And when the anger got beyond his endurance, he would force himself to go away for a time. It was the only way to prevent himself from murdering every bastard who laid his hands on her, and possibly her with them.

Nothing ever came of any of her liaisons. He never sensed her falling in love, feeling the kinds of things he liked to think she had felt with him.

He knew *everything* about her. Everything she did, everything she loved. And he knew her time was short. The deadline was approaching rapidly, the one those magicians had included in their spells. It had been driving him to desperation as it drew ever nearer. The so called Red Star of Destiny was due to eclipse Venus in a mere five days. And when it did, Elisabeta would cross to the other side, along with Tempest. He would lose them both. God, he couldn't bear the thought!

Although, in every practical way, he'd lost them both already. Unless . . .

Tempest wasn't in residence at the mansion now. She and her partners had taken off on one of their cases, and since he didn't sense any danger to them, he'd remained behind. And now he was glad he had.

He stood, brooding, at the arched windows of his parlor. The fireplace at his back was cold and dark. He didn't need it, didn't need warmth, sought no comfort, because there was nothing, really, that could grant it to him. Outside, a storm raged, the ocean dancing at its commanding touch, shuddering with the furious breaths of the angry wind. Lightning flashed, and the wind howled. He loved nights like this.

Vlad looked again at the newspaper, noting the location of the exhibit. The Canadian National Museum in Edmunston. Less than 200 miles away.

He could be there in four hours by car. Less, if he drove quickly.

But he was Dracula, and had far more efficient ways to travel. He pulled on his coat. It was long and leather, with a caped back, and in keeping with his mood, it was black.

He reached to the windows' center clasp, turned it and pushed the panes outward. Then he whirled, faster and faster. Like a cyclone he spun, as he focused his mind and altered the shape of his body.

When he soared into the night, into the storm, it was in the form of a giant black raven. He would find out soon enough whether the ring on display in Canada was his ring.

Her ring.

Stormy didn't know what the hell to do. She did know one thing. She was going to have to get her hands on that ring — because if it was *the* ring, she couldn't risk anyone else possessing it. Including Melina and her precious organization. She didn't know anything about this Sisterhood of Athena, and she didn't even consider trusting them. And not Vlad. God, not him.

That ring had some kind of power over her. That ring had brought Elisabeta to the surface, allowed her to take over again. And that ring, she was more certain than ever, must have been the one he had referred to in the tiny bit of memory that had resurfaced in her mind.

If he learned the ring was here, he would come for it. Nothing would stop him, if that was his goal. And God only knew what he would do with it once he had it. Use it, perhaps, to bring his precious Elisabeta back to screaming, bitching life inside her? She couldn't go back to that. Not again. She needed to be rid of the intruder, once and for all.

She needed to destroy the ring. Maybe that would do it. If the damn ring didn't exist, then its power, whatever that power was, couldn't exist, either. So that was the answer. She had to destroy it, melt it down and smash its gemstone to dust.

But first she needed a plan. She decided not to call Max and Lou on this matter. Not just yet. First, because they were involved with another case, one that had taken them out of the country, and second, because Max was far too protective of her. And this wasn't her problem. Stormy needed to deal with this on her own, without feeling the need to justify or explain or defend her decisions to her best friend.

So she filled her glass for the third time, and she soaked in the tub, and she thought and thought about how she might go about getting the ring from the museum, not for Melina, but for herself, and how she could do it without getting caught.

She fell asleep in the tub, her empty glass on the floor beside it, her mind reeling with scenes from the classic old movie *It Takes a Thief* and trying to ignore the other images that plagued her. Images of Vlad.

And then — in her dreams — it came. A memory.

Vlad had sent her to bed in the tiny cabin of the sailboat he'd used to make his escape after abducting her. He'd told her that they would reach his place on the Barrier Islands soon.

They must be there by now, she thought as she woke, and she wondered if she might be in his home already, because she didn't feel the gentle rocking and swaying of the sea beneath her. But it was pitch dark in this bedroom — too dark to tell where she was.

She rolled to one side, began to reach out in search of a lamp or something, but her hand hit a solid wall. Odd. They must not be in the boat anymore, because that wall was farther away from the bed than this. She ran her palm along the smooth wall and frowned. It was lined in fabric. Something as smooth as satin.

Blinking and puzzled, she moved her hand downward, then upward, only to find another smooth, satin-lined wall behind her head.

Something clutched in her belly, and she rolled quickly to the other side, thrusting both hands out, only to hit another wall. She was closed in tight on three sides, and a terrifying suspicion was taking root in her mind. Her breath coming faster now, her heart pounding, she pressed her palms upward. They moved only inches before hitting a satin lined ceiling.

I'm in a coffin! she screamed inwardly. *I'm trapped in a tiny box and God only knows what else! I'll suffocate!*

Panic twisted through her body like a python on crack, and she clenched her hands into fists and pounded on the ceiling, bent her legs as far as the space would allow and kicked at the bottom and sides. She shouted at the top of her lungs. "Let me out. Open this Goddamn box right now and get me the hell out!"

To her surprise, her pounding resulted in the ceiling above her rising with every strike, and she realized belatedly that, while she might be in a box, she wasn't locked in.

The lid gave when she pushed it, and she'd barely had time to process that fact when it opened all the way, as if on its own.

She could see at last, and what she saw was the man himself standing there, staring down at her. He looked harried, tired. His white shirt's top three buttons were undone, and his hair was loose and long.

Then he was reaching for her.

She slapped his hands away and, gripping the sides of the box, pulled herself up into a sitting position, swung her legs over the side, narrowly missing him on the way, and jumped to the floor. She gave a full body shudder, then snapped her arms around her own body, tucked her chin and closed her eyes.

He touched her shoulders. Her body reacted with heat and hunger, but she fought to ignore those things. "I'm sorry, Tempest. I fully intended to have you out of there by the time you woke, but I —"

She punched him. Hard. Straight to the solar plexus. It gave her a rush of satisfaction to hear his grunt, and when she opened her eyes and saw him stagger backward a few paces, it felt even better.

"Bastard."

"Tempest, if you'd let me explain —"

"How dare you? How dare you stick me in some fucking box like that? And why, for God's sake? What the hell were you thinking?" She drew back a fist and advanced on him, fully intending to deck him again, right between the eyes this time.

He had her by the forearms before she could swing, so she kicked him in the shin. He yelped but didn't release her.

"You know, that's what I like best about you freakin' vamps. You feel pain so much more than humans do."

"Enough!"

He shouted it, using the full power of his

voice — or she guessed it was full power, but maybe not, maybe he had a lot more he wasn't tapping into just yet. But either way, the sound was deep and as potent as if her head were inside a giant bell. It rang in her ears, split her head and temporarily deafened her.

She pressed her hands to her ears and closed her eyes until the reverberations stopped bouncing around her brain. Then, slowly, she lowered her hands, opened her eyes, lifted her head. He was still standing there in front of her, staring hard, anger glinting in his jet black eyes.

"I've told you, I'm sorry about the coffin. It was the only way."

She narrowed her eyes on him, about to cut lose with another stream of insults, accusations and possibly profanity, but then she caught a glimpse of the space beyond him, and she was shocked into silence.

Stone walls climbed to towering vaulted ceilings. Inverted domes housed crystal chandeliers. Sconces in the walls looked as if they could hold actual torches. The windows were huge, arched at the top, with thick glass panes so old the night beyond them appeared distorted. Sheet-draped shapes were the only furniture in the place. And a wide curving staircase wound upward and out of sight.

"This is . . . your place?" She swallowed hard as she took in the dust and cobwebs; then, turning slowly, she started a little at the sight of the two coffins lying side by side, both of them open. "Doesn't look as if anyone's used it in a while."

"It's been a long time since anyone has lived here, yes."

Blinking, she went to the nearest window, passing a double fireplace that took up most of one wall on the way. Wiping the dust from the glass with her palm, she stared outside.

The impression was of sheer height and rugged, barren rock. The moon hung low in the sky, nearly full and milky white. It spilled its light over cliffs, harsh outcroppings of rock and boulders jutting upward from far, far below. Beyond the cliffs, she could see grassy hills and valleys. But around this place, there was none of that. It was dark. It was bereft. Even the few pathetic trees that clung for their lives to the steep cliff-sides were scrawny and dead looking.

Stormy swallowed the dryness in her throat — she could barely do it. She was dehydrated, thirsty, starving and a little bit scared. This didn't look like any island off North Carolina.

"Where the hell are we, Vlad?"

2

Vlad kept his distance from the others who were visiting the museum. Mortals. Tourists. Groups of children being led about by young tour guides. He slipped into the Anatolian exhibit, which was housed in a room all its own, and stared at the ring in its glass case. Memories came flooding into his mind, into his soul, but he drove them back. It wasn't easy. He recalled taking the precious gem from his little finger and slipping it onto Elisabeta's forefinger, the only one it came close to fitting. He remembered how, within an hour, she'd wound it around with twine, to make it fit more snugly, and how seeing it on her made him feel proud and protective. It was large and strong and powerful on her small, delicate hand. It seemed to denote his claim to her. It seemed to mark her as his own.

"Sir? Excuse me, sir?" a woman asked.

Vlad blinked the memories away and

turned to face the uniformed woman who had approached him. He hadn't even been aware of her presence, much less of how much time had passed while he'd stood there staring at the ring.

"The museum is closing sir. You'll have to leave now."

"Ahh. Yes, of course."

She left him alone, and he turned again to the ring. It was the one. He'd found it at last. And yes, he would leave the museum — for now. But no power on earth would keep that ring from him.

He closed his eyes, turned and left the museum, but as soon as he stepped out into the fresh air of the night, he sensed something else, something he had not expected.

"Tempest," he whispered. And he turned slowly, scenting the air, feeling for her energy, certain she was close.

And she was. He began to move, barely looking, drawn by the feel of her. Like following the trail left by a comet's tail, he homed in on her warmth, her light, the sparkling energy that was hers alone.

He wouldn't get too close. He couldn't, not without running the risk of her knowing. In all these years, all this time, he hadn't come close to her, despite the temptation he could barely resist. And as long as he'd kept his distance, Elisabeta had slept. She'd been dormant, deep inside Tempest. Somewhere. He knew she hadn't left this plane. She hadn't died or moved on. She was still there. He felt her there. But she hadn't stirred.

As long as he stayed away from Tempest, he thought, she wouldn't. It was easier on Beta that way, or he hoped it was. Let her rest and bide her time. But time — God, time was running out for both of them. And now that he'd found the ring, he almost didn't dare to hope there could be a chance. Yet he couldn't help but hope.

So he followed her trail as her presence hummed in his blood, stroked his senses like a bow over the strings of a violin, until his longing for her vibrated into a pure, demanding tone. It was more powerful now, he realized as he drew closer, than it had been before. Even harder to resist, perhaps because he was allowing himself to move closer to her than he had in sixteen years. It drew him, drove him, until he stood on the sidewalk beside a hotel, staring up at the room where every sense told him she was.

God, it was all he could do not to climb the wall and go to her.

Always before, he'd been prepared to resist his own urges. Always before, he'd had time to steel himself before getting within range of her energy. But this had been entirely unexpected. He hadn't come here for this, for her. He'd come for the ring. His plans beyond that were uncertain. Without the scroll, the ring was useless.

Why was Tempest here? Had she come for the ring, as well? Why? How could she know?

He couldn't let her obtain it, if that was her goal. For her to possess it would be far too dangerous.

As he stood there, staring up at the room, Tempest stepped out onto the balcony, leaned on the railing and gazed out into the night.

He couldn't take his eyes from her. And his preternatural vision didn't fail him. He managed to drink in every detail of her face in a way he hadn't been close enough to do in far, far too long.

The blush of youth had faded from the body of the woman in which his love lay sleeping. In its place were the angles of a female in the prime of her life. Her face was thinner, her eyes harder, than they had been before. Her hair was still blond but not as pale; still short but less severe. Its softness framed her face and moved with every touch of the breeze. She still bore a striking resemblance to Elisabeta, her ancestor. He longed to bury his fingers in those sunlight-and-honey strands, to bury himself inside her; to feel her shiver under the power of his touch.

She wanted him.

God, he could feel her wanting him. Yearning for him. And she knew he was close. She sensed him, perhaps not as powerfully and clearly as he sensed her, but it was there. And consciously or not, she was calling out to him. She wanted him still.

He had to school himself to patience. He had to know why she was here, what she was doing. He'd waited sixteen years to be with her again — more than five hundred before that. Surely he could wait one more night. But not much more than that.

He was hungry. He needed sustenance, blood to satisfy his body and perhaps calm the raging desire in his veins. To keep himself from going to her, for just a little while longer. And then, in the early hours just before dawn, he would go after the ring.

And that was precisely what he did. But when he got to the museum, it was to find the window broken, the alarms shrieking, sirens blaring and the ring . . .

Gone.

■ ■ ■ ■

Stormy woke to the insistent sun beaming through the hotel room's windows and searing through her eyelids. She rolled over in the bed and hid her face in the pillows, but the memory of her dreams woke her more thoroughly than the sun ever could have.

She'd dreamed about Vlad.

But she hadn't dreamed about the two of them making love — which was odd, because she'd dreamed of *that* many times over the past sixteen years, never sure whether it had actually happened, or if it was just part of her senseless yearning for him. Or something more sinister — perhaps the longing of her intruder or one of *her* memories.

No. This dream had been more like a memory. Until the end. Then it had become a vision. He'd been standing there on the shores of Endover, where she had first met him. His castle-like mansion hovered on its secret island behind him, and the sea was raging in between. He'd been just standing there, staring at her.

Wanting her.

Calling to her.

The wind had been whipping through his

long dark hair, and she'd remembered — yes, remembered! — the way it felt to run her fingers through it. His chest had been bare, probably because, in her mind, that was the way she preferred to remember him. His chest. Next to his eyes, and that hair, and his mouth, it was her favorite part of him. She'd touched that chest in her dreams. She'd run her hands over it and over his belly. Had it ever been real?

It felt real. More real than anything else in her life.

She rolled onto her back and pressed her hands to her face. "God," she moaned. "Am I ever going to get over him?"

But she already knew the answer. If she hadn't been able to forget Dracula in sixteen years, it wasn't likely to happen anytime soon. He had a hold on her. Maybe it was deliberate. Maybe it was him messing with her mind, refusing to let her forget him, even while making her forget the details of their time together. Or maybe it was because of that other soul that lurked inside her. Because, though it had been dormant for a long time, Stormy knew that *the other* was still there. And if she'd begun to doubt it, Elisabeta's recent appearance had driven the truth home. She lived still.

But was that why she couldn't forget Vlad?

Or was it just because he was the only man who had ever made her feel . . . desperate for him. Hungry for him. Certain no one else would ever suffice.

And no one else ever had. Or ever would. She couldn't even climax with another man.

He certainly hadn't had the same issues, though, had he? He'd never made contact, not once in sixteen years. And it hurt, far more than it should. Some days she convinced herself it was because he truly *did* care about her. That he was keeping away to protect her from the inner turmoil Elisabeta would cause if he did otherwise. But most of the time she believed the more likely reason. It was, after all, Elisabeta, not Stormy, he loved. And since he couldn't have her, he couldn't be bothered with Stormy at all.

She closed her eyes, and revisited, mentally, the initial parts of her dream — and knew it had been a memory. A snippet of the weeks Vlad had erased from her mind. He'd taken her to Romania, not North Carolina, smuggled her there inside a casket. She'd awakened in his castle, furious with him.

But why? What had happened there? Why had he let her go? God, why had he ever let her go?

Groaning, Stormy dragged herself out of bed, shuffled across the room and kicked the clothes she didn't remember wearing out of her path. She went to the door and hoped, for the hotel staff's sake, that her standing order had been delivered on time.

It had. Outside the door was a rolling service tray, with a silver pot full of piping hot coffee and a plate with several pastries beside it. There were a cup, a pitcher of cream, and a container with sugar and other sweeteners in colorful packets. Beside all of that was a neatly folded — and hot off the presses, by the smell of the ink — issue of the daily newspaper.

Her order had been filled to perfection — assuming the coffee was any good — and delivered on time. She'd specified this be brought to her room every morning of her stay between 7:30 and 8:00 a.m., and that it be left outside her door so that her sleep wouldn't be disturbed.

Yeah, she was a pain in the ass as a hotel guest. But given what they charged for rooms these days, they ought to throw in a little extra service, the way she saw it. Not that they were throwing it in, exactly. She would be billed, she had no doubt. But the agency was thriving, so what the hell?

She wheeled the cart into her room, filled

the cup with coffee and snagged a cheese and cherry Danish. It wasn't Dunkin' Donuts, but it was the closest she could get at the moment. Then she sat down to enjoy her breakfast and unfolded the newspaper.

The banner headline hit her between the eyes like a fist.

BOLD BREAK-IN AT NATIONAL MUSEUM — PRICELESS ARTIFACT STOLEN.

"No," she whispered. But she already knew, even before she read the piece, what had been taken. The hole in the pit of her stomach told her in no uncertain terms.

And her stomach was right.

According to the article, the burglary had been a graceless smash-and-grab. Someone had kicked in the window of the room where the ring was on display, so they clearly knew right where it was. They had set off every alarm in the place but were back out the window and gone before the security guards even made it into the room.

It didn't seem a likely M.O. for Melina Roscova. Stormy would have expected more grace, more finesse, from a woman like that. But who else would want the ring?

The answer came before she had time to blink. Vlad. That was who.

She'd dreamed of him last night. Had it

53

been coincidence? Or had it been his real nearness making his image appear in her mind?

Did he have the ring? Just what kind of power did that thing have?

She shivered and knew that whatever it was, it frightened her. But she shook away the fear and squared her shoulders.

"One way to find out," she muttered. She finished the Danish, slugged down the coffee, and headed for the shower for a record-breaking lather and rinse, head to toe. But halfway through, she stopped. Because . . . damn, hadn't she fallen asleep in the bath last night? Why the hell didn't she remember getting out of the tub and into bed?

She frowned as she toweled down and yanked on a pair of jeans and a black baby T-shirt with a bad-ass fairy on the front above the words Trust Me.

"I must have been more tired than I thought," she muttered. "It'll come back to me."

Telling herself she believed that, she slapped a handful of mousse into her hair and gave it three passes with the blow dryer. "And that," she told her reflection, "is why I love short hair."

She stuffed her feet into purple ankle socks, and her green and teal Nike Shocks, then grabbed a denim jacket and her bag — a mini-backpack — on the way to the door. There she paused before going back to grab her travel mug off the night stand. She filled it from the coffee pot, snatched two more pastries and the business card Melina had left her the night before, then headed out the door.

She moved through the hotel's revolving doors and turned to tell one of the uniformed men who stood there to go get her car, but Belladonna was already there, waiting. She was parked neatly just beyond the curved strip of pavement in front of the hotel's doors, along the roadside. Had she called down last night and arranged for the car to be there, then forgotten doing it? That didn't seem likely, but between the drinks she'd had last night and the stress of being in the same city with that ring, much less Vlad, she supposed it was possible.

And that was as far as she allowed that train of thought to travel. She would deal with the burglary now. Just focus on that. The intricate and tangled web of her mind and her memory would only distract her. She had to see Melina Roscova. Because she had to find out what had happened to that ring.

My ring, a little voice whispered deep

inside her mind.

It wasn't Stormy's voice.

It was a four-hour drive to Athena House, or would have been if she hadn't gotten lost on the way, and stopped for lunch to boot. Stormy inched Belladonna's shiny black nose into the first part of the driveway and stopped at the arched, wrought-iron gate that had the word ATHENA spelled out in its scroll work. The gate was closed, but there was a speaker mounted on one of the columns that flanked her on either side.

She got out of the car and headed for the speaker. The big iron gate hung between two towering columns of rust-colored stone blocks. The entire place was surrounded by a ten-foot wall of those same hand hewn stones, and beyond the gate, Stormy could see that the house was built of them, as well.

Giant stone owls carved of glittering, snow-white granite perched on top of each column, standing like black eyed sentries to guard the place. Those glinting onyx eyes gave Stormy a shiver. Too much like Elisabeta's eyes, she supposed. And the notion of them sparkling from her own face, the way witnesses had said they did, sent a brief wave of nausea washing through her.

A speaker with a button marked Talk was

mounted to the front of the left stone column. Stormy poked the button. "Stormy Jones, from SIS, here to see Melina Roscova."

"Welcome," a feminine voice said. "Please, come in."

The gate swung slowly open. Stormy went back to the car, sat down on her black seat covers with the red Japanese dragons on them, which matched the floor mats and the steering wheel cover, and waited until the gate had opened fully. Then she drove slowly through and followed the driveway, which looped around a big fountain and back on itself again. She stopped near the mansion's front entrance and shut the car off. Then, stiffening her spine and hoping to God that Melina would admit to having stolen the ring herself, she got out and went up the broad stone steps to a pair of massive, darkly stained doors that looked as if they belonged on a castle, right down to the black iron hinge plates and knobs, and the knocker, which was held in the talons of yet another white owl.

The doors opened before she could knock, and Melina stood there smiling at her. "I know we didn't discuss a fee before, but I'll pay whatever you ask. I'm just so glad you changed your mind."

She continued babbling as Stormy's stomach churned, and she led the way through the house's magnificent foyer into a broad and echoing hallway, and along it into a library. As they walked through the place, they passed other women, all busy but curious. All between twenty and fifty, Stormy thought, taking them in with a quick sweep of her well trained eyes. All attractive and fit. *Really* fit.

"You certainly work fast once you make up your mind," Melina said, as she closed the library doors, and waved Stormy toward a leather chair. "Did you bring it?"

Stormy walked to the chair but didn't sit. Instead, she turned to face Melina, her back to the chair, and asked as calmly as she could manage, "Did I bring what?"

Melina's smile showed the first sign of faltering. "The ring, of course."

Disappointment dealt her a crushing blow. So much so that Stormy sat down heavily in the chair behind her and lowered her head. Dammit, she'd been hoping, but she didn't think Melina was acting. She drew a breath. "I don't have the ring, Melina."

"Well, what did you do with it?"

"Nothing." She forced herself to lift her head, to face the woman, who was, even then, sinking into a chair of her own, looking as deflated as Stormy felt. "So it's safe to say *you* didn't break into the museum and steal it last night," Stormy said.

"I didn't." Melina closed her eyes briefly. "I assumed you had. Figured you'd had a change of heart or . . . something."

"I didn't," Stormy said, echoing Melina's own denial.

"Then that means —"

"It means someone else has the ring," Stormy said.

Melina rose slowly, walked to a cabinet and opened it, then poured herself three fingers worth of vodka. Stolichanya. Good shit. She downed it, then turned and held the bottle up.

"No, thanks. I'm driving."

"Not for a while, I hope."

"No? Why wouldn't I be?"

Melina grabbed another glass and poured, then refilled her own. She capped the bottle and put it away, then walked across the room to hand the clean glass to Stormy. "Because I need your help. Now more than ever, Stormy. You have to agree to take the job."

"The job was to steal the ring," Stormy said. "Someone's already done that."

"Yes. And now the job is to find out who has it and take it from them. Before

59

it's too late."

Stormy was pretty sure she knew who had the ring. And she didn't look forward to going up against him, although it seemed she wasn't going to have a choice about that. Maybe with the money and resources of this Sisterhood behind her, she would have an edge. A shot, at least. God knew she couldn't let Vlad decide what to do with the ring. She didn't know what sort of power the thing possessed, but she sensed, right to her core, that whatever it was, it might very well destroy her.

Melina sighed. "I have to let my Firsts know what's happened, so we can begin the search."

"Your Firsts?"

"My . . . lieutenants, for want of a better term. Not to mention my superiors." As she said that, she lowered her head and wiped what might have been a bead of sweat from her forehead. "Stay for dinner. As soon as I have things squared away, I'll tell you everything I know about the ring. Everything, Stormy. Although . . ."

Stormy lifted her brows, and when Melina didn't finish, she prompted her. "Although?"

Melina shrugged. "I get the feeling you already know as much as I do," she said softly. "Why is that, Stormy?"

Stormy shrugged. "I never set eyes on that ring until yesterday, Melina. I think your imagination is working overtime."

Melina studied her for a long moment, then seemed to accept her words with a nod. "Will you help me?"

"You keep your word and tell me all you know — and I mean everything, Melina — and I'll do my best to find and . . . *acquire* the ring."

Melina smiled. "Thank you, Stormy. Thank you so much." She clasped Stormy's hands briefly.

Stormy felt a little guilty accepting such senseless gratitude from the woman. After all, she hadn't said anything about giving the ring to her. And she didn't intend to.

When the sun went down, Vlad rose from the crypt where he'd spent the day. The crushing devastation that returned the moment his mind cleared of the day sleep was nearly enough to send him sinking to his knees. But he fought it. All was not lost. It couldn't be.

To be so close — so close to having the ring — and then to lose it that way . . .

He could only reach one conclusion. Tempest. She must have the ring. She had

61

come for it, just as he had. And she'd beaten him to the theft.

So there was still a chance. He need only find her and —

She's gone.

The knowledge seeped into his mind, as real and as palpable as air seeping into a mortal's lungs. Tempest had left the city.

No matter. There was nowhere on earth the woman could go where he would be unable to follow. To find her. To feel his way to her. She would never escape him.

So he followed the trail she had left. A trail of her essence, woven with her yearning for him. And he found her.

She was behind the walls of a mansion, beyond a stone barrier and an iron gate marked by the word ATHENA.

He recognized the place for what it was — it wasn't the first he'd seen — a base for the Sisterhood of Athena.

They were involved with Tempest? With the ring? By the gods, how? Why? Why would Tempest entangle herself with the likes of them?

Vlad planted himself outside the tall stone wall that surrounded the place, though he could easily have leapt it. He didn't need to. His power over Tempest was strong enough that he could crawl inside her mind, see everything she saw, hear everything she heard. He could *feel* her thoughts.

And damn the repercussions. She'd stolen the ring and . . . what? Brought it to these meddling mortals? How dare she betray him that way?

No, he would do whatever was necessary to get to the bottom of this, to find the ring and get it back. So he made himself comfortable in the darkness beyond the walls of the mansion, and he slid as carefully as he could into his woman's mind.

3

Dinner was late at Athena House, but well worth the wait: a tender glazed pork loin with baby carrots and new potatoes. Enough side dishes to satisfy anyone, and the promise of dessert later on.

As she ate, Stormy tried to match the names she'd been given to the faces around her, but she determined she would never keep them all straight. There were three she knew for sure. Melina, of course. Then there was Melina's apparent right-hand woman, Brooke, with sleek, shoulder length red hair parted on one side, as straight as if it were wet. She looked as if she'd stepped off the set of a Robert Palmer video and was so thin Stormy wondered if she ever ate anything at all. She wore a tweed skirt that hugged her from hips to knees, with a buttoned-up ivory silk blouse. And third was Lupe, a shapely Latina who reminded Stormy of Rosie Perez every time she opened her mouth. She was five-two, way shorter than her two cohorts, and curvy as hell. She had full, lush lips and copper-toned skin. Her hair was longer than Brooke's, jet back, and curled as if it had been left out in a windstorm, and her brown eyes were like melted milk chocolate. She wore designer jeans and a chenille sweater that had probably cost more than Stormy's entire wardrobe.

Those three she remembered. And those three were the ones who went with her into the library when the meal had ended. And yes, Stormy thought, Brooke *had* eaten — about enough to feed a baby bird.

A fourth woman brought a china tray with matching coffee pot, cups, cream pitcher and sugar bowl into the room, set it down and left without a word.

"This place is . . . odd," Stormy said.

"Is it?" Melina poured coffee into four cups, took one and sat down. She took it with cream, no sugar, Stormy noticed. Smooth but strong.

"It feels like a cross between an army barracks and a convent."

"Because that's what it is," Lupe said with a grin and a combination Spanish-Brooklyn accent. She took her own cup, added four spoons full of sugar and sat back. Hot and sweet, but dark, Stormy thought.

She eyed the room. It was large, a towering ceiling and four walls lined with books and bound manuscripts, many of which seemed very old. The scents of old paper and leather permeated the place. At the farthest end of the room there was a table that stood about desk height. It might have *been* a desk, for all Stormy could tell, since it was hidden under a purple satin cloth. Antique pewter candle holders with glowing tapers stood on top, to either side of an aged leather book.

Stormy eyed the book, watching only from the corner of her eye as Brooke took her own cup of coffee, adding nothing to it at all. Dark and bitter.

She took her own with just enough cream to mask the bite, and just enough sugar to lull her into forgetting that caffeine could kick her ass. She smiled a little as she fixed it and thought that you could tell a lot about a person by the way they took their coffee.

Melina said, "We first learned of the ring in 1516, when a member of the Sisterhood acquired the journal of an alleged mage who'd lived a century earlier."

"The Sisterhood of Athena is that old?" Stormy asked.

"Older." Melina watched her staring at

the book.

"So this is the one? The old journal?" Stormy asked, stepping toward the book on the table.

"Yes."

She set her coffee cup down and moved closer, then reached for the book, only to pause when Brooke put a surprisingly chilly hand over hers. "It's very delicate. Be careful."

"Like she's planning to rip off the cover?" Lupe asked with a toss of her head. "Give it a rest, Brookie."

There was no question, the nickname was not a term of endearment.

Stormy looked from one woman to the other. They were opposites and maybe equals. There was tension there. But that wasn't her problem. She steadied herself and touched the book with great care, opening its leather cover and staring down at the brittle, yellowed pages within.

Words flowed across the pages in some foreign script, where words were even visible. Many had faded to mere shadows. She wanted to turn the page, but didn't dare, for fear it might disintegrate at her touch.

"It's not in English." After she said it, she realized she had stated the obvious.

"No," Melina said. "Many pages are missing or only partly there. Many more cannot be read, but we've translated those that can. It's written in a long-forgotten language, so some of the translations are piecemeal or educated guesses. But the journal does speak of 'The Ring of the Impaler.'"

Stormy nodded. She didn't bother trying to feign surprise. She'd never been a good actress. "Meaning *Vlad* the Impaler, aka Dracula."

"That's the conclusion we've reached, yes. The timing would have been right, and since it was found in Turkey, and the Turks were at war with the Romanians during Vlad's reign, it makes sense."

Stormy felt herself shiver. This *was* the ring Vlad had referred to sixteen years ago in the words that had so recently echoed in her head. If there had been any doubt, it was gone now. It was the ring he'd been seeking for more than five centuries. She forced herself to retrieve her coffee, to sip it slowly and not tremble visibly.

"And this journal . . . it says something about the ring?" she asked.

Melina moved past her to the aged book and opened it to a section marked with a blood red ribbon. "This is the reference," she said. "If you prefer, you can copy it out and take it to your own translator. But I can

68

assure you, you won't find a more accurate interpretation than ours. We use only the best linguists for this sort of thing."

"I believe you," Stormy said. "But if it's all the same to you, I'd prefer to copy it. Or better yet . . ." She dipped into her backpack, which she'd slung over the back of her chair, and pulled out a state of the art digital camera, tiny and light and packing 8.5 megapixels. "May I?"

Melina nodded, but her face was pinched. Stormy snapped several shots of the book, including close ups of the page to show the text as clearly as possible. Then she put the camera away and turned to Melina. "So are you going to tell me what it says?"

"Of course." The other woman moved behind the large table that held the book, and confirmed Stormy's suspicion that it was actually a desk when she lifted the purple cloth and opened a drawer. She removed a notebook and an eyeglass case. Then she slid the glasses on — gold framed bifocals in their stereotypical rectangular shape. She opened the notebook and began to read.

" 'At the prince's bidding, we imbued the ring with his bride's essence and created a powerful rite, which we transcribed upon a scroll. These were given to him, along with our instructions. When he finds the woman, he must place the ring upon her finger and perform the rite we created. At once the essence of the one he lost will return. Her mind, her memories, her soul, will be restored. Certain physical traits — mysteries to us but known to the prince, or so said our divinations — will return, as well. This was perhaps the greatest work of magic I have ever performed. The power of all of us together, the most accomplished mages of our time, was an awe-inspiring experience. And yet my heart remains heavy, for the work we did has a shadow side. The soul of the lost, while a part of the whole, is not the whole. For it to return, it must also displace. It is unnatural, and I fear the repercussions upon the whole, upon the innocent, and upon my own soul for my part in creating what I fear is a dire wrong. We did, however, set a way for the gods to subvert our work. A time limit, in the tried and true method of occultists from time immemorial. When the Red Star of Destiny eclipses Venus, the time of this spell will expire. And all parts of the sleeping soul — both the woman she was and her spiritual descendant — will be set free to begin anew.' "

Melina closed the book and lifted her head. She removed her glasses and folded them with care.

Stormy looked at the other faces in the room and realized this was the first time either of the other women had heard these words aloud. Brooke looked excited and intrigued, while Lupe seemed puzzled and troubled.

"So the ring has the power to bring someone back from the dead?" Lupe asked.

"Not the body," Melina told her. "Only the soul."

"Creating what? A ghost?" Lupe asked.

Stormy set her cup down. "It's a soul-transferal. The dead spirit comes into the body of a living person. It . . . takes over." She got a chill when she said it. "Correct?"

Melina nodded. "That's my best interpretation, yes."

"And by spiritual descendant . . . some sort of reincarnation?" Stormy asked, though she thought she already knew the answer.

"But wouldn't a reincarnation already *be* the dead woman's soul?" Lupe asked.

Stormy shook her head. "Not necessarily. Some theorize that when we die, our soul returns to meld with a greater one. A higher self. All the experiences are shared, and the higher self spins a new soul from its parts. That's the reincarnation. It's part of the whole, but not the same whole that lived before. A new individual."

Lupe nodded, as if that made sense to her. Stormy wondered how, when it had taken her sixteen years to wrap her mind around the notion. It had been explained to her by the hypnotist she'd seen in Salem, and she hadn't believed it at first. Hadn't wanted to believe that the enemy lurking within her was her spiritual ancestor. A part of her.

Now she had a whole new nightmare to wrap her mind around. Elisabeta was Vlad's bride. His wife. His dead wife, and she was already hiding in Stormy's body, waiting for the chance to take over. And the ring he had in all likelihood stolen last night could bring her back to raging life in Stormy's own body. It could give her full control.

"So the question is," she asked slowly, "what happens to the living person? The rightful owner of that body? Does she just get . . . booted out when Elisabeta takes over?"

Melina licked her lips. "How did you know her name was Elisabeta?"

Stormy's eyes flicked to hers quickly, then just as quickly away. "Come on. You said you've been observing my company for years. You must know vampires are an area of expertise for me."

Melina nodded but kept looking at Stormy for a beat too long. Then she sighed. "I don't know what would happen to the rightful owner of the body. But the rite spoken of in this journal could very well be a recipe for metaphysical murder."

"Not necessarily, though," Brooke said. "Some people, myself included, believe that two souls could conceivably co-exist within the same body, providing both agreed to it."

"It would be like having a split personality," Stormy said softly. "Constant conflict, fighting for control." She was speaking, of course, from personal experience. "It could never be over until one of them died."

"I disagree," Brooke said. "They could share. Perhaps even . . . meld, given time. Melina, does the rite say the person the soul resides in has to be a spiritual descendant?"

"No."

"It's obscene," Lupe said softly. "A slap in the face of the supernatural order, no matter how it works."

"Exactly," Melina said. "A lifetime ends when its time is over. That's the way things are supposed to be. You cannot interfere with that and think there won't be serious repercussions. And now . . ." She closed her eyes. "Someone has the ring."

"But what about the rite?" Stormy asked.

"Is the actual rite given in the journal?"

"No," Melina said softly. And as she said it, her eyes met Brooke's very briefly, then slid away again. "We don't even know if the rite exists anymore. It could easily have disintegrated, as so many pages in this journal have done."

"Could it be recreated?" Stormy asked.

Melina tipped her head to one side, studying Stormy a little too closely again. "Perhaps. A talented witch or sorcerer might be able to create a spell that would work. They could certainly try, with God only knows what sort of results. And no doubt there are some stupid enough or power hungry enough to want to." She shook her head in disgust. "Which is why we must get the ring out of circulation. It has to be secured. As long as it exists, there is the risk that an innocent life will be lost or altered beyond repair."

Stormy agreed. Particularly since the innocent life in question was her own. "What did that last part mean," she asked. "That part about the Red Star of whatever?"

"We don't know. We have no way of knowing what modern astronomers have named whatever star those old ones were referring to. Or if it was a star at all." Melina carried the notebook to the desk and put it into a drawer, then locked it. "That's it," she said. "That's absolutely everything we know. Brooke and Lupe, because they are second in command to me, are the only two here who know all this. And now you know it, as well." She moved across the room to Stormy. "Do you think you can find the ring and take it from whoever stole it?"

Licking her lips nervously, Stormy nodded. "I think I have to."

It had been so long. Far, far too long.

Elisabeta lived still. He sensed her, alive and aware, deep inside Tempest's consciousness. Waiting for him to rescue her.

And maybe the things he'd overheard while eavesdropping from deep within Tempest's consciousness were things that required him to take action. To see her. To speak to her. Or maybe he was only allowing himself to believe they did, because he couldn't be this close and not get a little closer. Close enough to touch.

The one called Melina — the leader of this little coven — suggested Tempest stay there at the mansion for the night, rather than driving all the way back to the city and her hotel. When Tempest agreed, he sagged in relief, because he couldn't wait much longer. He needed to go to her.

But he would have to be careful. As angry as he was that she would betray him by agreeing to help the Sisterhood of Athena steal the ring, he didn't want to traumatize her unnecessarily. He would, no doubt, be forced to do enough of that later. Soon, in fact.

He had no idea how she felt about him now. He didn't how she would react to seeing him again for the first time in sixteen years. But he could not leave without seeing her. So be it.

The bedroom to which she was shown had a minuscule balcony. Vlad stood beneath it, watching her shadow play against the curtains as she moved around the room beyond them. He tried to be patient when her movements stopped, but he didn't succeed. Instead, he leapt from the grassy lawn behind the Athena mansion, clearing the rail and landing softly on the balcony. And then he went still, listening and sensing for her in the room beyond.

The shower was running. The bedroom lights were turned off, but a sliver of illumination came from beneath the closed door of the adjoining bathroom. And so he waited there, aching, silent and bleeding inside.

Eventually the sound of flowing water

76

stopped. He waited, still and alert, watching her as she stepped into the bedroom wearing only a towel. And then she dropped the towel to the floor, and he swore his body caught fire at the sight of her, nude and damp and beautiful still. So beautiful.

She crossed the room, tugged back the covers, settled into the bed and closed her eyes.

She was tired; he felt that in her. And then she sensed something, someone near, might even have known on some deep level that it was him, lurking in the night, hungering. But it didn't trouble her enough to keep her from sleep. And he wondered briefly why she was so exhausted.

He had to know what she was doing. He had to know why she was involved with the Sisterhood of Athena, and what she planned to do with the ring if and when she found it. He'd overheard enough to be fully aware she intended to search for it on behalf of the Sisterhood. Did she honestly intend to hand it over to them? What could have instigated such an idiotic, not to mention disloyal, act?

He waited until he was certain she slept — it didn't take long. Then he slid the glass door open and moved silently into the room, up beside her bed.

For a long moment he stood there, just experiencing her. The scent of her, familiar and arousing, filling him. The sounds of her breath, moving softly, deeply, in and out of her lungs. The sight of her. Her once purely platinum hair had new tones, honey and gold, woven through with paler highlights. It was slightly longer than before, softer. And there were lines, tiny ones, at the corners of her eyes. He wanted to touch her, taste her, and the knowledge that the blankets and sheets were the only things covering her burned in him.

But he wasn't there for those things. He was there for information. And the ring.

He lowered himself into a chair, focused on her mind and crept inside, carefully. He didn't want her aware of his intrusion, nor did he wish to rouse Elisabeta, who still lingered. His eyes fell closed as he felt her exhaustion, and then he sank into her dreams.She was on a sailboat, lying on the deck, bathed by the light of a full moon so big it lit the entire sky and the sea beneath it. It painted her in its milky light. She wore a stretch of sheer white fabric that draped from one shoulder all the way to her feet.

She was smiling up at someone. It was with a little rush of shock and pleasure that he realized it was him. He was in her dream.

And he was moving closer to her, reaching out to her, telling her not to be afraid.

"I'm not afraid," she told him. "Not of you." And she tilted her head. "She can't get to me in my dreams. Did you know that?"

The real Vlad was surprised, as he watched her dream image of him react with a knowing nod. "It's the one place you're safe from her. That's why I come to you here."

Was it true? Was it real? It almost seemed as if she had dreamed of him before. Could it be true?

He had to put it to the test. Had to. He stepped out of her consciousness, so that he was looking at her lying there in the bed, rather than looking out through her eyes within her own dream.

"You will not wake. You will stay safe in the haven of your dream," he told her. "Do you understand?"

He felt her agreement, though she didn't speak aloud. He also felt her longing for him, wanting him, craving his touch. It was almost too much to resist, and yet . . .

"I have questions for you, Tempest."

"Yes."

He was sitting on the edge of his chair now, leaning closer to her. He couldn't stop himself from touching her, just a little. He commanded her not to wake with the power of his mind as he trailed his fingertips over her cheek.

She leaned into his touch, and she shivered a little with a rush of pure desire. So responsive to him still. Maybe even more so than she had been before.

"Tempest, why are you looking for the ring?"

"Have to find it. Said I would." She spoke the words aloud, startling him. But she remained asleep, lost in the throes of her dream. When he started to move his hand away, her smaller hand closed over it to press it closer to her face. Then, slowly, she moved it downward, over her neck, her collarbone, underneath the blanket to her breast.

He released a shuddering breath as his palm rubbed over warm, soft skin and the stiff peak pressing into its center. Softer than before, not as firm or perky, but warm and full. He told himself to take his hand away. She arched her back, and he couldn't do it. Instead he drew his fingers together on her nipple, pressing and rolling it to give her a taste of the pleasure she so craved.

"Why, Tempest?" he asked. "Tell me why?"

"Make love to me, Vlad."

"Talk to me, first. Answer my questions,"

he told her.

She twisted in the bed, pushing at the blanket until it slid and bunched up around her waist, leaving her upper body bare and fully exposed.

He shivered at the sight of her. Still so incredibly beautiful, with creamy skin almost begging to be touched. Hips a little wider than before, body a little fuller. It wasn't the body of a twenty-three-year-old now. It was a woman's body, and he burned with desire to bury his own inside it.

"Tell me why you have to find the ring." He cupped her untouched breast with his other hand, and squeezed and lifted it, then pinched the nipple softly, because he loved the way she gasped and shivered every time his fingers closed tighter on the hard little bud.

"If you have it, you'll kill me."

"I would never hurt you, Tempest." Another pinch. Harder this time. She sucked air through her teeth. Gods, he wanted her.

"Use your mouth," she whispered.

"Tell me why you think I'll kill you." He couldn't take his eyes off her breasts. He wanted to taste them. And he didn't have the will to do otherwise. He bent his head, squeezing her breast in his hand, so the nipple thrust upward, and lapped its tip with his tongue.

She gasped. "More."

He loved this part of her, this new part. The girl she'd been would have waited to see what he would do, how he would touch her, then reacted when he did. But the woman she had become told him exactly what she wanted. And it made him all too eager to comply.

"Tell me, Tempest, and I'll give you what you want," he whispered, his breath bathing her sensitive skin as he spoke.

"If you have the ring, you'll put it on me. You'll perform the rite." She arched her back. "Please, Vlad."

He closed his mouth around her nipple, suckled her deep and hard for a long moment. Her hands closed in his hair, and she held him to her. He bit down a little, and she arched against his mouth, silently begging for more.

He stopped. "Keep talking, Tempest. Tell me what I need to know."

Breathless, she whispered, "If you perform the rite, I'll die. My soul will go away. And she'll take my body. Take you." She pressed her breast to his lips, and he took it again, drawing on it, nipping and tugging.

She writhed beneath him, arching and moaning until the blanket fell to the floor at the foot of the bed, leaving her completely naked and exposed to him. Vulnerable to him.

Gods help him.

His hand slid over her body, across her belly, to the soft curls between her legs. She let her thighs fall open wide, arching her hips against his hand.

"What will you do with the ring when you find it?" he asked.

"I can't tell you. You'll stop me."

He slid his fingers between her folds. She was wet. Dripping, and so hot. "Tell me, Tempest," he whispered, and he thrust his fingers inside her.

She shuddered from her head to her toes, and pressed him deeper.

"Will you give the ring to the woman? Melina?"

"I don't know her. Don't trust her," she said. Then, "Harder!"

He drove his fingers into her more deeply, withdrew and did it again. "Tell me what you'll do with the ring."

"I'll . . . destroy it," she whispered.

He went still. Shocked. Destroy it? By the gods, she couldn't. She *wouldn't.*

Her eyes fluttered.

He saw it, knew she was starting to lose her grip on sleep, and called up the full power of his mind. "Don't you dare wake up, Tempest. Sleep. Dream. Enjoy."

She relaxed a little, and he rewarded her by sliding his fingers into her again. In, and then out. Over and over. "Give yourself to the pleasure, my beautiful Tempest. Give yourself to me."

"You'll hurt me . . . destroy me."

"If that's my will, there is no point in fighting it. Surrender to me, Tempest. Let go." He worked her body and her mind, bending to take her breast in his mouth again, in his teeth, using his thumb to torment her clitoris while his fingers drove deeper into her, until he felt her give way. She writhed and moaned as the orgasm gripped her, and he spoke to her mind, commanding her to remain asleep, to remember it all as no more than a pleasant dream. Her body jerked and shuddered with her release, and she whispered his name over and over as she came.

He caressed her until the last shivers finished, until the spasms eased and she calmed slowly back down. He stroked her body and, leaning close her ear, whispered that she was his, that her will belonged to him, and that she would trust him, believe what he told her and do what he bade her, always. He tugged the blankets over her body and tucked her in tightly.

"You've hurt me," she whispered. "You never came back to me, Vlad. You only came now for the ring. And now you have it!"

She was getting agitated. He soothed her, stroking her hair, her cheeks. "I don't have it Tempest. I didn't take it."

"You don't? You didn't? But you want it. And you have to know . . . have to know . . . Even Melina knows."

"Knows what?"

Her head twisted from side to side on the pillows, her eyelids beginning to flutter rapidly without quite opening. "You don't care, do you? You want to clear the way for her to come back, even if it means my soul. You want me dead. Nothing can hurt more than that."

"You will trust me, Tempest. Your will is mine. I own your soul. Know that, and stop fighting it. You'll do my bidding, whatever that might entail. But for now, sleep, Tempest. Just sleep."

She relaxed slightly, and as he continued petting her, rubbing her shoulders and neck, she calmed down, bit by bit.

"I love you, Vlad," she whispered. "I never wanted to. But I do."

He didn't know how to respond to such a declaration. It shocked him. He'd hoped, secretly, that she still harbored feelings for him, because it would make doing what he had to do easier if he could do it with her cooperation. But he'd never imagined those feelings could be so intense, especially since he'd erased her memory of the time they had spent together.

She rolled onto her side and relaxed as he gently urged her mind into an even deeper sleep, a dreamless, restful sleep.

He rose then, went into the bathroom, washed his hands of her scent, her essence, with no little rush of regret, and then splashed cold water onto his face.

He hadn't intended what had just happened between them. And yet, he'd learned far more than he'd ever hoped to learn. He knew now that she wasn't working for the Sisterhood of Athena — not really. She didn't know anything about them, didn't trust them any more than he did. He knew that she hadn't stolen the ring. But she intended to find the ring and destroy it, and he knew why. She feared that ring — feared wearing it would be the death of her soul, and would result in her body being surrendered to an intruder.

And so it would.

And he'd learned that she loved him. Tempest loved him, and it hurt her to believe that he didn't love her in return. That he would choose Elisabeta over her. Even if it meant her life.

Above all else, he'd learned something more vital than anything else. Tempest believed herself immune to invasion from Elisabeta in her dreams. But she was wrong. Elisabeta had been there. She'd heard, felt, experienced, all of it. He'd felt her there. Why she hadn't come into full control, he didn't know. It might be that she was too weak after so much time. Or it might be that she was waiting, listening, trying to learn the same things he was. Who had the ring and how to obtain it.

He could visit her as often as he liked. He could make love to them both, Tempest and Elisabeta, if only in dreams.

Was it wrong to visit Tempest's body this way? Probably. But it wasn't against her will — he knew her will, could sense it in her mind. But the will to make love to a vampire in her dreams might not be the same as it would be in her waking state.

Did he give a damn if what he was doing was right or not? Gods knew he'd done worse things in the centuries he'd been alive. And if this was the only way he could have her, so be it.

He knew he would return — night after

night if he could manage it. He was like an addict craving a drug, and having found a font of it, endless and undefended, he couldn't do less than take his fill.

Especially being fully aware just how little time remained. Four days. Four short nights until the Red Star of Destiny eclipsed Venus. And then they would both die.

Beyond the physical pleasure he would give, and eventually receive, as well — yes, why the hell not? Beyond those things, he would be able to keep himself fully apprised of Tempest's progress and her interactions with the Athena group.

He returned to the bedroom, leaned over her and whispered in her ear, "Remember me only as a dream, Tempest. Remember and know you will dream of me again. From now on, beautiful Tempest, your nights, and your will, belong to me."

"Don't go," she whispered. "Don't leave me again."

He leaned closer, pressed his mouth to hers, kissed her softly, deeply, and wished for more. And more. He had to leave. He had to find a victim, feed on hot, rich blood, before his will failed him and he took hers instead.

That would make him vulnerable to her. It would strengthen the already powerful bond and create a weakness in him. One that might make him falter in the things he needed to do.

And he could not falter. He had to move forward with his plan or all would be lost.

4

Stormy felt warm all over. She rolled onto her side to hug her pillow to her with a deep contented sigh and felt a smile tug at her lips. And then she came fully awake and the smile died. The sigh died. The warmth turned to a chill that shivered from her toes to her throat, where it caught and lodged.

Vlad had been there.

She sat up in the bed, scanning the darkness of the room around her. The balcony doors were closed, their curtains still, blocking out the night beyond them. She saw no one lurking in the shadows. The luminous red eyes of the digital clock beside the bed read 4:15. There were no other eyes glowing at her from the corners. She reached out, groping for the lamp just to be sure, found the switch after a couple of false starts, and turned it on.

Light flooded the bedroom. She saw no one. But she *felt* them: eyes on her, watching her. The sensation was so real, she spun around to look behind her, but no one was there. Even so, it felt as if someone was standing right behind her, breathing down her neck.

Shivering, hugging herself, she moved across the room to the French doors of the balcony and tested them. Locked. Swallowing the dryness in her throat, she went to the closet and closed her hand around the cool brass doorknob. She stiffened her spine and jerked it open.

But no one was lurking inside. Sighing in relief, she turned and moved to the bathroom, reaching in first to flip on the light, then scanning the room. She'd left the shower curtain open, but she glanced behind it anyway.

Nothing.

She left the bathroom light on when she retreated to the bedroom, though it was a stupid, childish thing to do. Dropping to her knees beside the bed, she gripped a handful of covers and lifted them so she could peer underneath. But there was nothing there except an expanse of the same carpet that covered the rest of the floor. And then she shook her head at her own foolishness. The very notion of Vlad hiding under a bed . . . It was ludicrous.

She was alone.

But he'd been there. She was sure of it. It hadn't been just a dream. She ought to know, she thought. She'd been dreaming of him for sixteen years. She'd never felt like *this* upon waking. She felt relaxed; fulfilled. *Sated.*

Swallowing hard, she moved to the French doors again, unlocked and opened them, then stepped out onto the balcony and faced the darkness.

"Vlad? Where are you?"

The only answer was the gentle whisper of the wind moving through nearby trees, and sliding around the eaves and the railing.

"I know you're out there, Vlad. And I know you want that damned ring. Don't you try to put it on me, Vlad. Don't do it. I'm warning you."

There was still no answer. She stood there for a long time as bits of the dream that wasn't a dream came back to her. She remembered the way he'd touched her, the way he'd made her body come alive, made it sing.

Don't be stupid! It was me he was touching, me he wants, not you! Never you!

The voice, familiar and hated, shouted the words inside her mind, and Stormy gasped, gripped her head and closed her eyes. *That* was who she'd felt watching her. Elisabeta! She was getting stronger again. Rising up again.

She closed her eyes, chasing away the shivers of fear racing through her body. She had to focus on what he'd said, not on what he'd done.

He'd said he didn't have the ring.

Had he been telling the truth? Maybe so. Because if he had it, why hadn't he put it on her last night? Why wait?

Perhaps because he still hadn't located the rite that went along with it. Maybe he was just waiting for the one missing piece, biding his time.

From now on, Tempest, your nights, and your will, belong to me.

She heard his passionate whisper, a command, not a request. She lifted her head, staring out at the night. "No part of me belongs to you, Vlad. Understand that. I'm not the young, cow-eyed girl I was before. And I've been working with your kind for long enough to know how to shield myself. My will is too strong to be broken by a vampire. I'm my own woman, and no man owns me. Not even you."

She thought she had told him she loved him last night. But surely he couldn't take that declaration seriously. Not when she'd been asleep, believing it all to be a dream.

"That was wrong, Vlad. What you did last night, making me stay asleep, and trying to convince me it was just a dream? It was wrong. You violated me."

To get to me! And he will again and again and again, and you'll have no say in the matter.

"Shut up, Beta!"

She felt no response from Vlad, swallowed hard and lowered her head. She'd loved every second of it. But that didn't make it all right. He hadn't asked. He'd only taken.

Given, actually. But still . . . She wondered briefly if she was truly angry that he'd touched her without asking, or was it more that he had denied her seeing him again when she'd longed for nothing else for all this time? He'd kept her asleep, used his power over her to keep her from waking up. She wanted to see him. She wanted to throw her arms around him and weep for joy. She wanted to tell him how much she'd missed him.

"Right. The man has come to murder me. Get over it, Stormy."

Because it was true. He hadn't come for her. He'd come for the ring, and for Elisabeta.

94

"Don't let it happen again," she whispered. And on some level, she was sure he was out there, somewhere, listening. "Just don't."

She went back inside, locked the French doors and crawled back into the bed, determined to get another hour or two of sleep before it was time to get up and face the day. He wouldn't come back again tonight, she told herself. It was too close to dawn for that.

She only wished she could be as certain about Elisabeta. The sleeping intruder had awoken, strong and ready for a fight. It wasn't one to which Stormy was looking forward.

She rolled over, punched her pillow and closed her eyes. And she did get the sleep she'd been so determined to get. But it was far from restful, and filled with more pieces of her missing memories.

Vlad built a fire in the giant hearth and yanked the dusty sheets from the furniture, making a place for them to be comfortable on the ancient but still sturdy chairs. He located food, canned stew with gravy, certainly not cuisine, but she declared it edible and proved it by devouring every bit. She was starved. The castle's caretakers, he told her, only came in one weekend a month, and though he'd phoned ahead to tell them to prepare a room for her, the supplies they'd left in the pantry were meager at best.

"I'm not the original Vlad Dracula," he told her at length.

Stormy looked at him quickly. "You're not?"

"No. I am . . . far older. But that's unimportant right now. I was centuries old, already, when my travels took me to Romania. I cannot help but think it was fate that led me there. To her."

"Elisabeta?"

"Yes."

He was intense, his eyes focused on the dancing fire that painted his face in light and shadow, giving him an even more frightening appearance. And even more beautiful.

"The prince, the real son of the king, had been killed in battle before he was out of his teens, his body left to rot, unidentified and unclaimed. His father never knew what had become of him, and by the time I arrived, he had been mourning his lost son for some years. I knew the young prince's fate. I'd heard it directly from the enemy who'd slain him. That man panicked when he realized he'd killed the prince, knowing the vengeance the king would wreak should he learn of it. So he stripped the prince of his clothes, obliterated his face and dragged his body into a stand of brush, never to be found." He lowered his head. "When I arrived, the king mistook me for his long-lost son. I didn't have the heart to kill the joy in the old man's eyes. I saw no harm in playing the role."

"I see." She didn't, not entirely, but she was eager to hear more of his story. About Elisabeta, the woman who terrified her, seeming to possess her at times.

"I'd been living as Prince Vlad for nearly five years when I met her. We married a day later."

She shot him a quick, searching look. "That's it? You met her and married her a day later? That's all you're going to say about your . . . courtship?"

Vlad lifted his brows, spearing her with his steady gaze. "What else is there to say?"

"I don't know. How you met her. Where. What made you fall in love with her. It must have been . . . intense, if you married her so quickly."

"Intense." He turned his eyes toward the fire, stared into the snapping flames. "That describes it as well as anything. The details . . . the details are unimportant."

"The details are the only thing that's important."

He shrugged as if it didn't matter, and she knew he wasn't going to share his private hell with her. Not now. And maybe not ever. "The outcome is the same, with or without my most intimate memories being spilled at your feet, Tempest. I was called into battle on our wedding night. Enemies had crossed our borders. I led our soldiers to meet them, but we were severely outnumbered. It was ugly. Bloody. Many died. I was struck down, but one of my men dragged me into shelter and left me there, safe from the sun."

She sighed, disappointed that he'd refused to go into detail about his time with Elisabeta. She sensed that he didn't trust her with that kind of power.

"Was it luck that your soldier put you under cover?" she asked softly. "Or did he know?"

Vlad glanced her way. "No one really knew what I was. But by then my father and my closest comrades were used to my nocturnal leanings. They all knew I detested daylight, took to my rooms whenever the sun was shining. They knew I slept by day and that disturbing my sleep was an offense of the most dire sort." He shrugged. "They may have suspected more. Gods know the villagers did. Rumors about my nature were flying, even then."

"So it was you, not the original prince, who inspired all the stories," she said softly.

"Yes. It was me."

She nodded slowly, then swallowed the

lump that came into her throat. "Some of them . . . are pretty gruesome."

He paused a moment. "I am not proud of the things I have done in the past, but I won't make excuses. I returned to the castle to find my new bride dead. And yes, I wreaked havoc on my enemies after that. I was brutal. Perhaps even insane, at the time. But it's done, and I can't undo it."

She drew a breath and shivered a little. "So you blamed them, your enemies, for her death?"

"It was well deserved."

"Did they kill her? Storm the castle while you were away and —" She broke off there because he was shaking his head. "How did Elisabeta die, Vlad?"

He set his jaw, fixed his eyes on the fire. "She received word that I had been killed in battle, and in her grief, pitched herself from a tower window."

At her tiny gasp, he shifted his gaze toward her again. She held her hand to her lips involuntarily and felt her eyes go damp.

"I'm so sorry," she whispered.

He shrugged and looked away.

"Why do you do that?"

"Do what?" he asked without looking at her again.

"Pretend it doesn't matter. That it doesn't

hurt anymore."

"It was a long time ago."

"And it's been eating you up inside ever since."

"Don't pretend to understand me, Tempest. You couldn't begin —"

"You've spent all these years waiting for her to come back to you, searching for her. Don't try to pretend this obsession of yours isn't based on unbearable pain, Vlad. It won't wash, not with me."

"My pain is not the subject of this conversation. You wanted to know about Elisabeta. I'm telling you about her."

"Not really," she said. "But maybe I can piece it together from the scraps you're willing to share. Go on, Vlad. Finish the story. What happened next?"

"Her body lay in the chapel. My dear friend Rhiannon had arrived in my absence. It was she who told me what had led to Beta's death. And she told me more, as well. She told me that Elisabeta would return to me in five centuries."

She nodded slowly. "I know of Rhiannon. She's well versed in the occult arts, or so the stories go. Magick, divination, prophecy."

"She was a priestess of Isis, after all."

"So you believed her."

"Believed her? Yes. But I was not convinced

Elisabeta's return would be enough. I wanted to ensure that she would remember me, that she would still be the woman I had loved. That she would love me again."

Tempest rose from the chair and moved to stand in front of him, staring down at him, blocking his view of the flames, so he had little choice but to look at her instead. "How could you do that?"

"I couldn't. But I knew of those who could. Rhiannon took her leave, and I had my father send horsemen into the farthest reaches, to bring back sorcerers, witches, magicians of every sort. I charged them with the task, and they assured me they had accomplished it. They gave me the ring from Elisabeta's finger, along with a scroll, rolled tightly and held within its circle. The told me they had somehow bound her essence to the ring, and that when she returned, I need only replace it on her finger and perform the rite contained in the scroll to restore her completely."

He went quiet and watched her face, her eyes, awaiting her response. She stared at him, her eyes moist. "And you think I'm her. And you think that with this ring and scroll, you can . . . make me remember the past?"

He nodded slowly. "I am not convinced you are her. Not yet. But if you are, then I think the rite would accomplish it, yes."

Stormy closed her eyes, lowered her head. Vlad rose to his feet and began to pace. "We were attacked after burying her, by the same army we'd been battling in the days prior to her death. Ambushed. Everyone was killed. The king, the villagers, the priests. Everyone. Even me."

She frowned, but then it faded as realization dawned. "But you revived."

"I did, just before sunrise. But my body had been searched, stripped of anything of value. The ring and the scroll were gone."

He moved past her, paced to the fireplace, bracing one hand on the huge stone hearth and staring into the flames. "I thought if I brought you here, to Romania, showed you the places she knew, your memory might return on its own."

"Not my memories," she said, her throat dry. "Hers. And so far that's not happening, Vlad."

"No. Nor would it, not in this castle. She never set foot here, as far as I know. No, it's the places she lived that I want to show you." He looked toward the window. "But dawn is coming soon. I must rest. Tonight I'll take you to the village. To my father's castle. To the places she knew. Perhaps . . . perhaps it will stir something to life."

"Oh, I've got no doubt. It'll probably stir *her* to life. She'll take over, and I won't have any control over my own body, my own actions. God, you have no idea what a horrible feeling that is, Vlad. I don't want to go through it again."

"If that happens," he said, turning slowly, "I'll take you away from whatever seems to have instigated it. I'll care for you until you return to yourself."

She did not for one minute believe his lies. "And will you also keep me from doing anything I wouldn't do, if I *were* myself?"

He stared at her but said nothing, and she closed her eyes, her face heating as she turned away from him. "When she takes over, Vlad, you know what happens. Between us. Are you going to make me say it?"

He still didn't respond. And she was under assault from within by the memories of the things she'd done during the episodes she'd spoken of. She'd flung herself into his arms. She'd kissed him, fed from his mouth with her tongue while moaning endearments in Romanian. She'd arched into him, pulled his hips hard against her and told him how she wanted him. Only it hadn't been her. It had been Elisabeta. Stormy had been no more than a silent witness. And yet she'd burned with the same desire the other woman felt for him.

"I need your promise, Vlad. Promise you won't make love to me . . . not unless you're certain it's really me."

He caught her shoulders and turned her to face him, then lifted her chin so that he could watch her face. "And if I *am* certain it's really you?" he asked. "Do you intend to take me to your bed then, Tempest?"

"I don't know. I don't know if what I feel for you is real, my own desire, or something she's planted in me. I just don't know."

"And you don't wish to engage in sex with me until you do," he said, completing the thought for her.

She swept her lashes downward. "I know you don't have to wait. You can take me any time you want to, either by brute force or by using the power of your mind to bend me to your will. I'm not even going to lie to you and say I would hate you for it. I want it. I crave it. But I'm asking you not to do that. I'm asking you to wait."

He caught a handful of her hair in his fist and tipped her head up, bent his head and took her mouth, but only briefly. It was a hungry kiss, and he swept his tongue into her mouth to taste her. Then he lifted his head away.

She was trembling. "Even if she takes over. Even if she begs you to take her."

"It would be a test of my control. One I cannot promise I will pass." He trailed a finger over her cheek and downward, tracing her jawline and then her neck. "But rest assured, Tempest, if I find out this is a game — if I learn you've been lying to me, trying to convince me you are my Elisabeta as other women have tried to do over the years — I'll take all you have and then some. I'll make you my slave, a mindless drone without a will of your own. You will exist only for my pleasure and only for as long as I will it."

She lifted her eyes to his and whispered, "Is that supposed to be a threat, Vlad? Because it doesn't really sound all that horrifying."

He lifted his brows but said nothing. Still, she saw the fire in his eyes and thought maybe it was for her, for once, and not the woman who possessed her.

She touched his shoulder, her eyes fixed on his. "I want to be whole again. I want to understand this thing, and more than that . . . I feel something for you, Vlad. Something powerful. And it's killing me that I can't tell whether it's my own emotion or hers. I want to sort this out, and for the first time I feel as if there might be a chance to do just that. So yes. I'll go with you to the places she knew."

He averted his eyes just as something came into them. He hardened his features. "It's not as if you have a choice, you know."

She lowered her head and turned away

quickly. "No, I don't suppose it is." She sighed deeply, wondering if she were insane to be feeling so much desire for a man who'd abducted her against her will. Though in truth, it hadn't been against her will. Not really. She wanted to be with him. She wanted to figure all this out. And if she really wanted to get away, she doubted even Dracula himself could stop her. She wasn't exactly helpless.

Slowly, very slowly, she faced him. "What if she does manage to return, to take up residence in my body? Have you wondered about that? What future could you possibly have together, either way? Vlad, you're a vampire. I'm not. I'm not one of The Chosen. This body can't be transformed. Have you considered what that means?"

He lowered his head sharply. "I will not consider the inevitability of finding my love only to lose her again. I cannot."

"Fine. Then consider this. If she comes back, Vlad, what happens to me?"

He glanced toward the windows. "The sun is coming. I feel it."

Stormy felt as if a blade had been sunk into her heart. It didn't matter to him what happened to her, she realized slowly. He didn't care.

Stormy hadn't expected to have a companion with her for the day, but she couldn't find a way to get out of taking Brooke along when she returned to the museum. Frankly, she didn't know why she bothered returning to the scene of the crime at all. She knew damn well who had taken the ring. Vlad. It had to be Vlad, no matter what he had said. Who else would want it? And she knew he was near. She felt him. How big a coincidence would it be that he was in town when that cursed ring was stolen? Too big, that was how big. He must have taken it. He was still determined to evict her from her own body just to bring back his lunatic of a wife.

It shouldn't hurt, but it did.

"That's the room, isn't it?" Brooke asked as they moved through the corridors of the museum. There was no yellow police tape, but the doors were closed.

"Yeah, that's it."

"Doesn't look like we're going to get a look at it from out here."

"Well, you never know."

Stormy glanced up and down the hall, and seeing no one, she gripped the knob and twisted it, then smiled. "Unlocked. What do you know?"

"Do you really think we —"

"It'll only take a minute. Look, why don't

you go on a little tour? I won't be long."

"No way. If you're going in there, I'm going with you."

Stormy frowned but quickly ducked inside the room, with Brooke right behind her. She closed the door and took a look around. As she did, she asked the question on her mind. "Melina doesn't trust me, does she?"

Brooke seemed surprised. "Why would you think that?"

"She sent you along. And you act like someone under explicit instructions not to let me out of her sight."

Brooke shook her head. "It's not Melina. It's me. I've . . . got a real interest in this case."

"Really?"

She nodded. "I find it fascinating. Are you telling me you don't? I mean, you do this shit for a living."

"Sure I do. That's why I'm in this business. But then again, so are you, in a way. You and this . . . Sisterhood."

Brooke nodded.

"So why the special interest in this case?"

Brooke shrugged and looked around the room, then pointed. "That must be how they got in, huh?"

Stormy eyed the window. A sheet of blue plastic had been affixed over it, probably just to keep out the elements until a crew arrived to replace the glass. She moved closer, lifting the plastic. The window glass was shattered, the remaining shards leaning inward. "Point of entry. Yes." She looked beyond the glass. "There's a ledge out here. I suppose the intruder could have climbed up there, worked his way along to this window and then come in." *Unless,* her inner voice whispered, *he just jumped up from the ground. It's only the second story. No challenge for a vampire.*

Brooke peered around her, but Stormy let the plastic fall back into place. "So again, I ask you. Why the special interest in this case, Brooke?"

The other woman met Stormy's eyes and maybe realized she wasn't going to evade the question quite as easily as she'd hoped to. She thought for a moment, then said, "It's not often I disagree with Melina on anything. This time I do. And I'm eager to find proof of which theory is the right one."

"It's important to you, being right?" Stormy asked. "Or is it her being wrong?"

Brooke shrugged. "I just want to know, one way or the other."

"Okay." Stormy filed that away and examined the room further. She spotted the surveillance camera mounted high in one

109

corner, and her heart beat a little faster. If only she could get her hands on a copy of that tape. What it *didn't* show would tell her as much as what it did.

Voices in the hall jerked her off that train of thought, and she held up a hand to tell Brooke to be quiet. Brooke's eyes widened and shot toward the door, but she stayed still and silent, and the voices passed, fading away.

"We'd better get out of here. I think we've seen all there is to see."

Brooke nodded, and Stormy moved to the door, pressed her ear to it for a moment, then opened it and, after a quick look up and down the hall, moved through. Brooke followed. No one saw.

"That's it, then? We're heading back?"

"Not just yet," Stormy said. "I want to get a look at the point of entry from outside."

They exited the museum, and walked down the sidewalk and around the corner to the side of the building where the broken window was located. As Stormy took in the street from end to end, not missing a single detail, she tried to make small talk. "So how long have you been with the Sisterhood, Brooke?"

"Eighteen years. How long you been in the supernatural investigation biz?"

"Officially? About sixteen years now. Max and I were teenage sleuths before that. Kind of the Scooby Gang of our town, you know?"

"That's funny." Brooke smiled, relaxing a little.

"You must have been just a kid when you joined this group, then, huh?" Stormy asked. She noticed a trash can that looked out of place. It was painted green and had a maple leaf symbol on it. It stood underneath a tree with a large, low hanging limb, right next to the museum building.

"Seventeen."

"Really? And what about Melina?" A person could have climbed from that trash can to the limb, she thought, and from the limb, they could easily make their way to the ledge.

"What *about* her?" Brooke asked.

"I'm guessing you two are about the same age, aren't you?"

"She's a year older. But she came in about a year before I did."

"Hmm."

Brooke eyed her. "What?"

"Nothing." Stormy had located other trash cans. They were green and bore the same logo. But they were not on the sidewalk. They were across the street, in a small

111

park, spaced at intervals along the walking path.

"Come on, that 'hmm' definitely sounded like something," Brooke said.

Stormy shrugged. "Well, I don't know. I guess I was just wondering how it is that she's the one in charge and not you. Does it go by seniority or . . . ?" Not one green trash can anywhere else on the street or on the sidewalk, Stormy noticed. They were all in the park. So someone had definitely placed that can underneath that tree. Deliberately.

A vampire would not need to move a trash can, climb a tree or inch along a second story ledge to reach that window. For the first time, she honestly wondered if Vlad had been telling the truth. Maybe he *didn't* have the ring.

"The former leader picks the new one. To be honest, Eleonore was grooming both of us to take her place. But she had to choose one or the other."

"And she chose Melina."

"Yes."

"That must have hurt."

Brooke shot her a look, her brows furrowed. "Don't be ridiculous. If I didn't like it, would I still be here?"

"I suppose not."

"So are you getting anything out here?

Any clues or whatever it is you Scooby-types look for?"

Stormy thought she was getting a lot. Mainly, a question. If Vlad didn't have the ring, then who the hell did? And why was it she suddenly felt more vulnerable than she already had, when she knew damn well no one was more of a threat to her than he was?

"What do you say we get some lunch, huh? And then maybe we'll pop by the police department and see if we can get them to drop any hints about what they've got on this case so far."

"You think they'll tell us anything?" Brooke asked.

"Not on purpose. Come on."

5

The day was unproductive, for the most part. Stormy knew now that it was possible an ordinary mortal, not Vlad, had stolen the ring. And she knew the police had the tape from the video surveillance camera, but not whether anything was on it.

Maybe the night would provide more answers.

She'd pleaded exhaustion and gone to her room early. But she wasn't tired. She was eager and afraid and excited and terrified. He would come to her tonight. She knew he would. The fear made sense. Not the longing. Never that, she told herself, knowing she was lying.

She opened the windows, one after the other, so the night wind whispered into the bedroom and the curtains sailed like ghosts. And she left them that way while she headed into the bathroom for a long, steamy shower. When she stepped out again, dried herself off and padded, naked, back into the bedroom, he was there. Waiting for her.

He sat in a chair, in the shadowy corner. She wasn't surprised or startled or even embarrassed to be standing naked in front of him. It felt normal, natural and expected.

"Hello, Tempest," he said softly.

She felt herself tense as she reached for a robe. "I knew you would show, now that the ring has surfaced. So tell me, Vlad, was it real, last night?"

He got to his feet and came to her, took the robe from her hands before she had a chance to pull it on. Her heart skipped and her belly tightened. And even then, she felt that foreign presence stirring, deep inside her.

"I like looking at you. Give me that, at least," he said, very softly.

"You know I can't, Vlad. You know what it would do to me." She stared into his eyes, wondering if he even gave a damn about that. "Even now, she's waking up, trying to take over. Just being close to you —"

"I know, Tempest. Believe me, I know."

"Of course you do. It's why you're here."

He seemed surprised but didn't let it throw him. "I've never been far from you," he told her.

That got her. True or bald-faced lie, her

heart went for it, and seemed to go soft and squishy in her chest.

"I've missed you so damn much," she whispered, a wrenching confession.

He bent his head and kissed her, wrapped his arms around her waist and pulled her nude body against his clothed one. His tongue delved into her mouth, and she took it, loved it, welcomed it, as she arched against him. But the *other* was coming alive, clawing her way to the surface, demanding possession of Stormy's own body.

She pulled free of Vlad and took a step back.

"I want you." His words were nearly a growl. And, she noted, he didn't say her name. She suspected he was speaking to Elisabeta, not her.

When she spoke, her voice was broken, trembling. "It wouldn't be me. You'd be making love to her. My body, her soul." She met his eyes, held them hard. "Maybe you wouldn't mind that so much. She's the only one you really want."

"Does it matter, Tempest? I don't think you would refuse me. And I know she wouldn't."

"Do it, then," she said.

She saw him frown. "Tempest?"

"Yes, it's still me, dammit. Do it. Take me

and see what happens. But I warn you, Vlad, if you put that ring on my finger —"

"I don't have the ring."

She went silent, staring at him, trying hard to see if he were telling the truth or lying. But, for the life of her, she couldn't tell.

"Please don't lie to me, Vlad. Please —"

"I don't have it, Tempest. I did come here for it. But someone else got there first. Until last night, I had assumed it was you."

She closed her eyes, wanting to believe him.

"I made a discovery last night, Tempest," he said softly. "And you know what it is, don't you? Elisabeta can't invade your dreams. Everything but that. Last night, I came to you in your dreams. And she didn't take over your mind. She couldn't. Your dreams are you own. Safe ground, apparently."

Stormy blinked her eyes open and stared at him. "But it was only my mind you invaded."

"No, Tempest. It was real. I touched you, kissed you. I wanted —" He closed his eyes.

"I didn't know getting a woman's permission was on your list of priorities, Vlad."

He lowered his head. "You still don't. It's only a token effort, really. I heard you, cursing me, just before dawn. I'm still unsure how much of it was sincere. But I think we both know I'm going to take you either way."

She didn't want to think about that, not now. "I don't think I believe you."

He looked her squarely in the eyes. "Refuse me and find out."

She lowered her eyes and didn't answer. Her body was screaming for him. She wanted to tell him yes, to take her in every imaginable way. She wanted to tell him no and enjoy being ravaged by his will rather than her own. She wanted. She just *wanted.*

"I brought you something." He reached over to a night stand and picked up something she hadn't seen there before. A videotape.

"What is this?" she asked as he handed it to her.

"The museum's surveillance footage from the night the ring was stolen. I liberated it from the police department."

Her brows rose. "Is there anything on it?"

"I don't know. I haven't viewed it. I'll leave that to you and ask you to tell me what you find."

She blinked, shocked by the gesture. "You're showing a hell of a lot of trust in me to give me this tape. What makes you think I'll tell you what's on it, though? My goal is to keep you from getting the ring, not to help you find it before me."

"View it. At least then you'll know I don't have the ring. I have neither the time nor the inclination to sit through hours of footage, nor easy access to audio-visual equipment. And if you choose not to tell me what you find, it will be a simple enough matter for me to command you to tell me, or simply invade your mind and read what is there."

"You want me to find it first, don't you?" She scanned him with her eyes narrow, wondering what he was up to.

"I don't care which of us finds it first. If it's you, I can take it from you without so much as exerting any effort."

"You're that sure of yourself. Of your power?"

He met her eyes, smiled slowly, evil lighting his face. "Where you're concerned? Yes, Tempest, I am. You'll do whatever I command."

He glanced at the bed. She did, too, and she knew what he was thinking. She was thinking the same thing. Her pride wanted to refuse him, but she told her pride to go to hell. She wanted him — it was a force she didn't even try to resist. Was he compelling her to feel this way, even now? Was it

Elisabeta's desire burning her up inside? Or could it be her own?

It didn't matter. She wanted him so much she was trembling with it. Her breaths came short and hitched, and her heart pounded. She walked to the bed, put the videotape on the night stand and peeled back the covers, then lay down, pulling them over her. She closed her eyes. "I'm going to sleep now, Vlad. And you are more than welcome in my dreams. You . . . you always have been."

He moved to the bed, sat on its edge. "Open your eyes, Tempest."

She did, and found his locked with them. "Don't blink, and don't look away. Just look into my eyes. Know my will. Feel my will. Do you feel it?"

"Yes," she whispered.

"Good. Close your eyes now. And sleep. Sleep, Tempest, sleep. Be alert, and aware, and remember everything — but sleep. And do not wake until I tell you to wake."

"Yes." She licked her lips as the last vestiges of control melted away from her hands. "Make it good, Vlad," she whispered.

She was asleep. And yet . . . not. Vlad was pulling the covers away from her, bending over her, touching her body, and she felt everything, all of it, but for the life of her, she couldn't move or respond. It was as if she were a marionette and he was holding her strings. When he wanted her to move, she did, but of her own will, there was nothing in evidence. Nothing.

His hands moved over her breasts, rubbing and squeezing them. And then his lips followed, and he kissed and suckled her. She wanted to clutch his head and hold him closer, but she couldn't do that. Her arms would not move. Not unless he told them to.

His hand slid between her legs. *Open to me,* he whispered inside her mind. And then her legs suddenly had the power to move, but only if they moved the way he'd instructed, to part, and when she thought they were wide enough and would have gone still, his will pushed them farther, wider, and she lay there, more exposed than she had ever been. He touched her then, explored her with his fingers, probed deep inside her, pinched her pulsing nub lightly, then harder.

She heard herself whimper in response to that rough touch, and to his teeth on her nipple, mimicking the motion of his fingers. Pinching, tugging. Hurting so deliciously that it felt good. She wanted to arch her back, to push her breasts up in offering. She wanted to wriggle her hips in time with the motions of his hand. But she was motionless. Paralyzed. Helpless.

And then he was sliding down her body, his mouth moving wet and hungry over her belly, her abdomen, before settling finally over her center.

The sensation was too much, and she would have tugged her thighs together to slow it down, but they would not budge. If anything, they opened wider — he made them open wider, made her hips tip upward to give his mouth even greater access. His tongue snaked out, lapped over her lips and then between them, and then deeper, plunging inside her. Too much. She wanted to draw back, to slow it down. Instead her body obeyed his will, not her own, and her hips thrust upward, grinding her mound against his mouth. He fed from her, licking her as if in a frenzy of hunger. His teeth scraped her, caught her and bit down just enough. And then his hands were on her, spreading her wider, laying her open to his plundering mouth. He ravaged her, and his puppetmaster mind made her own hands go to her breasts, made her own fingers twist her nipples and pinch them.

It was his will, all his. She was no more than a ragdoll, awash in sensation, with no ability to do or say anything in her own defense. He could do what he wanted, and that was precisely what he did. She would not, could not, resist or refuse. And God help her, she didn't want to.

His mind whispered to hers, *Give yourself to me. Come for me, Tempest. Do it now.*

Her body responded to his command, as he bit and sucked her harder than before, and forced her hands to pinch her nipples harder, until they throbbed and grew hot. She exploded at his command, and he plundered on, taking her while her body convulsed. She wanted to twist away, the sensations were so overpowering, and yet he wouldn't let her, made her lie there, open and utterly helpless to him, until he had taken his fill and reduced her to a shuddering, whimpering mass of sensation.

And then, even before the convulsions had stopped, he was moving up her body and sinking himself deep, deep inside her.

"Again," he whispered as he began moving deeper, withdrawing, moving inward again. "Move with me now."

She did, even though the actions brought too much sensation to bear. And the passion began building before it had even ebbed.

He held her, and drove into her over and

over, so deeply he drove the breath from her lungs. And this time, when he neared climax and she did as well, he sank his teeth into her throat, and he drank her essence, her blood.

The power of it nearly made her body shake apart with the release. It was above and beyond any orgasm she'd ever experienced. She felt everything. His body hard and pulsing, invading hers, filling her. His teeth embedded in the flesh of her throat as his mouth drained the very lifeblood from her body. She was his, utterly and completely his, and her mind and body exploded around him, because he commanded it. And it was powerful.

So powerful, in fact, that she woke from her lucid sleep to find him lying there, still inside her, on top of her, holding her, kissing her neck and licking at the wounds he'd left in her throat, even as he began moving again to rebuild the fire.

Elisabeta came to fierce, fighting life, and Stormy barely had time to whisper "No" before she was gone. Her time with Vlad was over. The invader had driven her out.

When her nails raked his back, Vlad realized she had changed. No longer responding only to his mind's suggestions, Tempest had instead taken control. She was moving frantically beneath him, making demands of her own, unspoken but clear in the movements of her body. He drew back to stare down at her, wondering how she had managed to escape the power of his mind, and he saw that her eyes were wide open and blazing . . .

. . . and jet-black.

"Tempest . . ."

"She's gone. And I won't let her come back. Not this time, Vlad. This body is mine." Elisabeta wrapped her arms around his neck to draw him more deeply inside her.

He drove once, twice, then closed his eyes and gave in to the passion that rose up in him. He was shaking with desire and need. And it didn't matter who owned the body any more than it mattered who owned the blood that he needed to stay alive. He took what he needed from anyone he pleased. He always had. This was no different.

And he took her. He took them. Elisabeta, Tempest, both of them. Neither would have turned him away. He wouldn't have cared if either of them had.

Harder and harder he rode her, until she was panting and gasping beneath him, her nails raking his back until the pain burned along every path she made, but it only enhanced his pleasure. The bed slammed against the wall with the force of his thrusts, and he pushed her still harder. He didn't care if he hurt her.

"Elisabeta!" He growled her name as he spurted into her, holding her hard and mercilessly as he drove to even greater depths and then held there, pulsing, throbbing, into her.

She grunted, perhaps in pain or maybe in pleasure. He couldn't be sure and told himself it didn't matter. Slowly he eased himself out of her, but he didn't lie there on the bed to embrace her. He got up. Got to his feet, began reaching for his clothes.

"I've come back to you, Vlad," Elisabeta whispered. She twisted in the bed like a contented cat, hugging the pillow, clutching the sheet. "And this time, it will be forever."

"Is she dead, then? Have you managed to evict her from the body without my help after all?"

Beta thrust out her lower lip, sitting up in the bed. "Why do you care? I'm the one you love. I'm the one you're meant to be with. Your wife, Vlad. I'm your wife."

"You don't have to remind me of that. I've been trying to find you again since you died, Elisabeta."

"But I didn't die," she told him. "Not completely. Your magicians and your sorcerers wouldn't let me die. They imprisoned my essence in some in-between state — they bound it to the ring. I couldn't have moved on even had I wanted to. But I didn't want to, Vlad. I didn't want to leave you. And I haven't."

She blinked those huge, dark eyes up at him, and he saw them fill with tears. "Vlad, why aren't you happy? Isn't this what you wanted?"

"It's all I've wanted," he told her. He put on his clothes, but she was still weeping, and he didn't have it in him to turn a cold shoulder to her. Even as unused as he was to showing affection, he couldn't remain cold. Not to her, not to his Elisabeta. He sank onto the bed and pulled her into his arms, holding her gently. "I've never stopped loving you, Beta. Nor stopped wishing you could return. But I have to know — is she dead?"

She stared at him, and he knew, before she even spoke, that she would lie. So he pressed his lips to hers to stop her from speaking at all, and as she melted in his arms and opened to his kiss, he entered her mind as easily as a warm knife through butter, and he read what was there.

But there were no specific thoughts, no answers. Just a sense of vehemence, hatred and fury that shocked him, and he drew away from her kiss as if burned by it. He also felt Tempest still there, alive, but trapped. Like a captive inside her own body.

"My love?" Elisabeta whispered. "Can't you stay with me? Just for a short while longer?"

"No, Beta. I must go. And so must you. Tempest's friends will be coming for her soon. They'll know what you've done unless you . . . recede. Go back to sleep inside her, and wait until the time is right."

Her lips went tight. "I won't. It's too hard to get control. If I release it, I might never get it back again."

"You will," he promised. "I'll help you. Don't you trust me?" He cupped her cheek. "Please, Beta. Let her come back to herself. Just for now."

She held his gaze, and for a moment he saw anger glittering in the depths of her eyes. But then she blinked it away, averted her face and nodded once. "All right. I'll do as you ask. For now."

She lay down in the bed, pulled the covers over herself, and closed her eyes. In a few moments her breath came slowly and evenly.

Vlad touched her face, her hair. "Tempest?"

She didn't reply, just kept on sleeping. He tried probing her mind but found it blocked to him. She'd taken refuge, put up the blocks she'd somehow learned to build — most likely by years of working with and for his kind — to keep him out.

Elisabeta. She wasn't the woman he remembered. But whatever she'd become, he knew he bore the blame. Imprisoned, trapped for hundreds of years — how could she not lose herself to fury and anger and . . . perhaps even madness?

"I'm sorry, Beta. I'm sorry for what I did to you. I promise I'll make it up to you, no matter what I have to do."

Pressing a kiss to her forehead, he rose from the bed and went to the windows and leapt to the ground, but never landed. Instead, he changed forms and flew as a nightbird over the walls of the Athena mansion.

6

He wanted another woman.

Elisabeta's borrowed heart felt as if it were slowly turning to a chunk of cold ice. Her prince, her husband, who had promised her eternal life, still wanted her, yes. But he wanted his precious Tempest, as well.

Well, she'd fooled him. She'd pretended to obey his wishes, to withdraw and allow Tempest to return to control. In truth, she'd only feigned sleep until he left the room.

But no more.

The woman whose body she possessed, Tempest, who called herself Stormy — the enemy — writhed within, struggled to regain control. Elisabeta felt her own grip weakening and knew she had to work fast. She had to do what was necessary and do it quickly. And she wasn't certain she trusted Vlad to do it for her. She had to do this on her own.

"You're not coming back," she told the

one she'd displaced. "Not this time."

Stormy dreamed. And more pieces of her past returned. Once again she was in Romania, in Vlad's castle.

Vlad carried an oil lamp from the great room, and led her toward the wide and cold stone staircase. The bannister was wood, solid and coated in dust. Not ornately carved, but beautiful in a rough and rustic way. He didn't take her hand as he led the way. She walked beside him, and when a piece of one of the stone stairs fell away beneath his foot and he had to grip the rail to keep from falling, she clasped his upper arm instinctively.

He looked at her, the lantern glow flickering between them, his eyes intense, as if he, too, felt the power that seemed to surge between them with any physical contact whatsoever. It surged even in something as innocuous as her hand on his biceps.

She had to lower her gaze from the burning intensity in his eyes. She shifted it to the lamp instead. "Maybe I should carry that, given that your kind are nearly as combustible as the lamp oil."

He lifted his brows but didn't object as she took the lamp from his hand. She held it by its slender neck, between the wide glass base and the sphere that held the oil. Its chimney was tall and narrow, sooty near the top. It was warm to the touch, unlike the man who'd been carrying it.

They resumed climbing the stairs and moved along a high-ceilinged corridor past arching doors that each seemed to be cut from a single slab of wood. Black iron hinges and knobs gave the place a gothic feel that was fitting, she thought. Pausing at one of the doors, he pushed it open wide and let her precede him with the light.

Its golden warmth spilled onto a huge canopy bed with sheer white curtains sur-rounding it. It was stacked high with pillows and covered by a thick comforter. And the room was remarkably dust free. She moved closer to the bed, noting the tall windows in the far wall, the thick red draperies held back with fringed golden ties. Bending, she ran a hand over the comforter and caught the freshly washed scent coming from the bed-ding.

"It's clean," she said, glancing over her shoulder at him.

He stood near the doorway. "I phoned ahead. Asked the caretakers to come in and make up a room for you. I hope it's comfort-able."

"It's fine." It was more than fine. It was darkly beautiful, like something out of a gothic fairy tale. She turned and held up the lamp to look around, noticing the ornate, ancient-looking furnishings, a rocking chair, writing desk and chest of drawers and wardrobe. There was a fireplace here, too, and she set the lamp on the mantle, and glanced into the hearth to see wood and kindling laid ready for the touch of a match.

He came closer then, removed the screen and took a long wooden match from a tin holder on the mantle. With a flick of his thumbnail on the matchhead, it flared to life, and he bent to light the kindling.

"You do mess around with fire a lot, for a vampire."

He shrugged. "I'm careful."

She nodded toward the windows. "What about those? Are the drapes thick enough to . . . ?" She let her words die as he turned to look at her, the question in his eyes.

"I hadn't planned to rest here with you, Tempest. Though if you would prefer me to, I —"

"No. No, that's not what I meant." She averted her eyes, shaking her head in denial, though it had been exactly what she had meant. She'd just assumed. . . . "Actually, I'll be grateful for the privacy. I have a lot of thinking to do. I just — I'm not used to sleeping by day, and the sun streaming in might keep me awake."

"I see." She was afraid he did. All too well.

He moved to the windows, untied the golden cords and tugged the draperies together, blocking out the graying sky beyond. "Better?"

"Much. But I could have done that." She dared to look at his face again and was surprised to see that his eyelids had become heavy, kept drifting closed. "Go on, go to bed. I can handle things from here."

He nodded but seemed hesitant to leave, even then.

"I'm not going to run away, Vlad. We made a deal. I always keep my word."

"That's good to know. Good rest, then, Tempest."

"You too. See you at sundown."

He nodded and left her alone in the room.

As the fire licked to life, the room grew brighter. Bright enough to let her explore it more thoroughly. There was a dressing table, and its surface was far from bare. There were a gorgeous silver hairbrush, comb and hand mirror lying on the top, and she wondered if they'd been there before or if he'd had them brought in for her. She wondered if they'd been Elisabeta's, then thought they would surely be tarnished with age if they had. Curious, she opened some of the drawers and found that they were not empty, either. A selection of undergarments — bras and panties, nightgowns and camisoles, and a few pairs of socks — filled them. Frowning, she moved to the wardrobe and opened its doors, wondering if she would find fancy dresses and gowns.

She didn't. Its hangers were filled with jeans and blouses, and a warm coat. Two pairs of shoes sat on a shelf — hiking shoes and running shoes. She picked up a shoe and looked at the number on the bottom. It was her size. The chest of drawers held sweaters and T-shirts. He'd definitely had these things brought in for her. And he knew her sizes, and her style.

Another door revealed a bathroom that was surprisingly modern, at least in comparison to the rest of the castle. Indoor plumbing must have been a more recent addition. The tub was old, claw footed and deep. The sink was a pedestal model, the toilet a huge one that must have been manufactured in the fifties. All the fixtures were brass and shining. Towels and washcloths, all clean smelling, were stacked on a shelf. And a small stand with a mirror behind it and a stool in front held bottles and jars — familiar ones.

Hair care products, moisturizer, soaps and razors, and a supply of makeup. All her brands. All her colors.

My God, how did he know so much about her?

Stormy wasn't sure whether to be touched that he'd gone to so much trouble, taken so much care, to provide for her comfort, or creeped out by the fact that he seemed to have dug into her life — or maybe her mind — so deeply without her knowledge.

Maybe she was a little of both.

She would have loved a shower, but that wasn't an option. No showerhead. Sighing, she put the stopper into the tub and started a bath running. Then she went back into the bedroom to choose a nightgown. The one she pulled out was long and white and flowing. Perfect attire for the heroine in a gothic novel, stranded in a strange castle in a foreign land with a vampire for a host. Why not?

The bath relaxed her; the nightgown felt heavenly against her skin. She hadn't expected to be able to sleep at all, but when she crawled into the bed, she knew she would. The mattress was covered in a downy featherbed, and her body sank into it as if she were sinking into a cloud. So comforting and warm, with the down-filled comforter snuggling her and the pillows cradling her head. She thought it would put the most hopeless insomniac to sleep. She sank into slumber as soon as she'd pulled the covers around her shoulders.

She slept for a long time. Deep, uninterrupted, blissful, restful sleep.

Until the dream came.

In the dream, she wasn't herself. She was someone else. Elisabeta. Oh, it was Stormy's body, her face, but the other woman's eyes lived in it. She was standing on the edge of a cliff, getting ready to jump.

Stormy felt as if she were inside the body of the other woman but not in control. It was as if she was just along for the ride. But she knew everything Elisabeta knew, felt everything she felt, as she stood on that precipice, high above a thundering waterfall. The night sky above her was dotted with stars, and behind her, grasses and wildflowers spread out as far as she could see. But her gaze was drawn to the woman again. Somehow she could see her, even though she felt trapped inside her.

Elisabeta wore a simple dress that reached to her feet. There were grief and loneliness, a great yawning emptiness, inside her, filled only with pain beyond human endurance. It hurt so much. Stormy felt it. She ached with it.

I've lost everyone. Everyone I ever loved. I have nothing left.

The Plague, Stormy thought slowly. Elisabeta's family had been taken by the Plague. Her mother. Her father. Her brothers. Her baby sister.

"Alanya." Stormy whispered the baby's name as it floated into her awareness. "She was only two." Her throat went tight, and she felt tears burning in her eyes. Tears . . . for Elisabeta.

There was something else wrong with the woman. Woman? No, she wasn't even that. She was barely more than a girl. Her mind was awash with overwhelming emotions, and her body — her body was weak and sick. She'd been growing weaker for a long time now, and she knew, deep down, that whatever was wrong with her would get no better. She saw no need to go on living, suffering from a mysterious malady that would surely kill her anyway, now that her family was gone.

She's one of The Chosen, Stormy realized. One of those mortals with the Belladonna Antigen — the only ones who can become vampires. They always weaken and die young, but God, not that young.

The Undead sense that kind. They watch over them, protect them. Where was her protector now? Stormy wondered.

She heard a shout, glimpsed a man on the opposite cliff. But it was too late for him to stop her.

"I'm finished," the tormented girl whispered.

She opened her arms and rocked forward, just let go. Her body fell, and Stormy fell with it. The pounding foam and rocks below jetted toward her at dizzying speeds, and her stomach felt as if it had stayed behind on the ledge.

And then something was shooting toward her, a person, arrowing through the sky. His body hit hers, driving the breath from her lungs, and then he turned, putting himself beneath her. When they hit, she swore she felt his bones crack before the water swallowed them both. She heard his grunt of pain. He'd broken her fall. He'd kept her from dying. And then water embraced them, and for a moment everything was icy cold and pitch-black.

But then there was a shout.

"He's mine!" the tormented, grief-stricken young thing shouted, and in an instant it was as if Stormy was staring straight into Elisabeta's eyes. The woman spoke without moving her lips. *He's mine, and I have nothing else. You will not keep me from him.* She closed her small hands on Stormy's throat and squeezed.

When Stormy had woken that dark night so long ago, she'd found herself clawing at the hands on her throat and choking, struggling to breathe. But there were no hands there. She had gagged and struggled as the dream clung to her, then sat up and finally sucked in a desperate breath. The sensation of being strangled faded as if it had never been.

But she soon realized that she wasn't in the big, soft bed anymore. She wasn't even in the castle.

She was sitting up in a grassy field that stretched out forever and was bordered by distant forest. The wind was wafting over her, gentle, not harsh, but cold, and it carried a peculiar dampness that wet her skin. There was a roar in her ears, one that sent a chill to her bones. Slowly, she got to her feet and turned in a half circle, and then she went still and sucked in a breath.

Because there was nothing, just empty space at her feet. Across the yawning, rocky chasm, a waterfall thundered and plummeted into the river below, and a huge cloud of wet mist rose up to engulf her.

"Oh, God. Oh, Jesus." She took a step backward, away from the edge, hugging herself and dragging in breath after breath of precious air. Her body was shaking. Her throat felt bruised, her lungs tight. God, it was so real! Elisabeta had been choking her. And somehow she'd made her way out here, to the very place she'd seen in her dreams.

Lifting her head, she shot a panicked glance at the night around her. But there was no one.

She was alone.

Not alone, she thought. *Not exactly. The enemy is inside me.*

Pressing her hands to her head, she waited for her breathing to steady and her heart to stop racing. Gradually she recovered, and the dizziness — no doubt from being strangled half to death — faded.

Could she have died? Was it possible for an invasive presence to kill her from within her own body? It felt as if it was.

And she didn't feel alone, even now. She felt watched.

The sky was dark, and she was disoriented. She'd slept for what felt like hours in the cozy bed. Slept like the very dead. But she didn't know whether morning had simply not yet arrived, or whether the day had passed and it was night again.

She wanted to call out for Vlad. And even as she told herself how ridiculous a thought that was, she knew that didn't change it. She craved him like a drug. Or maybe Elisabeta did. She only knew she wanted him, there, with her, right then.

And then, suddenly, he was.

His hands closed on her shoulders from behind. He turned her slowly to face him as his probing, unreadable eyes searched her face. "Tempest?"

Her throat tightened. A sob tried to rise, and she clenched her jaw, closed her eyes tight to prevent the tears, and held her body stiffly.

"I woke to find you gone," he said softly. "What happened? How did you get here?"

"I don't know," she whispered, and it was an effort to get the words to pass through her constricted airways. "I just . . . I don't know." And then she lost it. She couldn't hold herself stiff and strong for another second. She let her body go, let it do what it was longing to do: fall against his strong chest, rest in his powerful arms while her own wrapped around him and held on hard. She lowered her face to his shoulder, and she let the tears come.

As the memory faded, Stormy struggled to wake up but found it impossible. She knew on some level that she wasn't really trapped in some dark nightmare in which she was imprisoned in a lightless, airless tomb.

The tomb was her own body. The cold stone walls were keeping her from the controls in her own mind. She couldn't hear or see or move. But she sensed that her body was moving, awake and walking around just as if everything were normal. Except someone else was behind the wheel.

Elisabeta.

Bitch. Give me back my mind!

142

She fought, strained against the darkness. And it seemed to give. Elisabeta must be weakening. But she was fighting, too, and she was stubborn. Stormy pushed harder, clasping a shred of control and then holding on for dear life.

The darkness gave way all at once.

It was like breaking through the surface of a mirror-still lake. First there was nothing, and then, everything. All her senses came to full, screaming life at once. She could suddenly see through her own eyes and feel her own limbs, and for a moment she had no balance or sense of orientation.

Stormy found herself standing near the windows of her room in Athena House, wearing only her robe, her knees weak, her body lurching a little as she sought balance. She blinked her vision into focus. What she saw stunned her to the core.

The large, sparkling ruby ring. She held it in one hand, poised on the tip of her finger, and even as what she was seeing hit her, she was sliding the ring on farther.

She went motionless and stared at her hands, willing them to stop moving. She was holding the oversized ruby stone in her right and was about to slide it onto the forefinger of her left.

A scream was ripped from her chest as

she flung the ring across the room. It hit the wall and then the floor, bouncing, tumbling, then coming to a stop, its red stone facing her like some demonic eye.

Her bedroom door crashed open. Melina lunged inside. "Stormy! What's wrong? What happened?" She scanned the room, wide eyed, as the sounds of others pounding down the hallway toward the room reached them.

Stormy gasped for breath, wondering what the hell to say, how to cover, when Melina spotted the ring and gasped. "Is that —"

"Jesus," Brooke muttered from the doorway. "Where the hell did that come from?"

"I don't know. I don't know!" Stormy's knees buckled, and then Lupe was beside her, sliding an arm around her waist before she could sink to the floor. Stormy hadn't even realized Lupe had come into the room. She was strong, way stronger than Stormy would have guessed from looking at her. She supported her firmly, and moved Stormy backward until her legs touched the bed. Stormy sank onto it gratefully, her entire body trembling. Lupe stayed close, her eyes sharp, missing nothing.

"Was it the Impaler?" Melina asked. She didn't look at Stormy as she spoke. Instead, her eyes remained riveted to the ring. "Has he been here?"

"No. Of course not," Stormy managed to mutter. It was a lie, but what was between her and Vlad was none of their business. She dragged her gaze away from Lupe's then and frowned as the raging waters of panic began to calm. "Why would you jump to that conclusion?"

She noticed Melina and Brooke and then Lupe looking toward the French doors, which were not quite closed. A breeze came through the gap, fresh and cold, pushing the curtains with its breath.

Slowly Melina turned to face Stormy. "It makes sense, doesn't it? Vlad needs a body for his dead bride to come into. Maybe he's chosen yours," she said. "Are you sure he wasn't here?"

"I think I'd know if Dracula had paid me a nocturnal visit, Melina. That's not the kind of thing that could exactly slip by me." She was careful to keep the left side of her throat away from their prying eyes. His marks would still be there, would remain until sunlight touched her skin.

"He's powerful enough to make you forget," Brooke said. "From what I've read, he can shapeshift, and his thrall is impossible to resist."

"Not for me. I've been working with his

kind for sixteen years, don't forget."

"Where did the ring come from, then?" Brooke asked. "How did it get here?"

Stormy let the defensive attitude slide off her shoulders. "I . . . I don't know how the ring got here. I woke up and it was here, that's all."

"On the floor?" Melina asked. She was moving toward the ring now, reaching for it, and it took everything Stormy had not to knock her aside and snatch the ring before she could. She knew that urge wasn't coming from her own mind, not entirely. It was also coming from Elisabeta's. She flinched forward as Melina closed her hand around the ring and picked it up.

"In my hand," Stormy said. "I was sleep-walking or . . . or something."

Lupe's eyes narrowed at the "or something" part, but she didn't make any comment.

"When I woke, I was standing, and the ring was in my hand."

Lupe muttered in Spanish and crossed herself.

"That must have been terrifying," Melina said.

"Someone must have brought the ring," Brooke said slowly. "You didn't see anyone? Hear anything?"

"No. Nothing," Stormy insisted.

Brooke thinned her lips. "It didn't just appear here all by itself."

"I didn't say it had."

"Get off her, Brookie," Lupe snapped, stepping closer to Stormy in a way that was almost protective. "Maybe we should search the grounds," she said, possibly in an effort to change the subject. "We can check for signs, make sure whoever it was isn't still here. Give Stormy time to gather herself. I'll brew some tea. Chamomile, some valerian, maybe a little lavender, and we can talk."

Melina nodded. "You're very wise, Lupe. Safety first, analysis later." She turned to Brooke. "Rouse a handful of the girls and search the house, top to bottom. I'll take another group and search the grounds."

"I'll get started on the tea," Lupe said. And then she moved closer to Melina and held out her hand. "Maybe I should hold that for you until you get back. Just in case you run into . . . whoever."

Melina opened her palm and eyed the ring.

Brooke met her eyes. "I can hold it, if you want," she said.

Melina shook her head. "Lupe's right, it'll be safer here with her while we search. We'll decide what to do with it later." She handed the ring to Lupe, who closed her fist around it, nodded and dropped it into her bathrobe pocket. Then she turned to Stormy. "You should come to the kitchen with me. You shouldn't be alone right now."

"Thanks."

The four of them walked into the hallway. Melina and Brook headed down it in opposite directions, each intent on gathering troops to conduct a search. Stormy wasn't worried. Vlad was long gone by now.

But had he been the one to leave the ring with her? How else could it have ended up in her bedroom?

A voice inside asked if she needed to be hit over the head before she accepted the truth. He'd released her from his thrall and kept making love to her, knowing full well that would rouse Elisabeta to life. And then he'd given her the ring to put on. To drive Stormy out, to kill her.

He wanted her dead.

Why did she still want him so much?

She moved as if her legs were made of lead, down the stairs beside Lupe, who glanced nervously behind them and then said, "They know about you, Stormy."

She was so stunned she almost stumbled. Lupe's strong, tanned arm shot out to steady her. Stormy swallowed and gripped the railing. "They know what?"

"Come on." Lupe closed a hand around her forearm and picked up the pace, leading her to the bottom of the stairs, then through the mansion and into the oversized kitchen in the back. She ran water into a metal teapot and set it on a burner to heat. Then she reached into a glass cabinet and took out a china teapot, cups and saucers.

"What is it they supposedly know about me, Lupe?" Stormy asked.

"They know about you and Vlad. That he abducted you sixteen years ago, held you for a couple of weeks — time you don't remember. And . . ." She met Stormy's eyes, searching them and seeming hesitant. Then she gave her head a shake, went to a cabinet and flung open the doors. It was filled with jars, all of them labeled and packed with herbs. She scooped herbs from several of the jars and poured them into a cheesecloth sack with a drawstring closure.

"And what?"

"I'm getting to it, okay? This isn't easy. Saying it out loud sounds freakin' insane. But . . . they think you're the one. Elisabeta Dracula. Or her reincarnation or something."

"They think?" Stormy sank into a chair,

shaking her head. "And what do *you* think, Lupe?"

"Damned if I know." She yanked the drawstring tight and dropped the sack of herbs into the china teapot. "I've seen the portrait — photos of it, at least. In our file on Dracula."

"You have a file on him?"

She shot Stormy a look that clearly said she wasn't supposed to have revealed that and wasn't going to elaborate. "It would make sense. Him abducting you, I mean. If he thought you were her."

Stormy lowered her head, shaking it.

"That's why Melina hired your firm to find the ring. She knew she would have a better chance of finding it if you were helping. You have a connection to it. A special interest in it. It's yours, if their theories are true."

"I promise you, Lupe. I am not Elisabeta Dracula. I'm Tempest Jones."

"Yeah?" She sighed. "So then how did you get the ring?"

"I don't know."

The teapot whistled. Lupe grabbed it and poured the steaming water into the china pot. The fragrance of the herbs wafted into the room with the steam. "Okay. So what's on the videotape?"

Stormy's head shot up, her gaze snapping to Lupe's.

"I saw it on the night stand. What is it, anyway? Did it get there the same way the ring did, or . . . ?"

Stormy held up a hand. "I don't know if I want to discuss the tape. Not . . . yet, anyway."

"You don't trust me." Lupe shrugged. "Can't say I blame you. I mean, you don't know me. And you don't have any clue what I risked to tell you what I just did. If they find out . . ."

"They won't."

She smiled a little, lowered her head and put the china cover onto the teapot. "It needs to steep for a while." Then she met Stormy's eyes. "You've got more right to this than anyone else," she said, taking the ring out of her pocket and holding it up.

Stormy shook her head. "It's safer if you keep it away from me. At least until we destroy it."

"Oh, we can't destroy it," Melina said from the doorway.

Both women jerked in surprise and turned her way. Stormy had no idea how long she'd been standing there, how much she might have overheard, nor did Lupe, judging from the look on her face.

"But you told me the ring was dangerous," Stormy said. "That if it fell into the wrong hands . . ."

"It *is* dangerous. But legend has it Elisabeta's soul is somehow bound to that ring. If that's true, we have to set it free. With the ring, we can perform an exorcism. And then we can destroy the ring once and for all."

She reached out a hand, palm up and open. "Until we can do that, I think it best we put it into the vaults." She slid her gaze to Lupe's, then back to Stormy's, and it was open and reassuring. She fingered a chain she wore around her neck, tugging it from beneath her blouse. There was a silver key at the end. "I'm the only one with access, Stormy. Nothing will happen to the ring there. I promise."

Stormy thinned her lips, and finally she nodded. "All right."

"Good." Melina kept her hand out, and Lupe put the ring into it. "I'll take it to the vaults right after dawn."

"Why after dawn?" Stormy asked.

Melina licked her lips. "Just as a precaution."

That wasn't entirely true. Stormy knew it wasn't. Someone must have seen something. Someone knew Vlad had been there, or maybe Melina was as adept at spotting a lie

152

as Stormy was. Either way, they knew there had been a vampire around, and they were not going to risk him seeing where they put the ring.

"Call us when the tea is ready," Melina said. "I need to check in with Brooke's group." She left them, taking the ring with her.

Stormy started to follow, but Lupe stopped her with a hand on her shoulder. "You have some time," she said. "There's a VCR in my room, if you'd like to use it. No one has to know."

"Thanks."

Lupe nodded, leaving Stormy to wonder why the girl was helping her, whether it was a trick, a trap or honest assistance. And then she knew it didn't matter. She was on a path here, and she wasn't going to get off until she found where it led.

Stormy thanked her and headed into the next room after Melina. "Melina, just one thing."

Melina turned to look at her.

"This . . . exorcism. Do you know how to perform it?"

Licking her lips, the other woman shook her head. "No."

"Do you know anyone who does?"

"No, not offhand. But I'm sure we can

153

find someone."

"You don't need to. I . . . I know someone. Probably the best — maybe the only — person for the job."

7

Stormy returned to her room to make the call. Of all the vampires she'd ever encountered — and there had been many — Rhiannon was the one she was least fond of. She'd never been 100% certain just why. But there was something else. Rhiannon had helped her. She'd been there, in Romania. She'd been the one to return Stormy to her home, to Max and Lou and her old life. How it had happened, why, she didn't know. And maybe part of her was grateful while the rest of her resented being separated from Vlad. Even though staying with him would probably have killed her.

And still might.

Max liked to believe Stormy's dislike of Rhiannon was because she and Rhiannon were a lot alike, but Stormy didn't buy that. Sure, Rhiannon was tough, full of herself and fearless. But she was also, Stormy knew, dangerous. More dangerous than the others she'd known. Except, perhaps, for Dracula himself.

She hated to bring the haughty vampiress into this mess, but there was no denying her powers or her skill. No one knew more about this type of thing than she did. She'd been a priestess of Isis. Besides, Rhiannon knew the backstory. More of it than Stormy did, at this point. And she knew Vlad, and for some reason she had tried to help before.

Stormy slid her PalmPilot from its case. The contact list was password protected, and she changed the password weekly. This week it was DRAC-2006. Yeah, he'd been on her mind big time even before she came here and ran into him again. Then again, he always was. Still, lately it had been worse.

She used the stylus to enter the password and opened her file of confidential contacts. She had a direct number for Rhiannon's cell phone, complete with voice mail. She never knew what time zone her vampire contacts might be in. Nor did they.

Stormy was taken by surprise when Rhiannon answered on the second ring.

"Well, well, well," she said when she picked up. "If it isn't the spunkiest little mortal I know. It's been a long time, Stormy Jones."

"I'd be real impressed by your psychic

156

skills, Rhiannon, if I didn't suspect you had caller ID."

Rhiannon laughed. It was slow and sexy. "Don't belittle my powers so quickly. I imagine I can tell you why you've phoned."

"Fine, I'll play." Stormy crossed the room, picking up her videotape on the way, and sank into the cushioned and elegant chair near the French doors. "Why am I calling?"

"Because the deadline is approaching. Time is running out."

She blinked, then frowned. "Deadline?"

Rhiannon was quiet for a moment.

"What deadline, Rhiannon? Does this have to do with that Red Star of Destiny shit?"

"I . . . I assumed you knew. Vlad hasn't contacted you by now to tell you?" she asked, her voice very low and way more gentle than Stormy had ever heard it. That alone was enough to shake her.

"No, Vlad didn't tell me about any deadline. But if it involves me, I think I have a right to know, don't you?"

"There's no question. I wouldn't even consider keeping this from you, though he, apparently, is foolish enough to see some benefit to it. Tell me this. Do you know the rest yet? That ring you're searching for, do you know what it is?"

"How do you know I'm searching for a ring?"

Rhiannon sighed. "I keep very close tabs on you — and on Vlad, as well. This situation — it's coming to a head, I'm afraid. Tell me, do you know about the ring?"

"Yes. I know that if it's put on my finger and some rite performed, Elisabeta will return, and it will probably cost me my life. That's what I'm trying to prevent."

"Good. It helps that you're aware of that much, at least. But there's more. Stormy, the magicians put a time limit on the magick they used to ensorcell the ring. If Elisabeta's soul hasn't been restored to life by the time the Red Star of Destiny eclipses Venus, they said, the magick would die. Elisabeta would be free."

"So I've heard." Stormy turned the video in her hand, wishing for a machine right now, here in her own room.

"They included all the women she had ever been or would ever be in the wording. If you *are* her reincarnation, Stormy, and the deadline passes, you, too, would be . . . set free."

"Meaning?"

"Dead."

Stormy went icy cold. She'd been afraid that was what the cryptic words in the

158

journal had meant, but to hear them confirmed chilled her to the bone.

"Don't panic yet, child. There's still time to prevent it."

"I'm not prone to panic, Rhiannon. And I'm no child."

"Compared to me, you're a newborn."

Stormy lowered her head. "When is this Red Star of Fate —"

"Destiny."

"Whatever. When does it eclipse Venus?"

"Once every five and a half centuries or thereabouts."

"And that would be when?"

"Midnight on Tuesday," Rhiannon said.

"You're shitting me." Stormy closed her eyes, feeling as if the words had been a hammer blow to her gut. "Tomorrow's Monday," she whispered. "So I'm going to die in two days and Vlad didn't even bother to tell me?" She was going to kill that undead bastard herself.

"Apparently."

"What if we had the ring?" Stormy asked quickly. "Do you think you could exorcise her spirit from me if we had it?"

"Of course I could. There's no question."

Stormy nodded. "And would that prevent my untimely demise?"

"I can't be certain, Stormy, but I believe

it would. Call it an educated guess, if you wish. But there is no one *more* educated in this area than I. Not alive, at least."

Stormy nodded, knowing it was true.

"You have the ring, then," Rhiannon said.

The woman never missed a thing, did she? "Yes."

"Does Vlad know?"

"He's in town," she said. "He knows the ring is here, that someone has it, but I have no idea if he knows it's me." *Yeah, I wish. I know damn well he's the one who brought that cursed thing here tonight.*

"Then you have nothing to worry about. It's too near dawn now, but I can leave at sunset and come to you. Where are you, Stormy?"

"Edmunstun," she said. "It's in —"

"New Brunswick. Canada. Gods, tell me you haven't got yourself entangled with that nest of Athena vipers."

Something cold seemed to waft from her words, chilling the blood in Stormy's veins. "Why do you say that?"

"By the gods, you have, haven't you?"

"They're the ones who tipped me off that the ring was in town. They tried to hire me to steal it, actually, but someone beat me to the punch. I agreed to help them find it, and it turned up in my room."

"Your room where?"

Stormy swallowed, because her voice was getting hoarse. "Here at Athena House."

"Are you using their phone? By the gods, child, it's probably tapped."

"No. I'm using my cell." She was getting a very bad feeling, a dark foreboding in the pit of her stomach.

"They're not to be trusted, Stormy. Especially not one called Brooke, if she's still among them."

Stormy blinked, and her throat went utterly dry.

"Where is the ring now?"

She could barely move her lips. She glanced at the window, saw that the sun had risen. "By now Melina and Brooke are putting it in a vault for safekeeping."

"By the horns of Isis, Stormy, go after them! Now!"

Stormy snapped her cell phone closed and was halfway to the bedroom door before she realized she still had the videotape in her hand. Belatedly, she shoved it under the mattress, then headed back to the door and raced down the hall.

She met Lupe halfway down, gripped her arm.

"Where are the vaults?"

Lupe's eyes widened. She shot a look

down the stairs and then whispered emphatically, "I'm not allowed to tell you that. Only a handful of the women here know where they are, even fewer how to —"

"Don't give me that bullshit. You're third in command, after Brooke and Melina. I know you know. Get me there."

Lupe stiffened her spine, shook her head. "No."

"Dammit, Lupe, there might be a problem."

"Might be?"

"Just trust me on this. I have to —"

"I'll go. But I'm not taking you." She turned away.

"But —"

Lupe whirled to face her again. "Dammit, Stormy, do you have any idea what happens to women who betray the trust of the Sisterhood of Athena?"

Stormy went still, her eyes widening a little at the grim tone in Lupe's voice, the expression on her face. "No," she said. "I don't. What happens to them, Lupe?"

Lupe stared at her, and her eyes said volumes, though her lips didn't speak a word. "Never mind. Come with me." She led Stormy down the stairs and through the mansion, into the library. "The phone in here has a two-way radio function. There's another in the vaults." She leaned over the phone, reaching out to hit a button, but before her finger touched down, a crackling sound came from the telephone's speaker.

Frowning, Lupe hit the "speak" button. "Melina? Brooke? Is that you?"

She released the button, her eyes seeking Stormy's. Stormy strained her ears to listen, and then the crackling came again, along with a single quiet word.

"Help."

"Melina?"

Stormy leaned past Lupe and hit the button herself. "Melina? What happened? Are you all right?"

She released the button, and when no answer came, she hit it again. "Melina, where is the ring?"

She waited. No reply. Then she shot a look at Lupe. "We have to go. And I think under the circumstances, you won't get into too much trouble for taking me with you."

"I could. But at this point, I'm willing to risk it. Come on."

8

Stormy followed Lupe through the mansion into the sunroom that had been added on at the rear, a room that was like a tropical rain forest. Enclosed in glass, filled with plants and trees, fountains and a bubbling hot tub, and paths that wound amid them all. She barely had time to appreciate the ingenious beauty of the indoor paradise before they were exiting through a glass door and heading along another path. This one led through an even larger paradise, an outdoor garden that seemed to cover acres.

The entire area was heady with the almost overpowering scent of countless flowers. Above them, between the colorful limbs of flowering trees, was a broad expanse of sky painted orange and pink by the sunrise. The path they took wound and branched until Stormy wasn't sure she could find her way again without an escort. At the center of the garden, or what Stormy presumed to be the center, stood a giant granite sculpture of the goddess Athena. She stood proudly, an owl on her shoulder, a staff in her hand and a crown of stars encircling her head. Her stone robe flowed from one shoulder to pool around her feet and drape in places over the square base on which she stood. The base had been chiseled with twisting vines, and a few real ones had begun to creep over it. The entire image was utterly amazing.

"My God," Stormy whispered.

"God*dess,* you mean." Lupe knelt in front of the statue's base, which was at least four feet high, and touched one of the leaves that were carved there. Immediately a part of the base slid outward, along hidden tracks in the ground.

Stormy gasped, shocked. She hadn't even realized there were seams in the granite, they were so cleverly hidden by the pattern of the vines.

"This way," Lupe said, and she walked into the black void behind the chunk of stone.

Swallowing hard, Stormy followed, and as soon as she stepped inside, the stone slid home again, blocking out any light.

"Stay still a second," Lupe said. Stormy was surprised to feel Lupe's hand, palm flat against her shoulder, as if to ensure she obeyed.

Then there was light, and Stormy blinked in the sudden brightness before she realized Lupe was holding a glow-stick in one hand. Lupe held it out ahead of her, and Stormy saw that they were standing at the top of a set of stairs that vanished downward, into the darkness, plunging deep into the earth.

"You guys take this secrecy shit seriously, don't you?"

"We have to. Follow me." Lupe started down the stairs.

It was a long flight, with a hundred-yard tunnel at the end of it, and a door at the end of that. When they finally reached the door, Lupe punched a code into a numbered panel mounted to it, and the door opened.

She led Stormy inside, closed the door behind her and hit a switch. A light came on near them, then another and another, each one revealing more of the incredible room they had entered.

Room? It was more like a mini-stadium: huge and round with a concave ceiling. And the entire thing was lined in books. Hundreds — no, thousands — of them. Perhaps tens of thousands. She couldn't even begin to examine titles or subjects; she only got a sense of great age, and that could have come as much from the musty smells of old paper and leather as anything else.

"What *is* this place?" she asked in a whisper. Because it seemed appropriate to whisper in there.

"The Library of Athena," Lupe said. "There's barely a subject we can't research here. We have a hundred women employed at a separate facility, transcribing the books into computers, one by one. They don't know who they work for or why they're doing what they are. They just type and save, or scan the ones that are solid enough to withstand it."

"That's probably wise. If there were ever a fire —"

"There was, once. At our library in Alexandria."

Stormy blinked, stunned. "That was . . . ?"

"This way," Lupe said. She crossed the vast room, and at the far end, she took a book from one of the shelves and reached into the space left behind. The shelf behind her swung open to reveal a hidden doorway. "Follow me."

Stormy followed her into the shadowy dimness, down another set of steps — a smaller one this time — and at the bottom there was a far smaller room. It was square, and its walls seemed to be made of rows upon rows of small doors in various sizes. One section held tiny doors, another slightly larger ones, and another, still larger ones. Some were tall and narrow, others short and wide. Each one of them had two things in common: a lock and a number.

Two of them were very different from the others. Both were tiny. And both stood wide open.

The room was dark and shadowy; the only light came from the still-open doorway into the stairway. But as Stormy stood there, staring at the two tiny open doors, her mind racing with the possibilities they suggested to her, she heard a moan and tore her eyes away from the little vaults.

"Melina!" Lupe shouted. And then she was darting into a dark corner of the room, falling to her knees beside the limp form that had to be Melina.

Stormy joined her there, kneeling on the other side of the fallen woman. She lay on her back, eyes closed, and the dark blotch on the right side of her forehead looked suspiciously like blood. Stormy touched her cheek, patted it. "Melina. Wake up, come on. Tell us what happened."

Melina's eyes fluttered. "The ring," she whispered.

"That's right, the ring. Where is the ring?"

Melina's eyes opened. She tried to focus on Stormy, then on Lupe. Her eyes grew wider. "Oh, God, the ring!" She sat up rapidly, then swayed to one side, but Lupe gripped her shoulders and held her upright.

"Easy, Melina. You're hurt. You're bleeding."

"Help me up. Hurry."

Lupe and Stormy flanked her and helped her to stand. As they did, she stumbled a few steps forward and stared at the open doors. Then her hand flew to her neck in search of something. A key, Stormy recalled. She'd worn it on a chain, but it wasn't there.

"The key. God, she took the key."

"No. Look, it's right here." Lupe bent and picked up the broken chain with the silver key still on it. "And here are the others." She scooped up another ring, this one huge, with more keys than Stormy could have counted.

"I don't get it. Look, someone better start explaining some things to me, and fast," Stormy said. "What happened down here, Melina? And where the hell is Brooke?"

"Brooke." Melina lowered her head. "Oh, God, Brooke. What the hell is she doing?"

"That's what I'd like to know," Stormy muttered.

169

Melina lifted her head, met Stormy's eyes and nodded slowly. "We came down here with the ring. I was going to use my key, the master key, to open vault number one." She nodded to the first tiny door that stood open. "That's where all the other keys are kept. I'm the only one with the master key."

As she said it, Lupe replaced the giant key ring in its vault and closed it. She used Melina's silver key to turn the lock, then handed it back to her. Melina eyed the broken chain. "She hit me with something," she said softly. And she lifted a hand to the back of her head. "I turned around to face her, and she hit me again. I went to my knees, felt her yanking the chain from my neck. She took the master key and . . . I don't know. I lost consciousness."

"Where was the ring at that point?" Stormy demanded.

"In my hand." Melina lifted her hand, opened her palm and blinked at its emptiness, her eyes wet. "I can't believe Brooke would betray me — betray the Sisterhood."

"She took the ring, didn't she?" Stormy asked.

"She . . . must have."

"But why? What the hell could she want with the ring? Unless it's just the value of it," Stormy said. "She could sell the stone.

It's probably priceless."

"It's not money she's after," Lupe said softly. She was staring at the second of the two little doors, the one that still remained open.

"What was in that vault?" Stormy asked.

Lupe looked at Melina, who looked to the open door. Her face changed. It was overcome with something that looked a lot like fear. She moved closer and peered inside, but clearly there was nothing there.

"What was in that compartment?" Stormy demanded.

Melina pursed her lips.

"I can only guess," Lupe said. "But if it was what I think it was . . ." She turned to her mentor. "It was, wasn't it? We have to tell her, Melina."

Sighing, Melina lowered her head. "The rite."

"The . . . *rite?*" It took a moment for the meaning of the words to sink into Stormy's brain, and when they did, she damn near gaped. "The rite that's supposed to be used with the ring? The one that's supposed to restore Elisabeta to life? It's been here all along? And now Brooke has it?"

"It looks that way, yes." Melina closed the door. She didn't lock it.

"But why? Why the hell would you keep

171

something like that from me?" Stormy demanded.

Melina averted her eyes. "You're an employee, hired to find the ring. You had no need to know —"

"Don't give me that bullshit, Melina. You knew about my connection to that ring and to Elisabeta. That's why you hired me. My fucking life is in the rifle sights here, and you had the only bullet. You should have told me."

"It wouldn't have mattered."

"No? You don't think so? It's *my* life, Melina. Shouldn't that have been my call?"

Melina sighed. "I'm sorry, Stormy. I did what I thought was best. I hope you can believe that."

"Yeah. What was best for you and your damned Sisterhood, maybe."

Melina only shook her head. "Let's get back to the manse. We've got to get to the bottom of this."

"You're damn right we do," Stormy said.

Brooke sat in a darkened room in an empty house a few miles away from Athena House. The torn, ragged remnants of curtains that remained in the windows were drawn as tightly as they could be, dimming the early morning light. The only other source of illumination came from the flickering candle that stood on the small round table before her. The other items on the table included a round slab of balsa wood, on which was painted a series of letters and numbers, an upside down wine glass, a pad and a pen.

Brooke had two more items to add. She took them from her pockets now and laid them within the pool of light at the base of the candle. The carefully rolled parchment, bound by a length a yellow ribbon, and the ruby ring. The Ring of the Impaler.

She took a few deep breaths and placed her fingertips on the bottom of the wine-glass. "Elisabeta Dracula, I am calling you. Speak to me, Elisabeta. I've done as you asked the last time I contacted you. I have the ring and the scroll."

At first nothing happened. But Brooke was patient. The reward Elisabeta had promised her was enough to instill patience in her. She repeated her words and waited some more. Eventually she felt a breeze rush into the room. She saw it in the way the candle flame flickered, felt it icy cold on her face. She closed her eyes as was her custom. The wineglass began to move, only slightly at first, but then its motions grew stronger, until it was gliding over the smooth balsa wood in sweeping arcs and circles. When it stopped, Brooke opened her eyes to look and see what letter the glass covered, wrote it down and began again.

The spirit board spelled out: G-O-O-D.

"What do you want me to do now?"

G-E-T the spirit spelled. Brooke took one hand from the glass to jot down the letters of her target. The glass was moving quickly now, and in a far more agitated manner than it had before. T-E-M-P-E-S-T.

"And do what with her?"

P-U-T-R-I-

Brooke frowned at the letters and kept scribbling as fast as she could, even while keeping one hand on the glass, which was flying over the board now. It barely paused on one letter long enough for her to ascertain which one it indicated before sliding to the next.

N-G-O-N-H-E-R

Brooke's pencil fell from her hand and rolled to the floor. She bent to get it, removing her other hand from the wineglass to reach for it, snatched the pencil up and reached for the glass again.

And then she just sat there, staring. Because the wineglass was moving again, still spelling. All by itself — she wasn't even touching it.

A door slammed, but no one was there.

P-A-Y-A-T-T-E-N-T-I-O-N

"I'm sorry. You . . . go ahead." She looked at the notepad and read what she had written there. PUTRINGONHER. Put ring on her.

"You want me to get Stormy Jones and put the ring on her finger. Yes? But she's not going to let me do that, Elisabeta."

F-O-R-C-E

"Yes, yes, I understand."

P-E-R-F-O-R-M-R-I-T-E

Brooke nodded, but disappointment was rushing through her now. There was still nothing about *her*, not a word about how Elisabeta would keep her promise to grant Brooke the gift of immortality in repayment for her help.

"I understand," Brooke repeated. "I take her, put the ring on her and perform the rite. By force, if necessary. It's very simple." She cleared her throat. "And after I do all this, assuming I can pull it off, what happens then?"

I-L-I-V-E

"I got that, Elisabeta, but what I want to know is, what happens to me? You promised me immortality. So when do I get it. And how?"

A-F-T-E-R

Brooke frowned, disappointment washing

through her. She didn't trust this Elisabeta, had suspected a trick from the beginning. "No," she said slowly. "No, I don't think so. You need to tell me now. Tell me how it's going to work or the deal's off."

The icy wind returned, blowing harder now than before. It blew so hard that a shutter slammed outside the house and the door burst open. The candle went out, and the wind kept coming.

Brooke rose to her feet. "I'm not asking you to do anything. Just tell me, that's all. Tell me how it can happen!"

The wind increased. Her hair whipped, tugged against her scalp and tangled in the air. The candle tipped over and rolled across the floor. But there was no response from the board.

"You were one of The Chosen, Elisabeta. But I'm not. So how can I gain immortality? How is it possible?"

Still nothing.

"At least tell me this much, Elisabeta," Brooke shouted into the wind. "Why does it have to be Tempest's body? She's not one of The Chosen either. So why her? Why?"

The wineglass shattered, exploding outward as if some unseen force inside it had expanded all at once. Brooke jumped, emitting an abbreviated shriek of alarm. Then the wind died utterly. The entire house went silent, still as a tomb. Elisabeta was gone.

Brooke calmed herself and went through the house, opening the ragged curtains, putting everything back the way it had been before. "I don't think I trust this bitch," she said slowly, thinking aloud. "I think she's promising me the one thing she knows I want more than anything else just to get me to help her return to the land of the living.

"Well, I'll be damned if I'll let her give *my* reward to Stormy Jones when I'm the one doing all the work to earn it."

As she picked up the pieces of the broken wineglass, then tucked the spirit board, the candle and the scroll into the small bag she'd brought along, she mulled everything over in her mind. Clearly Elisabeta knew how to make an ordinary mortal immortal. She must know, because she would have to do that very thing to Tempest Jones once she took control of her body. Otherwise she would just end up dead again in a few years. But she'd been very clear about her goals. She wanted to return to life to reclaim the vampire she loved, and then to live with him forever.

Tempest did not have the Belladonna Antigen. She was not one of The Chosen.

So there had to be a way. But if Elisabeta

succeeded, then what reason would she have to make Brooke immortal, as well, as she had promised to do? What was to stop her from using Brooke to get what she wanted and then just ditching her, leaving her high and dry?

Brooke wanted immortality for herself. She craved it. Sought it. Had risked everything to get it, and this was not the first time. She would do whatever it took.

There was one last item to put away. She picked the ring up from the small table and looked at it. Smiling slowly, she slid it onto her finger.

"Well, will you look at that?" she whispered. "It's a perfect fit. Maybe we'll just try doing this my way, Elisabeta. What do you think about that?"

Still wearing the ring, she took the scroll from the bag, carefully loosened the ribbon that bound it and unrolled it. She would perform the rite, just as Elisabeta demanded. She would just make one little substitution. "Now," she said as she read, "let's just see what we need for the ritual."

When they helped her back into the house, Melina refused to go to her room, heading instead toward the breakfast room, where a dozen or more women were sitting around, sipping coffee and munching fruit and pastries.

They went dead silent, every eye on Melina. And no wonder, Stormy thought. She was a mess. "We've been compromised by one of our own," Melina said. "That puts us all at risk. We're going to Plan Q. Immediately. Don't delay, unless you know something that might help me trace Brooke."

There was a collective gasp when she said Brooke's name. No wonder. She had been second in command here.

"Move," Melina said.

And the women scattered, just like that, heading out of the room like a bunch of third graders in a fire drill.

"So what's Plan Q?" Stormy asked.

"Quit the premises. They'll be cleared out of here in twenty minutes, along with their notes, any personal items that might identify them as part of the Sisterhood, their computers, every sign they were ever here."

Stormy raised her brows. "Impressive."

"We drill for this," Melina said. "Though I never thought it would happen for real. Never." She blinked what might have been fresh tears from her eyes. "Where's Lupe?"

As soon as she asked the question, Lupe appeared with a first-aid kit in one hand

and an ice pack in the other. Melina held up a hand, shook her head. "We don't have time for that."

"Yeah, we do. You'll be more useful without that blood running in your eyes every time you frown too hard. Sit down."

Melina sighed, but she sat. "We need to search Brooke's room. And her laptop. We need to go over it, as well. And —"

"And we will." Lupe handed Melina the ice pack. "Press that to the lump on the back of your head. I'll deal with the front." Melina obeyed as Lupe opened the kit, took out a gauze pad and soaked it in antiseptic. Then she began dabbing at the wound on the front of Melina's head.

Stormy was still furious, but she needed action, not anger. For now. But she also needed reason. None of this made any sense. For a while she'd thought Brooke might be the one who stole the ring, but why would she leave it in Stormy's own room, only to steal it all over again?

She remembered the tape, the one Vlad had brought her. She had yet to view it. "I need to change clothes," she said. "And then I'll . . . meet you in Brooke's room."

"Wait for us in the hall," Melina said. "Don't go into her room on your own."

Stormy stared at her, not believing the

woman was still issuing orders. But *she* was not one of the Sisterhood's devoted little robots. "I'm not waiting for anyone. If you're not there when I'm ready, I'll start without you. But before I go, there's something you probably should know. I put in a call this morning to a woman I thought could help us in exorcising Elisabeta's spirit and freeing it from the ring's hold over it. She'll be here tonight."

Lupe paused in dabbing at Melina's head and turned to search her face.

"Who?" Melina asked.

"A vampiress by the name of Rhiannon." Their eyes widened, and Stormy felt a rush of satisfaction. "Yeah, I thought you might know her. She sure as hell knows you. I have to say, I'm rather interested to hear *what* she knows."

She turned and left the room, then headed up the stairs against the tide of women coming down, bearing backpacks, suitcases, duffel bags. It was a mass exodus. And it was fast and orderly.

By the time she reached the second floor, the stairs were clear, and she could hear vehicles outside, doors and trunks slamming, gears shifting and motors humming.

Stormy went to her room, thrust her hand under the mattress and pulled out the videotape. Answers. She needed answers, and she needed them now. Privately. She was no longer so sure she could trust Melina and the Sisterhood. Certainly Rhiannon didn't. Maybe she had good reason. She'd certainly been right about Brooke.

She took the time to change her clothes, discarding the nightgown in favor of jeans, a T-shirt, a pair of ankle socks and her teal and green running shoes.

She took the tape with her to Lupe's room, and barely took time to notice the darkly stained woodwork and earthy green bedding and drapes, before she spotted the tiny, outdated TV-VCR combo on a stand in one corner. She closed the door and turned the lock — she wanted privacy for this. At least until she knew what she was going to find. She realized that she was trying to protect Vlad, even though he was most likely trying to help Elisabeta kill her. And that, more than anything else, told her what she was expecting to find on the tape.

She was a fool where he was concerned.

Stormy put the video into the slot, hit the Power button, pushed Play and watched as a slightly snowy image of the ring in its display case filled the screen. The time stamp in the lower right corner read nine p.m. According to the police reports, the

182

alarms had sounded around 1 a.m., so she located a remote, sat on the bed, and hit the Fast Forward button. Then she waited and watched the time stamp until she got close.

Finally she hit Play again, set the remote aside and leaned forward on the bed, her eyes glued to the screen.

Right on cue, she saw something. Bits of something flying into the frame. Glass, she realized. The museum's window had just been broken. And a moment later, a small form stepped into reach of the camera's eye.

Not a vampire. Vampires didn't show up in photos or on videotape. This form was mortal, and clearly a woman. Small and slight. She wore a black turtleneck, with a little black knit cap covering her hair. She kept her face turned away from the camera, and she didn't waste any time. She yanked the plexiglass cube from the display, took the ring from its tiny pedestal, dropped it into her jeans pocket, and then turned right back toward the window and walked out of the frame. For just an instant, as she moved off the side of the television screen, Stormy glimpsed the full length of her, from her head to her teal and green running shoes.

She caught her breath. Groping for the remote, eyes still on the screen, she rewound, stopped, then played the tape again, but this time she hit the Pause button at the moment when those shoes appeared, ever so briefly.

Teal and green Nike Shocks.

She rose to her feet and stared down at her own shoes. Teal and green. Nike Shocks. She'd bought them for running.

"It's not possible," she whispered. "I *couldn't* have. . . ."

But even as she said it, she remembered how she'd fallen asleep in the bathtub at the hotel that night but awakened in the bed. She remembered the clothes she didn't think she'd worn, littering the floor in the morning, and the way her car hadn't been in the garage where the valet had parked it.

She closed her eyes, disbelieving even now. But she knew she couldn't deny what was being shown to her in black and white. And as she watched the entire theft again, she recognized her own form, her own clothes. But not quite her own stance and stride and manner. She had taken the ring. But she hadn't been the one in control when it happened.

"Elisabeta," she whispered.

She pressed her hands to her head and fell back onto Lupe's bed, closing her eyes. And even as she did, a flood of memories came. Memories she had thought were lost to her forever.

"This is the place," Vlad said in a voice that was oddly hoarse. He'd taken her to the mouth of a cave near the edge of the falls, below the Romanian cliffs where Stormy had found herself only a short time ago, shown her the cave where Elisabeta had helped him find shelter for the night, and now he had brought her to the place where the two had consummated their love, all in an effort to make her remember. To become Elisabeta.

She only wanted to get to the truth and be rid of the woman.

"I had gone to the cliffs that night for the same reason Elisabeta had," Vlad told her. "To end my life. Oh, I wouldn't have flung myself from the top, as she did. I planned to await the sunrise there by the falls, the most powerful place I knew. But when I saw her, when she pitched herself from the brink, I felt compelled to save her."

"And so you did?" she asked.

He nodded. "I propelled myself like a missile, through the air, and wrapped myself around her to break her fall before we hit the rocks and water below."

Stormy didn't really look at the spot where he'd stopped walking. She was looking at him instead, and seeing what he tried to keep hidden: a pain that was almost beyond endurance. It was in everything about him. His walk had become less the powerful, confident stride she'd grown used to. His usual stance — shoulders broad, back straight and chin high — had softened, as if the steel inside him were gradually melting. And his eyes — the hurt that roiled in his eyes was something even he couldn't disguise.

"I was injured, broken. She helped me into the cave, stayed with me there, and I told her my secrets. Told her what I was, what she was. One of The Chosen. I told her I could cure the illness that was taking her life, but only if she would be mine forever. And she agreed."

"So two suicide cases meet one night and decide to get married? Vlad, don't you see how messed up that is? You didn't even know each other, and neither of you was in your right mind."

He glared at her. "No one has ever questioned my sanity, Tempest." The tone held a warning.

"Sane people don't kill themselves, Vlad."

"You have no idea what it's like to live for thousands of years. To live alone."

"No, I don't, that's true. But I know lots of vampires, Vlad, and most of them aren't walking into the sunrise, no matter how old they are."

Forcing herself to tear her gaze from him, she looked at where he'd brought her after the cave. It was a tiny grove of trees, with a circular patch of wildflowers and grasses amid them. It was private, quiet and beautiful. And she knew it was the place where he and Elisabeta had consummated their love.

One night. It was all they'd had.

Moved to tears herself, she put a hand on Vlad's shoulder. "I'm sorry this is so difficult for you."

He swung his gaze toward her. "Don't pity me, Tempest. I don't want that from you. All I want —"

"Is for me to remember. I know." She licked her lips and stared at the area around her, but no memories came. Nothing was familiar. "Has it changed much?"

"The trees are bigger. Some have died." He nodded toward rotting black stumps amid the stand of hardwoods. "Others have sprung up to take their place," he said, pointing out the spindly saplings that arched their backs as if standing up straight were too much of an effort. "Other than that, no. It's almost exactly the same." He brought his gaze back to hers, searched her eyes. "Don't you remember anything? Anything at all?"

"I'm sorry," she said. "I don't."

"You have to. You will."

She saw the desperation in his eyes just before he reached for her, and felt a quick jolt that might have been fear, or maybe desire. Or some twisted mix of the two. She didn't have time to analyze it, because he pulled her hard against his chest, snapped his arms around her, one hand going to the back of her head to keep her from turning away. And then he was kissing her.

And, God help her, she loved it. Wanted it — and more.

He opened his mouth over hers, then closed it slightly, as if he were devouring her taste. And when he used his tongue, she went hot right to her toes. Every coherent thought, every rational argument that this was a bad idea, fled her mind. The only thing that remained was sensation. The way he made her feel: wanted, desired beyond reason. It was heady, and it was too powerful to resist. That this man, who could have any woman he wanted, wanted her. And she wanted him, too. Had, from the moment she'd set eyes on him, and maybe even before that.

She twisted her arms around his neck and opened to him, kissed him as passionately, as hungrily, as he was kissing her. God, it was going to be so good. So incredibly, unbelievably good.

He laid her down in the grass, pushing the nightgown from her shoulders, baring her breasts to the night, to him. He slid a hand between her shoulder blades to hold her up to him. And then he kissed her breasts, suckled them, gently at first, but with growing hunger, until he was nipping and tugging, making her gasp and pant and arch her back.

Lowering her down, he slid over her, his mouth moving over her collarbones, his lips tasting her neck. She tipped her chin up to give him room and whispered, "God, Vlad, I want you so much."

"And I want you, Elisabeta."

It was like being doused in ice water. She went stiff, then drove her hands between them and shoved at his chest.

He stopped kissing her and lifted his head, his eyes glowing with passion and beginning to cloud with confusion. She could feel how aroused he was — he was hard and pressing against her thigh.

"Get off." She shoved him again.

"Tempest —"

"Exactly. I'm Tempest. I'm Stormy Jones. But that's not who you were making love to just now, is it, Vlad? That's not the woman you want. It's her. Elisabeta. Not me."

"You can be her. You will be. Don't you

see that?"

"No. No, I'm not, never was and never will be. She's trying to take over my body without my permission, and just now, Vlad, you came damn close to doing the same thing. Using me so you could have her, or fool yourself into believing you had her. You don't want me at all, do you?"

He rose slowly, pushed a hand through his hair, paced away from her. "If I've hurt you, I'm sorry."

"No one hurts me," she said, sitting up and tugging her nightgown over her. "I'm way too tough for that, Vlad, so don't beat yourself up over it. I'm not some needy suicide case like your child bride was. Not even close." She got to her feet and started off through the forest.

"The castle is this way, Tempest."

Leave it to Dracula to ruin the perfect, pissed off, overly dramatic exit, she thought. Worst of all, if she turned around now, he was sure to see her tears. Because despite her denials, he had hurt her. Way more than made any sense whatsoever. She was an idiot where he was concerned.

"I need a minute. Go on ahead. I'll catch up."

"There are wolves."

"Yeah, well, I'm good and pissed off, so if they know what's good for them, they'll keep their distance." She strode off into the trees, just far enough to give herself the privacy to wipe the tears away. She waved a hand to create what she hoped was a drying breeze and blinked to get rid of any residual moisture. And she breathed, deeply and slowly, to try to convince her tight airways to open up a bit.

Finally she turned and, holding her head up, walked back to where she'd left him. And found him waiting there . . . with another woman.

She turned, and Stormy blinked as the question rolled from her lips. "Rhiannon?"

Rhiannon frowned at her, then shot her eyes back to Vlad. "You've made her cry already?"

"No one makes me cry," Stormy denied.

Rhiannon gave an exaggerated toss of her long, jet-black hair. She wore a floor-length dress that hugged her willowy form's every curve and might have been made of velvet. "This one could make the sphinx weep. There's no shame in it." Then she dismissed Vlad with a wave of her hand and turned to face Stormy. "I heard you'd been abducted by the Prince of Darkness himself. Thought I'd better . . . see for myself."

"I never knew you cared," Stormy muttered.

Rhiannon lifted her brows at the sarcasm in her voice. "I don't, particularly. But you happen to be one of those rare mortals I would, on occasion, lift a finger to help." She examined her own nails as she said it. They were long and bloodred. "Given that you're a friend of several of my dearest friends, I couldn't just leave you to fend for yourself."

"Fending for myself is what I do best."

"Maybe so. You do have a reputation for being tough — for a human. But be realistic, Stormy. It's not as if you could hold your own against Dracula."

"You might be surprised," Vlad said softly.

Rhiannon glanced his way, and when she looked at Stormy again, it was with speculation in her eyes. "Then perhaps I've come to rescue the wrong party? No matter. Vlad, could we please have this conversation in more appropriate surroundings? Traipsing through the wilds of Romania collecting nettles in the hem of my Givenchy gown is not my idea of a happy reunion."

"If I'd known you were coming —"

"Which begs the question, why didn't you? You're getting slow, Vlad. Not to sense another vampire making her way to you? It's disturbing. Makes me wonder just what has you so thoroughly . . . distracted."

He didn't reply, just began walking back toward the castle.

9

Footsteps in the hall let her know the others were on their way to begin the search. She was out of time to dwell on this, and she had to fight down the wave of nausea and the surreal feeling that made her dizzy. God, she'd been a fool sixteen years ago, to let herself fall in love with a man who didn't want her, except as a vessel for his dead lunatic of a wife.

But she'd been young then. She was older now, wiser, far stronger. And yet she was still a fool. She still wanted him. Still loved him.

She had never thought she would be one of those women she'd always secretly pitied. The type to fall for the wrong guy, to hold on to a man who didn't care a thing about her. Damn him, he was as stupid as she was, to cling for all these years to his obsession with a woman he'd barely even known.

She steadied herself, ejected the tape from

the machine, shut the power off and took the video back to her room before going to join Melina and Lupe in Brooke's room.

Her entire day was spent searching. They searched every nook and cranny of Athena House, searched the grounds and the basement, searched the nearby towns for any sign of Brooke. They started to examine Brooke's computer, but it proved to be no easy task, since the entire machine was password protected.

In fact, they were still trying to break into her files when the sun went down.

The three women were huddled around a desk in the mansion's library — not the secret, hidden one, but the one in the house itself. They were leaning over Brooke's laptop as Stormy tried keying in everything anyone could think of as a potential password. She looked up from her work to see that dusk was painting the sky beyond the windows in muted tones of plum and purple. She nodded stiffly, her decision made, got to her feet, and made a show of stretching the kinks from her back and shoulders.

"I need a break," she said.

Melina and Lupe frowned at her, but she stuck to her guns. "Keep trying if you want.

I'm going to get some air."

She left them there, thinking they surely had as good a chance of breaking the code without her as they did with her. They knew Brooke, after all. Stormy walked tiredly through the mansion, toward the back doors and out them. Then she circled the house until she stood on the grassy lawn underneath the bedroom she'd been using. Because that was where Vlad would come tonight. To her window. As soon as he woke, she thought.

She needed to talk to him. She needed to tell him about Brooke, and the missing ring and the rite. She had accused him of stealing the ring. Had even believed he might have been the one to leave it in her room, somehow stirring Elisabeta to life, knowing she herself would try to put it on. And though she knew that was his ultimate goal, she also knew he hadn't done it.

She wanted to tell him she'd been wrong about that. Despite everything, she felt compelled to tell him. And even if that wasn't logical, the rest was. She needed all the help she could get to find Brooke, and she knew that, with his powers, he would be more help than anyone else. Once they found the ring, she would find a way to keep it from him, to remove its curse and render it harmless. Right. All in the minuscule amount of time remaining.

She could keep her heart out of this and use her head. She *could*. She had to. Her life depended on it.

She hadn't explored this part of the lawn before. It bordered the gardens and featured a mammoth weeping willow tree whose tendrils dragged the ground on all sides. Curious, she parted the veil and stepped inside.

"I knew you'd come," a voice whispered.

But it wasn't Vlad's voice. It wasn't the voice of a vampire, and it wasn't the voice of a man. It was a woman's voice.

She rose from the concrete bench that sat at the base of the tree. Around them, the tendrils of the willow moved with the breath of the wind, whispering their secrets, whispering a warning. It seemed to Stormy they were urging her to turn and run.

"Brooke?" she asked. But the woman who stood there wasn't Brooke, though it was Brooke's body. This woman didn't stand like Brooke, didn't hold herself the same way. And her eyes were black as jet.

"Not anymore," she said. "Don't you recognize me, Tempest? I was sure you'd know me. We've been so close for so long, after all."

Stormy felt a cold chill race down her spine, and her gaze slid down to the woman's hand, where the ruby ring glistened from her finger. She tried to swallow, but her throat was too dry and too tight. "Elisabeta?" she whispered. "But . . . how?"

"How is unimportant," she said with a bright smile. "Aren't you relieved, Tempest? I didn't have to take your body from you after all."

Stormy took a single step backward, sensing danger. "Yes. Very relieved."

"Well, you shouldn't be." Elisabeta took a step closer, and Stormy backed up again. "I'm going to kill you anyway, Tempest. You've been sleeping with my husband, after all. And I don't intend to let you continue being a distraction to him."

She reached behind her and, in a flash, brought a huge blade around in front of her, then lunged.

Stormy dodged the blow but tripped over a root that thrust upward from the ground and fell on her back. A second later the other woman was straddling her, raising the blade over her head to bring it down on a collision course with Stormy's chest.

Vlad couldn't believe what he was seeing. A woman was leaning over Tempest, bringing a knife down toward her with furious force. He lunged toward them, even as Tempest jammed the heel of her hand into the woman's chin, snapping her jaw closed and her head backward so hard she tumbled off, rolling onto the ground, face down. And then Tempest scrambled to her feet. She kicked the woman in the rib cage as hard as she could, so hard the woman's body rose from the ground. Tempest delivered a second kick, flipping the woman onto her back. This time the knife went sailing through the air to land in the grass several yards away.

Tempest advanced, and Vlad thought she intended to kill the stranger. And then the woman on the ground spotted him, frozen there, amazed and unable to look away. She lifted a hand toward him. "Help me, Vlad. Please, don't let her kill me."

That voice. And those eyes.

He blinked in shock; then, as Tempest surged forward, he gripped her shoulders from behind, stopping her.

Tempest whirled on him, her eyes blazing with anger. "She tried to kill me just now!"

"Who is she?" he asked, his voice a whisper.

The woman on the ground struggled to sit up. "It's me, Vlad. It's Elisabeta. Don't you know me? I'm your wife."

He narrowed his eyes. "How . . . how could this . . . ?"

"Her name is Brooke," Tempest said, and she was a little breathless. "She's part of the Athena group. Vlad —"

His gaze was drawn to the woman, the stranger. His bride? Could it be?

Tempest gripped his shoulders and jerked him around to face her. "Listen to me, Vlad. I took the ring from the museum. It was me."

"You?"

"Yes, but only because she was in control. Elisabeta took over. I didn't even know until I woke this morning to find her running the show again. She was about to put it on me."

He frowned, searching her face.

"We were going to put it into the vault, where it would be safe. But Brooke stole it and also the rite, which was here all the time, locked away. Brooke thought somehow it could give her immortality for herself. She must have performed the rite."

He couldn't stop looking from her to the strange woman with the familiar voice and eyes. "So my Beta lives . . . in that body. Not in yours."

Tempest stared at him for a long, long moment. He felt her eyes on him but didn't meet them, because his gaze was focused on the other woman.

"Yeah, Vlad. She's not in my body anymore. She's not going to take over every time you get close to me."

Elisabeta sent him a watery smile, and his heart contracted in his chest. It was a familiar smile. So much about her was familiar.

"It's been so long," she whispered. "I love you, Vlad. I've always loved you. I need you now, more than ever before. Please don't desert me, not now."

"I would never desert you, Beta."

"I'm hurt. *She* hurt me."

He moved forward, reaching out a hand, and Elisabeta took it and let him help her to her feet. She brushed herself off.

"Poor thing. I shouldn't have done that, huh, Vlad?" Stormy asked. The sarcasm in her tone was clear, and, finally, he looked her way. She was furious. "I suppose I should have just let her sink that blade into my heart." She shrugged. "Then again, you're doing a pretty decent job of that all by yourself."

She turned and started to walk away.

Vlad released Elisabeta's hand.

"Vlad!"

He glanced back to see his bride sinking

to the ground again, bending nearly double and hugging her own middle, where Tempest had kicked her hard enough to fracture her ribs.

He looked to Tempest again, then back to Elisabeta.

"Go ahead," Tempest said. "Look, this is over as far as I'm concerned. She's out of me. That's all I wanted. The rite has been performed — successfully, by the looks of things. I'm not going to die. What you do with her is totally up to you. I could care less." She sent a glare back at Elisabeta. "But if you come near me again, I'll fucking kill you. No question. And no one, not even Dracula himself, will stop me. Got that, bitch?"

Elisabeta didn't answer, just sank to her knees, weeping.

"Yeah, that's what I thought. Brooke would have decked me for that." She met Vlad's eyes. "Not that she doesn't deserve whatever your innocent little bride there did to her, Vlad, but you might want to find out what happened to Brooke before you two head off on your delayed honeymoon."

She spun on her heel and strode toward the house.

Vlad needed time to process what was happening here. How could Elisabeta be alive in the body of this woman, this Brooke?

But right then, he could only focus on one thing. His wife was hurt, and she needed him. He couldn't just walk away and leave her lying there in the grass, bleeding and broken. He *couldn't*.

He let Tempest go and turned to Beta. He slid his arms beneath her, picked her up and carried her away, off the grounds of Athena House.

The pain lancing her heart was almost too much, Stormy thought, as she walked firmly and purposefully into the mansion. Just inside the doors, she stopped, then stood gripping the doorframe, waiting for the weakness to pass from her knees. She'd never wanted anything the way she wanted him. But she'd been deluding herself. For sixteen years she had hoped that Vlad would realize she was the one he wanted. That he would be with her if he could.

But now that he could, he had chosen to be with Elisabeta, instead.

"Fine," she said, lifting her head and swiping away the tears with an angry hand. "I hope they fucking rot together. I'm done with this."

"That's the tough little mortal I've grown to . . . tolerate."

She blinked past the hot moisture in her eyes to focus on Rhiannon. The vampiress stood halfway across the sunroom, between two tropical plants, with the steam from the hot tub forming a misty backdrop. A photographer couldn't have posed her more effectively, as she stood there in a dress of paper-thin red silk, draping from her shoulders to the floor.

"Now stop the weeping and tell me what's happened."

Stormy sniffed and shook her head. "It's over, that's all. I'm sorry you came all the way out here for nothing."

"Did I?"

Stormy nodded, stiffened her spine and lifted her chin. "Yeah. You were right about Brooke, Rhiannon. How did you know?"

"We'll get to that. What has the little traitor done this time?"

"Stolen the ring. And the scroll. Turns out the damned Sisterhood had it all along, locked up in a vault. I guess our pal Elisabeta decided Brooke was an easier mark, because she's taken over *her* body now."

Rhiannon's eyebrows arched. "Elisabeta is corporeal?"

"Sure as hell felt corporeal when she tried to kill me a few minutes ago."

Rhiannon gasped, but Stormy waved a

hand. "Don't worry. I kicked her ass and sent her packing."

"Well, that goes without saying, doesn't it? And where is Vlad?" Rhiannon asked.

"Last I saw him, he was carrying her away. Probably helping her lick her wounds. I'm done with the both of them."

"I only wish that could be true. For your sake, if not for Vlad's."

Stormy shook her head. "It *is* true. I'm packing my shit and leaving. I no longer have any reason to stay involved in this mess. Let him deal with her."

"Stormy, it's not over." Rhiannon stopped speaking then and turned toward the doorway from the sunroom to the main part of the house. "We have company."

Before she finished speaking, Melina and Lupe appeared. They came to an abrupt halt when they spotted Rhiannon.

"Well," she said in her menacing purr — a purr that could become a growl without warning. "We meet again. Hello, Melina."

"Rhiannon."

Lupe just stared, her eyes wide but watchful. Finally she managed to tear her gaze from Rhiannon's to focus on Stormy. Then she frowned. "What happened to you?"

"Later. Did you manage to get into Brooke's computer files?"

"Yeah. The password was *immortality.*"

Rhiannon sniffed. "Brooke has been obsessed with obtaining it for quite some time," she said. "And I suppose part of the blame for this mess belongs with my friends and I, for not telling you of her duplicity long ago."

"The Stiles incident," Melina said. "We found her notes in her computer, only a few minutes ago. She had planned to steal the formula Frank Stiles developed — the one he believed would make an ordinary mortal, immortal."

"Yes." Rhiannon waited, saying no more.

"Would it have worked?"

It *had* worked. Stormy knew that, because the vampires had used it to save the life of Willem Stone. And they'd learned how to recreate the formula, so that he could live as long as any of them. But she hadn't known the Athena group had been involved in any way with that case.

"Stiles is dead now, according to all reports," Rhiannon said. "So apparently his formula didn't work as he'd hoped."

Melina nodded slowly, sensing, perhaps, that there was more to the story than what she was being told. Stormy knew instinctively that Rhiannon would never reveal the secret of Willem Stone. And she thought she knew why. The Sisterhood would likely see him as a breach of their precious supernatural order. They might decide to do something about it.

"Why didn't your friends tell me, if they knew Brooke was trying to steal the formula? They must have known that was a betrayal of everything our order stands for."

Rhiannon shrugged. "You'd have to ask them."

"Why didn't *you* tell me, Rhiannon?"

She shrugged. "Because I don't trust any of you any more than I trust Brooke," Rhiannon said. "Besides, does it really matter at this point?"

"What else was in the files?" Stormy asked. "Anything about the ring or the scroll?" She told herself she no longer cared, but she thought a new topic might break some of the tension mounting in the room.

Melina nodded, allowing herself to be distracted for the moment. "Brooke believed that when Elisabeta returned to life, she would return with some means of gaining immortality. Speculated that she might somehow imbue the host body with the Belladonna Antigen that Brooke believed Elisabeta had possessed during the course of her natural lifetime, enabling her to become a vampire."

"That wouldn't do Brooke any good, though," Stormy said.

"Brooke thought it would," Lupe said. "She was convinced Elisabeta could co-exist with another soul in the same body. She was willing to share her own body in exchange for eternal life." Lupe lowered her head. "My God, she intends to put on that ring and perform the rite. She means to bring Elisabeta into her own body."

"She's already done it," Stormy said.

The other two women gaped at her. She nodded and went on. "I just ran into her outside. Only she wasn't Brooke. She was one hundred percent Elisabeta. And I don't know about you, but I *know* that one. I've lived with her for a long time now, and I know damn well she has no intention of sharing that body with Brooke."

"She couldn't if she wanted to," Rhiannon said. "Two souls cannot long occupy the same body."

"Mine did," Stormy said. "She's been living in me for years."

"Yes, because the ring kept her from moving on. Brooke has no such anchor. She's surrendered her own body. In your body, Tempest, Elisabeta could only lurk and wait and occasionally take control. She wasn't strong enough to drive you out, and the power of the ring kept her from moving on. But Brooke has given herself over. Her own soul will shrivel, weaken and fade."

"How soon?" Melina asked.

"Melina?" Lupe was searching her mentor's eyes, her own huge and brown and full of questions.

"How soon?" Melina repeated, ignoring Lupe's unspoken question.

Rhiannon shrugged. "A few days, at most."

"Can we save her?"

"Why would we want to?" Lupe all but shouted her question. "Melina, she betrayed us. She betrayed the Sisterhood. She hit you over the head and left you lying there. Why would you want to help her now?"

Melina lowered her eyes. "I don't expect you to understand."

"No one could understand. It doesn't make any sense," Lupe said.

"To me it does." Melina looked to Rhiannon again. "Can we save Brooke?"

"Only by exorcising Elisabeta. And only after releasing the hold the ring has over her, so she can move on." Rhiannon lowered her head.

"I thought the ring's hold was dead, now that Brooke has performed the rite," Stormy said.

"Not entirely, I fear," Rhiannon replied. "If we free Elisabeta from Brooke's body, chances are the ring would still keep her from moving on as she should. She might very well return to your body, Stormy. The ring's powers are that strong. We need to be sure."

"What if we can't do it?" Stormy asked.

Rhiannon bit her lip. "Then they'll both die. Brooke will move on, and Elisabeta will once again be trapped by the power of that ring. Stormy, it's your body Elisabeta needs. You are her spiritual descendant, I am convinced of this. You're spun from the same collective soul. What she's done, it's like . . . like performing an organ transplant between two incompatible patients. It cannot take. It cannot last."

Stormy lowered her head. "Well, good luck with that. I'm out of here. This no longer concerns me."

"I'm afraid it does, Stormy."

Stormy met Rhiannon's eyes, praying the vampiress had no rational argument to give.

"She'll realize soon enough that Brooke's body cannot hold her. And when she does, she'll come for yours. She still has the ring and the scroll."

And Vlad, Stormy thought. She has Vlad, too. And if he realized his precious wife was dying in Brooke's body, that she needed *hers* to survive, he might very well come for it himself.

Tough as she was, she knew she wouldn't stand a chance. Not against both of them.

"And there's the deadline. If her soul isn't at peace, either fully re-established in a living body or fully relieved of the burden of physical life, she'll die. And so will you, Stormy. Tuesday. Midnight."

Stormy closed her eyes, lowered her head. "Fine. I'm in. But I'm not interested in saving Brooke. She got what she asked for, as far as I'm concerned." She recalled Lupe's words earlier, about her having no idea what would happen to her if Melina found out she had shared the Sisterhood's secrets with Stormy. "And from what I understand about the Sisterhood of Athena's rules and regs," she went on, "she's going to end up being executed anyway. Am I right about that?"

Melina gaped briefly, then looked away, refusing to answer.

"So I'm right on that one. There's no point. No one leaves this organization. And I'm not interested in freeing Elisabeta, so her soul can move on to eternal bliss. All I want to do is kill the bitch. Once and for all. I want her dead."

210

"It amounts to the same thing," Rhiannon said.

"Then let's do it."

"We're going to have to get her here," Rhiannon said. "We need to convince Vlad. And I think, Stormy, that you are the only one who can do that."

She lowered her head. "He won't listen to me."

"I think he will." The vampire shrugged. "I've been wondering, Stormy, why it is I like you, when I have little tolerance for most of your kind. And I've come to the reluctant conclusion that it's because you remind me of myself."

Stormy met the woman's dark eyes. "Is that a compliment?"

"Well, it was. But I'm wondering now if I was wrong about that. Because, frankly, I would never stand by and let some other woman walk away with the man I loved. I would fight."

Stormy sighed. "I've been fighting Elisabeta for sixteen years."

"Yes, you have. So what's one more night?"

She thought about that for a long moment; then, finally, she nodded, knowing Rhiannon was right. She was going to love Vlad forever, win or lose. She might as well give it one last try. Pride be damned. Her life was on the line here. "What do you want me to do?"

"Go to him. He's staying at a house, a vacant one, two miles north along this very road. I sensed his presence there when I arrived. Go to him, Stormy. Talk to him. Make him see that this is the only way."

She licked her lips, then nodded. "I think I'll walk. I could use the air."

10

As Stormy walked in the clear, warm night, she felt the rush in her mind as more of Vlad's blocks fell away and more memories of her time with him sixteen years ago returned.

She and Vlad had returned to the castle with Rhiannon, to find Rhiannon's mate, Roland, there waiting for them. Roland had, she recalled, coaxed Stormy into taking him for a drive into the local village for a proper meal. Partly to give Rhiannon time to speak to Vlad in private, Stormy suspected, and partly to give Roland time to speak to her; to ascertain for certain whether Vlad was holding her against her will. She had assured him that wasn't the case.

But as they'd driven back, along the winding road to the castle, she'd seen something that had hit her hard. A meadow, with an old foundation crumbling in one corner. She'd stopped the car and gotten out, compelled beyond reason. And then she'd blacked out.

When she roused again, Roland had been carrying her into Vlad's castle. And then . . .

She felt weak, sick, achy. Her body was limp, her head down, supported against Roland's shoulder, and her eyes refused to stay open for more than a heartbeat at a time.

"What the hell happened?" Vlad demanded.

"Damned if I know, my friend."

Vlad took her from Roland as he spoke, then turned and carried her into the castle. He laid her on the chaise, hands going to her cheeks as she felt his senses probing her mind. "Tell me everything, Roland."

"Of course. We had dinner, talked a bit. She seemed perfectly all right. Healthy, strong. But on the way back here . . ." Roland paused, and Stormy forced her eyes open in time to see Vlad shoot him a look, one that begged the rest of the tale.

Rhiannon sucked in a breath. "By the gods, Roland, what happened to your face?"

Roland touched his own face, and for the first time Stormy noted the four long scratches that ran from high on his cheek nearly to his jaw.

"Roland?" Vlad prompted.

"I don't know what happened, Vlad. She stopped the car and got out, hurrying into a meadow to examine an old foundation. I went after her, naturally. She seemed . . . distressed. Kept saying, 'She's coming.' And then . . . then she changed."

"In what way, Roland?" Rhiannon asked.

"In every way," Roland whispered. "Her voice, her stance, her scent. The color of her eyes turned to black, and she began speaking in a language I do not know. But I'm certain it was Italic."

"Romanian," Vlad said softly. He was stroking her hair now, leaning in close to watch her face, willing her to come more fully awake with his mind. She felt it but was too weak to obey. "It's happened before." Vlad looked away from Tempest only long enough to glance at the other man. "She put those scratches on your face?"

"Yes, when I tried to keep her from running off into the forest." He frowned. "She was strong, Vlad. Stronger than a mortal should be."

"It's exactly as Maxine described," Rhiannon said. "Is this an example of how your precious Elisabeta's spirit is melding with Stormy's own? By taking control from her? By attacking a friend?"

He continued stroking Stormy's face, her neck. "Wake up, Tempest. Wake now."

"Vlad, I do not remember your bride as being either violent or strong," Rhiannon said. "This is more like some kind of possession."

He shook his head. "Beta is confused and frustrated. Five hundred years she's been trying to find her way back to me. And now that she thinks she has, Tempest insists on fighting her."

"Perhaps for good reason."

Tempest blinked slowly and opened her eyes more fully. "I'm . . . I'm okay." She sat up slightly and pressed the heel of her hand to her forehead, closing her eyes tightly. "I remember seeing a foundation in a meadow and feeling compelled to explore it more closely. I pulled over, and Roland and I —" She stopped there and shot a look at Roland, then quickly lowered her head. "I did that to your face. I'm sorry."

"I don't believe it was you at all, Stormy," Roland said.

"It wasn't. Not really." She glanced at Vlad. "What made her come through so strongly?"

Vlad shook his head in apparent bewilderment, then glanced at Roland again. "Where was this foundation?"

"Off the main road, if you can call that dirt track a road," Roland said. "About a half mile down, where the forest ends, there's a large meadow with the foundation of a house in one corner."

Vlad closed his eyes and said nothing.

"The house," Tempest said softly. "It was her house. Elisabeta's."

"Yes, it was." Vlad looked at Rhiannon. "Do you still think I'm wrong?"

"In so many ways," she replied. "If this invading spirit is that of Elisabeta, Vlad, she is not the woman you remember. She has changed, warped, twisted."

"You're the one who is wrong."

She met his eyes, then moved closer to Tempest, leaned over her, clasped her hand. "Come back with us, Tempest. Let me find a way to exorcise this creature from you once and for all."

Tempest sat up and swung her legs around to put her feet on the floor. She looked at Vlad, searched his face. He couldn't seem to hold her gaze. Guilt? Did he know full well what he was doing to her? she wondered. Did he know Rhiannon was right?

"It will be dawn soon," he said softly. "There wouldn't be time to leave tonight, even if she wanted to."

"Dawn has no impact on her, Vlad," Roland said. "Our jet is waiting at the landing strip fifteen miles from here, with instructions to take her home should she show up asking to leave, with or without us." He looked at Tempest again. "You can go if you wish it,

Stormy. We'll join you as soon as we can."

Vlad pushed his hands through his hair and paced away. "Dammit, why won't you stay out of this?"

"Because you'll destroy her, Vlad," Rhiannon said. "How many more of these episodes do you think she can withstand? Look at her!"

He whirled on her, his eyes blazing. "I'll destroy *you* if you continue to interfere!"

Roland stepped between the two, and Vlad hit him, a single, powerful blow that sent the man sailing across the room, where he hit a stone wall and sank to the floor. Rhiannon launched herself at Vlad then, growling like a wildcat as she swung both fists into his chest and put him flat on his back as surely as if he'd been hit by a wrecking ball.

She came on as he struggled to get upright. But then Tempest was on her feet, shouting, her voice deep and strong, despite the weakness still invading her body. "Stop it! Stop it now, all of you!"

Rhiannon froze and turned slowly to stare at her. Vlad remained where he was, on his back on the floor, and Roland lifted his head, but not his body, from where it had come to rest.

"Don't you think it should be up to me whether I leave or not? And how I decide to deal with this presence? It's my problem, after all. My life. Why are you all arguing over what

I should do when the decision is no one's —
no one's — but my own."

She crossed the room to where Vlad lay on
the his back and extended a hand to him. He
took it, searching her face. She knew full well
he had no intention of letting her go, not yet.
Not until she remembered. He was obsessed
with his damned dead bride. But Stormy had
her own reasons for staying. She needed to
solve this thing.

And she hoped he would come to his senses
and decide to let Elisabeta go at long last.
That he would come to love *her,* instead.

She helped him to his feet, then turned to
walk away from him, and knelt in front of Roland. "Are you all right?"

He nodded, and she helped him up, as well,
frowning as she cocked her head to glance at
the back of his. "He has a bit of a gash here,
Rhiannon. You should bandage it before you
rest. Do you two have a place to stay tonight?"

Her meaning was clear in her tone, she
thought. They were not to stay here.

"We have accommodations on the jet. Quite
luxurious ones, actually." Rhiannon came to
check Roland's head wound as she spoke.
She touched it, and Roland sucked air through
his teeth. Rhiannon shot Vlad a narrow-eyed
glare. "I should kill you for this."

"No one's killing anyone," Tempest said.

"You two should go if you want to make it to the jet before sunrise."

"And you?" Roland asked.

Vlad watched her, awaiting her answer, and she knew damn well he would keep her with him by force if he had to. Or anyway he would try.

"I'm staying," she said. "One more night. I gave my word." She turned to Vlad. "Just as you gave yours that you'd see me safely back home after that. And I'm holding you to it, Vlad." She also knew he had no intention of letting her go until he was damn good and ready. But she had to at least pretend to believe. God forbid he should ever realize what a fool she was to have fallen for him so hard.

Stormy turned back to the others. "I'll be fine. You see?"

"Oh, I see, Stormy. But do you?" Rhiannon had her fingertips pressed to Roland's head to keep it from bleeding. "Do you understand who you're dealing with? This is Dracula, child. And if he decides to keep you here, no power on earth will set you free."

She blinked, then turned to Vlad, her eyes probing his. "I trust him," she lied. "He'll keep his word."

"And if he doesn't?"

She shrugged. "Then it'll be my mistake,

won't it?"

Rhiannon scowled at her. "God save us from spunky mortals with more courage than brains," she muttered. "Courage won't help you in this, Stormy."

"It's never let me down before."

Sighing, Rhiannon seemed to give up. "If someone can locate a bandage, we'll be on our way."

Vlad nodded toward a cabinet visible just through an open door at one end of the room. "I always have a supply on hand."

"As do we," Rhiannon snapped. "But we left ours on the jet, never dreaming we'd have need of it here — in the home of my own sire."

"Sire?" Stormy asked with a gasp. "Vlad, you . . . you're the vampire who made Rhiannon?"

"I am. Though there are times when I sorely regret it."

Rhiannon left, then returned in a moment with adhesive strips and gauze, which she applied to Roland's head. Then she took his hand, and, without a goodbye, they headed for the door.

Rhiannon stopped there and turned briefly, but she spoke to Tempest, not to Vlad. "If you're not back in the States in a reasonable period, we'll be back." She slanted a look at Vlad. "And we won't be alone."

"Oh?" he asked, his tone sarcastic. "Bringing along an army of vampires, are you? Enough to set Dracula straight?"

"I won't need to bring them, Vlad. There are vampires everywhere. More than an antisocial creature like yourself could even imagine. And while they are different, there's one thing they pretty much have in common. One value we all share, by unspoken mutual agreement. We don't do harm to mortals or meddle in their lives. And we don't tolerate rogues who do."

"You protect The Chosen. Isn't that meddling?"

"Tempest is not one of The Chosen."

"And yet you're here, meddling."

"I'm here to prevent you from destroying her. And in the process, yourself."

Vlad averted his eyes. "Doesn't matter."

"Yes, Vlad. It does." She sighed and opened the door, walked through and, without looking back, spoke to him one last time. "What you've done this night will not be undone. Goodbye, Vlad."

He didn't respond, only watched as the door banged closed, apparently on its own, and then turned to Tempest. "Thank you," he said.

"For what?"

"For trusting me."

"Do you think I'm an idiot?" she snapped. "Hell, Vlad, I don't trust you as far as I can

222

throw you. Not when I know perfectly well whose side you're on in this . . . this war of mine. I just wanted to get rid of them so we could get on with this. I still think the answers to my issues might lie here, in this place and, maybe, in you."

His face turned angry. He took her arm and started for the stairs. "Tonight," he said, "we share the bed."

"Fine by me."

She knew he saw what she tried to hide. The flash of desire, of longing, of hunger in her eyes. She wanted him, even now.

She shuttered the desire, hid the ripple of delicious fear, buried them both in sarcasm. "You'll be dead to the world in twenty minutes, anyway."

"But very much alive again come sundown, Tempest."

She stopped halfway up the stairs, turning to spear him with her eyes. "Are you trying to frighten me into running away, Vlad? Into taking off as soon as you sleep, finding that jet and begging its pilot to take me home?"

He stared into her eyes. "Believe me when I tell you, frightening you away is not what I want."

"Then knock it off with the idle threats, okay?"

"My threats, Tempest, are far from idle. And

I don't think you will mind at all when I carry them out."

Vlad carried Elisabeta, in Brooke's body, to the house a few miles away where he'd holed up for the night, and where he'd sensed the presence of a mortal upon waking this very evening. Even without his heightened senses he would have known that someone had been there. There had been shards of broken glass on the floor. Curved, as if from a wine glass. And the small rickety wooden table had been moved, and bore the soft drippings of a recently burned candle. A black candle. Which suggested workings of negative magick.

The scent that lingered was that of a woman.

This woman, he realized now. Though not precisely this one. She was different now. She was *Elisabeta* now.

He took her into the house, but not down the basement stairs to where he'd set up a secure haven. Instead, he carried Elisabeta into the back part of the house, where a sofa was covered in a filthy sheet. Then he yanked the sheet away, relieved that the fabric beneath it appeared far cleaner.

"Here now," he said, lowering her down onto the cushions. "Just rest. Are you still in pain?" He lifted her blouse to just below her breasts, to see the bruises already darkening the skin that covered her ribs.

"It's . . . it's better now," she said, her accent slighter than it had been. He supposed she'd had sixteen years of listening while she lived inside Tempest.

"I forgot how much it hurts to be . . . alive," Beta said.

He frowned as he drew his gaze from her bruised ribs to her face. Her meaning, he knew, went beyond the physical pain she had been dealt this night.

"Is it as bad for you?" she asked. "Pain, I mean. Hurting?"

"Worse."

"Worse?"

He nodded, lowering her shirt again. "In vampires, sensation is magnified. Pain included."

"God, how will I bear it?"

His eyes shot to hers. "How will you —"

"But you heal fast, don't you? Every ache and pain goes away as soon as the sun comes up. And when you wake again, you're as good as new. That's the way it works, isn't it?"

"Yes."

She nodded. "It's starting to feel better." She smiled at him and tried to sit up a little.

"When will you do it?"

"Do what, Beta?"

"Change me, of course. I want you to make me immortal. A vampire, like you."

He stared at her, shook his head slowly as what she was saying became clear to him. And only then did he realize what he hadn't before. He smelled it on her, sensed it on her. The Belladonna Antigen. But it was different somehow. Weak. Thin. Altered in some way.

Brooke had not possessed it before. Of that he was certain. Had The Chosen been so close, he would have sensed it at once.

"It has to be done in just the right way, Beta. At just the right time."

She clasped his shoulder and drew herself nearer to him, brushing her lips over his jaw and cheek. "When will that be?"

"I don't know." Her mouth slid around to his, and for a moment he kissed her. But then he clasped her shoulders and held her while he tugged his mouth from hers. "Beta, we have to talk."

"But I've missed you so, Vlad. I don't want to wait."

"It won't be long. But if you want to be made over —"

"All right." She pursed her lips, then turned so that she was sitting up on the old sofa and leaned back against it. "What is it you need to know?"

He nearly sagged in relief. "Tell me about Brooke."

Her head came up, eyes narrow. *"Brooke?"*

"It's her body you're using, Beta. I need to know about it. She . . . wasn't one of The Chosen. I'd have known if one were that close."

"Oh, no. Do you mean . . . ?"

"No, love, no. I sense the antigen in you." He stared at her. "I suppose you must have brought it with you somehow."

She smiled. "Maybe I did."

"But it's not full blown, Beta. It's not strong. I'm not sure it's quite the same. The transformation might not work."

"Or it might."

"If it fails, you'll die, Beta."

She blinked rapidly. "Well, we don't want that." Then she frowned at him. "Are you sure you're telling me the truth, Vlad?"

"Why would I lie?"

Shrugging, she watched his face carefully. "Because of her, of course."

"Who? Brooke?"

"Tempest."

He shook his head. "She no longer has anything to do with this."

"She does if you're in love with her. If

you've decided you'd rather be with her than me. I've waited five hundred years, Vlad."

"You didn't wait at all, Elisabeta. Not even three days. You believed them when they told you I'd been killed on our wedding night, and you flung yourself to your death."

"A living death," she whispered. "Trapped, like being buried alive. You did that to me."

"I was trying to save you."

"You destroyed me. All so you could have me back again. If you've decided you don't want me now, after all I've been through . . ."

"I haven't. I'm telling you the truth, Beta. We need to take some time, be sure you'll survive the change before we proceed." She didn't argue, so he pressed on. "Where is Brooke now?"

Beta sighed. "She's here, Vlad. Cowering inside this body. But she will not remain long. This I know."

"How do you know?"

"I simply do." She held his gaze; then, lowering her eyelids to half mast, she lay back on the sofa, her hands going to her blouse to open its buttons. "None of it matters. Not really. I'm here now. We can be together at last. The way we've both been waiting to be for all these years." She rose from the sofa, trailing her fingertips over his face. "Take me now, Vlad. Take my blood. Make me immortal."

He licked his lips, staring at her as she pushed the blouse apart, baring her breasts — no, some other woman's breasts. And he *did* want her. But he bent to snatch the sheet from the floor and draped it over her. "Not yet. You're not strong enough. There's something . . . not right."

Something changed then, in her eyes. Something dark came into them and shadowed her face. She backed away from him, and, moving so quickly he didn't seen it coming, she yanked out a blade she'd had hidden somewhere in the clothes she wore and drew it swiftly across her palm.

"Beta, don't!" He reached for her, but she danced away. Then she lifted her hand. Scarlet blood welled in her palm. His eyes fixed on it, and he couldn't look away as she moved closer again. And then she pressed her palm to his lips.

Hunger raged in him. He hadn't fed sufficiently in far too long. He had been obsessed with this situation to the exclusion of everything, including his own needs.

He closed his eyes, tasted the blood from Elisabeta's hand, and the bloodlust swelled in him. He gripped her wrist and licked a hot path over her palm, taking every droplet.

And then he drew away, his eyes narrow. "It's partly your blood, Beta. The Belladonna Antigen, the thing that made you one of The Chosen when you lived in your own body, it's there. But just barely. It's still partly Brooke's blood, coursing in your veins. She didn't have the antigen. You know this."

"How would I possibly know?"

He shook his head. "It doesn't matter. I know. She didn't have it, or I would have sensed it the moment I set foot in this town, much more so on the grounds of Athena House. She didn't have it, and now that you've taken possession of her body, she does. But only slightly."

"It's enough. It has to be enough. Make me over, Vlad. Make me what you are." She stared up at him, her eyes pleading.

"It wouldn't work. Not like this."

She lowered her head and turned away from him. "I don't believe you."

"Beta, I'm telling you the truth. If I try to change you now, this body you've stolen will simply die. I'm sure of it."

"I didn't steal it! It was given to me." Blinking, she turned and stared up at him. "Do you still love me, Vlad? Do you still love me at all?"

"I'll always love you."

"Then prove it to me." She moved closer, slid her hands, one of which was now wrapped in a handkerchief, up the front of his shirt, tugged at the buttons there. "Show me you love me and not her. Do it now." She reached up to kiss his neck, to bite it and tug at the skin there. "Prove it to me," she whispered, pressing her hips to his.

Vlad closed his eyes, his hands lowering to her shoulders and then to her waist.

She tipped her head up for a kiss, and he couldn't refuse her, not with the longing and hope he saw in her eyes. He kissed her. Her fingers twisted in his hair. She sucked his tongue, drove hers into his mouth and kissed him with a fervor he'd never felt in her before. And when she broke the kiss, she pressed his head to her throat. "It *is* me you love. I knew it. Take me, darling. It's been so long."

Very gently, he pulled free of her.

"What's wrong, my love?" She blinked up at him, searching his face. "Is it this body? Is it not to your liking?"

"No, it's not that." There was nothing unattractive about the body Elisabeta occupied. Brooke's body.

"I can't do this. Not now, Beta. You're far too weak." And even as he said it, he felt like the worst kind of hypocrite. He'd taken women before. But not like this. In the past, when he'd needed to feed, he'd lured women to him, used the power of his mind to ease every inhibition in theirs and then ascertained the depths of their desire.

Sometimes he only drank. Other times, he took them in every imaginable way, but only if he sensed that, deep down, they wanted it. And always he left them with no memory of what had transpired.

This was different. He couldn't reach Brooke's mind, because Elisabeta was in control of it. He couldn't test her desire, because Elisabeta was ruling her body. But she would be aware. A captive inside her own body. He'd heard Tempest describe it enough times. And even he, even Dracula, wouldn't stoop so low. He'd never needed to.

"I do not understand you. What could be wrong with —"

"It would be a rape, Elisabeta. It's not your body. Brooke —"

"Who cares about Brooke? She will be dead soon enough. She is not coming back, Vlad. It won't matter at all."

He frowned down at her.

"I have what I needed from her. A body. I would have preferred the other one but —"

"How can you sure Brooke's soul will leave this body?" he asked. Partly to change the topic, and partly because he needed to know exactly what was happening.

"I do not know *how* I know, only that my soul has taken this body, fully taken it. I can feel her weakening, even now. She will be dead in a few days. She will move on to some other realm. She cannot last."

"Why not?" Vlad asked. "You did. You lasted years inside Tempest's body, even though she was in control."

"Yes, but I *could not* move on. I was bound, Vlad, by the power of the ring."

"I see."

"If that little bitch would simply have died as she ought to have . . . But I do not wish to talk about her. Or even to hear her name again."

He frowned. "She's a part of you. A part of all of this."

"I hate her," she said. "I wish her dead. When I am a vampire, she will be my first kill." As she said it, she smiled slowly, but her smile froze, perhaps at the look of surprise she must have seen in his eyes.

"Oh, Vlad, darling, don't look that way. Death is not horrible. I used to think it was, when I was young and naive. I howled in pain when my family died of the plague.

My brothers. My baby sister. I wanted to die with them. But now I understand so much more. Death is . . . it's a lie. There is nothing to fear in it. When you kill someone, they do not stop existing. They only . . . move out of the way." She sighed, smiling wistfully. "To be a vampire — it must be like being a god," she whispered.

"No, Beta. It's not like being a god."

"Oh, but it is. I've been paying attention all these years. Tempest, she deals with your kind all the time. You never die."

"We can die, just as anyone else can. Only the means are different. Fire, or loss of blood, or sunlight —"

"You can read minds. Influence the thoughts of mortals."

"So can some mortals," he said. "There's nothing so godlike about those skills."

"Vampires have the power of life and death in their hands."

"As does any criminal with a handgun," he told her. "We're not animals, Beta. We don't kill simply because we can."

She frowned up at him. "I do not remember this side of you."

"What side?"

She shrugged. "Vlad, this is not who you are."

"Not who I was, perhaps. But, Beta, it's

been centuries. Perhaps I've changed."

"It's more than that. You refuse to make love to me, and it has nothing to do with the simpering ghost of a spirit still clinging by a strand to this body. It's *her.* It's Tempest."

"She has nothing to do with this. I told you, I've changed." He studied her. "You've changed, too."

"Yes, well, being imprisoned for a few centuries will do that to a person." She turned and started across the room toward the door.

Vlad gripped her shoulders to stop her. "Where are you going?"

"If you will not change me, Vlad, I'll find some other vampire who will. Trust me, I know where to find them. I learned a lot while I was trapped inside Tempest Jones."

She pulled free, but he gripped her arm again. "Dammit, Beta, don't leave like this."

She turned so fast that he didn't see it coming, didn't see her hand drawing the knife she'd tucked into the pants she wore. But he felt it. The blade sank deep into his belly.

Vlad's entire body erupted in pain. His eyes went wide, then bulged as he clutched his middle and fell to his knees.

"Well, what do you know? You were telling the truth about that much, at least. You *do* feel pain more intensely than mortals." She tipped her head to one side. "Is it true, what Tempest believes? That the older the vampire, the more heightened his senses? Because, if it is, that must *really* hurt."

She shrugged, then dropped to her knees so she was at eye level with him again. He struggled to speak but couldn't form a word. The pain was too much.

"I can help you, Vlad. I can bandage that up for you and feed you from my own body. *If* you will transform me. Make me what you are, what I was born to be."

"It would kill you," he told her. "I can't be the cause of that, Beta."

She shrugged and got to her feet again. "Then . . . goodbye."

11

The front door slammed open, and Vlad lifted his head, trying to blink past the red haze of pain to see who was there. And then he knew, even before he saw her. He *felt* her.

Tempest. Her wide eyes swept the room, came to rest upon him, where he knelt on the floor, clutching his belly and bleeding, and then turned their full fury on Elisabeta.

"What the *hell* did you do?"

Elisabeta turned from where she'd been standing, and studying Vlad as if she'd never seen a bleeding man before. She faced Tempest, and her stance became stiffer. "Why are you here?" she asked. "Can't you see that my husband and I are having a long overdue reunion?"

"Yeah, I can see that."

"She has a knife, Tempest." Vlad managed to force out the words.

"I see that, too," she said. Then she

stepped and turned, and lashed out with one foot, then the other. The two kicks were delivered powerfully, rapidly. The first sent the blade flying from Elisabeta's hand, and the second connected with her borrowed jaw.

Beta's head snapped back, and her body jerked before she hit the floor. Tempest didn't bother with her any further. Instead she turned and hurried to Vlad. Dropping to her knees, she gripped his blood-soaked shirt in her hands and ripped it open without taking time to unbutton it. He saw the way her lips thinned, the way her eyes flickered when they fixed on the wound in his gut. But she didn't give her reaction any more time than she'd given Beta. Instead, she tugged off the shirt she wore, revealing the T-shirt she had on underneath. She balled up her white button down shirt and held it to his belly.

"Press it to the wound. Press it *hard,* Vlad."

Behind her! He started to speak a warning, but before he made even a sound, Tempest sprang up, turned and slammed the heel of her hand to Beta's chin, then the other hand, then the first again, in a rapid fire assault that had Beta's head snapping like a punching bag. With the final blow, blood spurted from Beta's nose.

Beta shrieked, clutching her face and backing away. "*Tarva!* Bitch!" she cried as she blinked in shock at the pain and the blood on her hands. "I will kill you! I swear I will kill you if it's the last thing I do."

"Yeah, I'm worried about that. I couldn't fight you before, Elisabeta. You were inside me. But you made a big mistake getting out, getting a body, because I *can* fight you now, and I damn well intend to."

"You'll never win."

"I already have." Tempest reached for her, gripped her arm and tugged her away from the door.

"Tempest," Vlad managed. "What are you going to do with her?"

She looked down at him, her eyes filled with what looked like blatant disbelief, but before she could answer, Elisabeta bit her hand, and when she jerked it away with a gasp, Beta whirled and ran from the house as fast as Brooke's legs would carry her.

Tempest lunged as if to give chase, then stopped herself, turning slowly back to him. "I should let you bleed out, you know that?"

He nodded once, slowly. "Give me a few more minutes and I'll oblige you."

"Shit."

He fell backward, too dizzy to remain on his knees, as retaining consciousness became

239

a struggle.

Stormy wished for her car and the heavy duty first-aid kit she kept in the trunk. In her line of work, it didn't pay to be without one. Vampires were bleeders. A lot of them were friends. And most of the people who knew of their existence would just as soon see them all dead.

But she'd decided to walk tonight, so she didn't have her car. She was just going to have to make do. She did have some supplies in her backpack.

She raced through the house in search of a kitchen or bathroom, glancing at her watch on the way. Not even eleven yet. There was a lot of time before dawn, when his wound would heal on its own. A lot of time — he could be dead before the sun rose.

Kitchen. Excellent, the water faucets worked. She peeled her T-shirt off over her head, and used her teeth to tear off the short sleeves. Then she put it back on, and soaked the sleeves in water.

Back in what she presumed to be the living room of the broken down house, she saw Vlad trying to get to his feet and shook her head. "Stay down. Just . . . stay down, or you'll make it worse."

"I thought . . . you'd gone after her."

"And leave you to die? I'm pretty pissed at you, but not quite that much." She sighed. "Sit down. Lean back against the wall there and let me see how bad it is."

He sank down, leaning back on the wall as she pushed his shirt off his shoulders and began wiping the blood away with the wet cloths. It didn't matter that she had no soap or antiseptic. It wasn't an infection that would kill him — it was the bleeding. But she had to be able to see the wound.

"Where did you learn to fight like that?"

"Hmm?" Kneeling, she straddled him and tried to quell the queasiness that washed over her at seeing so much blood coating his rippled abs.

"Martial arts moves," he said. "Flawlessly delivered."

"I'm a black belt in Tae Kwon Do."

Her hands were shaking as she continued to wash away the worst of the blood. It didn't do a lot of good, because there was more coming.

"I didn't know."

"I imagine there's a lot you don't know, Vlad. You couldn't possibly have watched my every move for the past sixteen years. Here," she said, pressing the wads of cloth to the wound. "Hold this tight."

He did, but she could see it was hurting him. As old as he was, he probably felt a splinter in his finger the way she would feel a knife wound. God help him. It was nothing compared to what was coming.

She'd dropped her mini-backpack by the door when she'd come in, just before she'd dropped Elisabeta close beside it. She went for it now, brought it back to where he lay and dug around inside. She might not have a full blown first-aid kit, but she wasn't entirely without resources.

Being prepared had become a way of life for her.

She pulled out a small packet that contained curved needles and silk thread. Vlad spied the needle when she took it out of the pack, averted his eyes and swore.

"I know. It's going to hurt like hell, but if I don't stitch this up, you won't last until dawn. I don't see any other way to stop the bleeding."

He nodded. "I know. It's all right, go ahead."

"I intend to."

She bent closer, pinched the edges of the still-bleeding wound together and jabbed the needle through his skin. Vlad's entire body tensed, and he sucked air through his teeth.

"Sorry," she muttered and quickly knotted the silk and prepared to make a second stitch.

It would only take six. Three would be plenty for a mortal, but this was a vampire. She couldn't leave any space between one thread and the next or the blood would just seep through.

"I wasn't going to hurt her, you know. I just wanted to take her back to the mansion."

"For what purpose?"

She jabbed the needle in. "Rhiannon's there. She says Brooke and Beta will both die if things aren't dealt with. She says Brooke's body is incompatible. That the soul won't *take*."

"She needs *your* body."

"Yeah. Fortunately, you're in no shape to deliver me to her right now."

He lifted his brows, forcing his eyes to focus on hers.

She averted hers, noting that he didn't deny that had been his intent all along. She put the stitches as close together as she could and tried her best to ignore the pain she was causing the man she loved beyond all reason.

By the time she finished, he was trembling. She cleaned the blood from his skin, watching the area she'd sewn up to see if the blood would still manage to escape. It didn't. She covered the wound with a gauze square from her purse and stuck it in place with the tiny roll of adhesive tape. Then she sat back on her heels. "Done."

She looked at his face when he didn't respond, and alarm shot through her. His eyes were closed. He lay still. The pain must have been tremendous to make him lose consciousness. Unless this was from the blood loss. Unless he was . . .

"Hey." She smacked his cheeks. "Come on, Vlad, talk to me."

He blinked but couldn't seem to stay focused, and his eyes fell closed again. "Sorry."

"Not your fault." She shrugged. "Well, actually, it's entirely your fault."

Barbs were lost on him at the moment, though. She slid an arm beneath his shoulders, raised him into a more upright position. "Come on, we need to get you off the floor and into your safe room, wherever that is."

"Safe room?"

"I know you have one. You people *always* have one. So where is it, Vlad? Where have you been spending your days?"

"Oh." He pressed his lips together, swallowed. "Downstairs. There's a room in the basement."

"Isn't there always?"

She stepped in front of him, sliding her hands underneath his arms. "I'm going to help you get up, okay?"

He bent a leg to press his foot flat to the floor and gripped her shoulders with his hands. "I'll try."

"Here we go." She lifted and pulled him forward, and he rose up, only to fall against her chest. She nearly went over backward but managed to keep her footing. She held him hard and told herself this was not the time to think about how much she wanted him pressed against her. Bare chested and needing her. Just not needing her quite like this.

"Easy. Okay, I've got you."

Vlad lifted his head, easing his body's weight from her, but she knew he wasn't strong enough to stand on his own. She pulled his arm around her shoulders. "Lean on me, Vlad. I'm stronger than I look."

"Stronger than I ever knew," he said.

"Stronger than I ever was. I've been working with people like you for the last sixteen years. Have to try to keep up."

He leaned on her, though not as much as she thought he should have, and pointed the way while she walked him to the stairs. She had to hold him close to fit them both down the basement stairs side by side, and he almost fell once. She gripped him hard, held him up with an arm locked around his waist, grunted with the effort.

Eventually they got to the bottom and through the door into the private room. The room was small and Spartan. A king-size four-poster bed, neatly made, took up most of the space. No windows, of course, so it was dark as a dungeon. She supposed windowless rooms were a plus in the vamp real-estate market. She yanked back the bedcovers, then eased him down until he was sitting on the edge of the mattress.

"Can you manage to get the shirt off, Vlad? There's no point ruining the sheets."

"I can manage."

"All right. I'll be right back."

He held up a hand. "There's no need. I'll be fine here until morning. Just . . . lock the doors on your way out."

She scowled at him. The remark stung, but she told herself this was no time to let her hurt feelings interfere with what had to be done. "I said I'll be back." Then she hurried up the stairs into the main part of the house. She locked all the doors, checked the windows and commandeered a candle

246

she found on a shelf. She always carried matches in her bag. On her way back down, she locked the cellar door, then returned to the hidden little room and locked its door, as well, after she entered.

And the entire time, she was still stinging over his eagerness to get rid of her. But she congratulated herself on not stopping to cry or to lick her wounds. His were more serious right now. Besides, this wasn't about her broken heart. It was bigger. Elisabeta had to be stopped. Stormy's life depended on it.

"All secure," she said when she re-entered the saferoom and lit the candle.

He was still sitting on the edge of the bed. His shirt was pushed down off one incredible shoulder, and that was all. A small red stain showed through the bandage on his belly.

"Damn. It's bled a little more." She set the candle on a stand and moved close to him, stood between his thighs. "Don't move. Just let me do this."

Vlad closed his eyes and obeyed her, remaining motionless as she slid his shirt down the other shoulder, her hands running over him as she did. She couldn't quite deny herself this small pleasure. Her palm skimmed over his shoulder, down his arm, over the firm swell of his biceps and all the way to his wrist. She tried not to feel anything in reaction to the sensation of his skin sliding beneath her palm, her fingers, but she responded anyway.

She slid the shirt's one remaining sleeve over his hand and set it aside. "I'm going to ease you back now. I don't want you to try to do anything, Vlad. You tense up your abs, and that's going to cause the bleeding to start again. All right?"

He nodded.

She got onto the bed behind him and put her arms around him. "Now just let your weight fall against me. No straining. Just relax against me."

She helped to guide him, and once she supported his upper body's weight in her arms, she lowered him slowly and slightly sideways, until his head rested on the pillows.

She got up then. His knees were bent, legs still over the side of the bed. She tugged off his shoes, peeled off the socks, tugged the covers back still farther, and then lifted his legs onto the bed. Finally she pulled the covers over him.

"There. Comfortable?"

He nodded. His eyes were closed again.

She moved up to stand beside the bed,

lifted the covers to check the wound, but didn't see any sign of further bleeding. At least no more had seeped through the makeshift bandages. She walked to the other side of the bed, climbed up onto it, being careful not jostle it too much, and sat with her legs folded to one side.

He opened his eyes. "You don't have to stay."

She nodded. But she wasn't really listening to him. She was thinking and trying construct her argument. "I know your kind, Vlad. I know more about your kind than any mortal you've probably ever met. Some of my best friends are vampires. You understand?"

He nodded, though all she could see was the back of his head from her current vantage point.

"You're going to die before morning," she told him.

He rolled onto his back and blinked up at her. "I don't think —"

"You're going to die. You've lost too much blood. Look at you. You can barely keep your eyes open. I stopped the bleeding, but you don't have enough to keep you going until dawn. I can see that." She pursed her lips. "You won't make it unless you let me help you. Let me . . . do what needs to be done."

His eyes sharpened slightly, plumbing hers. "You would do that for me? Even after . . . ?"

"After you chose her over me? Look, Vlad, I know you'd rather it was her, here with you, helping you right now."

"If it was, I'd be dead by now. She's . . . she's confused, Tempest."

"She's insane. As I've been trying to tell you all along." She closed her eyes, sighed. "We have to be practical. You need blood. I've got plenty. So let's just do this thing." She turned her arm, palm up, and stared at her wrist. Then, with a nod, she held it out to him. "Go on."

"It will . . . it will create a bond."

"You drank from me already, remember? And yeah, it did create a bond. It's how I knew you were in trouble when I got close to this place tonight. I felt it, your pain." She bit her lip for a moment, averting her eyes. "Frankly, I don't think what I feel could get much stronger, anyway. I'm like a fly in a spiderweb. But don't worry. I'm not going to let you destroy me." She lifted her wrist toward him. "Go on, do it."

Vlad ignored her proffered wrist, reaching up to cup her nape instead. He drew her downward, closer to him.

Halfway down, she resisted, and he stopped pulling her closer but didn't let her back away, either. Her face was only a few inches above his. And she wanted him so much it hurt. It hurt like nothing had ever hurt before.

"Not like this," she whispered.

"Like this, Tempest. *Just* like this."

Stormy closed her eyes and let him move her until her face was only a breath away from his. His lips brushed her cheek and then her jaw. She shivered in anticipation as his mouth slid to her neck. His fingers spread into her hair and caressed her there, his touch as soft as a breath. He kissed her neck, and she sighed, because it felt so damn good. She stretched out her legs and lay there beside him, her chest on his, her throat resting against his mouth. Involuntarily, she arched her neck, wanting him, *needing* him, to take her.

He whispered her name against her skin, and then she felt his mouth open to suckle her there. And finally there was the shock of pain as he bit down. She gasped, but the piercing hurt was brief and delicious in a forbidden way. And then he was drinking her, and her body shivered its response.

It was like sex — every part of her alive with pleasure at the sensations of his teeth sinking deeper into her flesh, of his tongue caressing, of the gentle and then more aggressive sucking of his mouth as he fed at her throat. She couldn't bear it. The sensations built, and every muscle in her body coiled and tightened as she yearned for release.

And then he was moving, rolling her onto her back, his own body moving over hers. He was still feeding from her while his hand shoved its way down the front of her jeans.

"Vlad . . . you shouldn't move or . . . oh, hell."

She stopped speaking, because his fingers were sliding into her. And he had to know then, if he hadn't before, what he was doing to her. How hot and wet and hungry she was. For him. Only for him. He worked her with his hand, and she spread her legs shamelessly, craving what only he could give her.

Then he found the nub that pulsed and cried for attention, and rubbed it with his thumb. He bit down harder at her throat, and pressed and rolled that tender, aching bud harder at the same time, as his fingers slid in and out of her. She climaxed in an orgasm so powerful she thought it would melt the flesh from her bones.

On and on it went. She went rigid, then

began to shake and spasm and moan. She arched her pelvis to his hand and tipped her head back until her chin was pointing straight up at the ceiling. And he was merciless. He was inside her, owning her body, his teeth in her throat, his fingers in her vagina. And he wouldn't let go. He just kept working her, making her come, the sensations going on and on and on. The intensity didn't fade. Rather, it built, until her body was jerking and shivering so much it hurt. She was literally thrashing on the bed as he kept pushing her, forcing the pleasure that was almost beyond endurance. And even the pain was good. But it was too much. Too much.

Still, he kept on, until she screamed for mercy.

Finally, finally, the sensations peaked and began to ebb. He withdrew his fingers and then his fangs from her. He stopped drinking and instead kissed her neck in a way that was almost healing in its tenderness. And then he eased onto his back again, keeping one arm around her and drawing her onto her side, so that she snuggled against him.

She was weak from the power of that orgasm. And perhaps from the blood he'd taken, as well. And she was still feeling the shivery aftereffects of the climax. She'd never felt anything like that before. It was beyond human. They'd shared blood before, but Stormy knew, despite her denials, that each and every time it happened, the bond between them would become more potent, more powerful. She was making all of this harder on herself. Everything she did lately was self-destructive and stupid.

And yet she loved it. She loved *him.*

Lazily, Stormy reached down and drew the covers over them, and as she did, she checked the bandage. A little more blood stained it than had been there before. But not a lot, and she knew hers had replenished him. He would be all right.

But would *she?* Would she ever be all right again?

She felt dizzy, sated, weak and utterly compliant. He could do whatever he wanted to her tonight, and she knew she wouldn't resist, not after that. He'd devoured her will along with her blood. Not that she'd had a hell of a lot to begin with, where he was concerned.

She lowered her head to his shoulder. "Thank you, Vlad," she whispered. And then she fell asleep in his arms.

Elisabeta was confused and hurting when

she left the house where Vlad was staying. She'd stabbed him — stabbed her beloved husband! She could hardly believe she'd done it. But he would be all right, surely. She had been angry, told him goodbye, but she hadn't meant it. And after all, he was immortal, a vampire. He would be all right.

She couldn't focus on any other alternative — she had more than she could deal with just . . . just *living.*

She wasn't used to the intricacies, much less the full blown sensations, of being incarnate again. And she'd lost touch with how fragile life could be. Oh, she had felt the stuff of living several times since her death, but only briefly, when she'd managed to take control of Tempest's body. Now she was inhabiting a body all her own. Brooke was trying to take it back, but her efforts were pathetic, at best. She was no threat. Already she was weakening.

But God, the sensations!

That *tarva* Tempest had *hurt* her. Blood had spurted from her nose, and pain had exploded in her face. It hurt for a long while after their fight. She was not accustomed to physical pain.

And there were other things. An unfamiliar pang in her stomach rumbled until she realized it was hunger. But she wasn't sure how to deal with that. She hadn't had to make her own way in the physical world in a very, very long time. More than five centuries. But she had found that if she searched her mind, she could access the knowledge Brooke had acquired during her lifetime, just as she had been able to access Tempest's storehouses of information.

There was *money* in her pocket, Brooke's memory told her. There was a twenty-four-hour grocery store a mere mile and a half away. She could purchase food there.

It seemed a very long walk to Elisabeta. She was tired long before she made it there, and by the time she did arrive, she was almost too tired to want to eat anymore. And another urge had made itself known, demanding to be dealt with. Fortunately Brooke's knowledge included the finer points of public restrooms, and Beta was able to find and use the one within the small grocery store. But it felt odd and disgusting. She'd forgotten some of the less pleasant aspects of physical existence.

She nearly jumped out of her skin when the porcelain bowl seemed to come to life all on its own the instant she rose from it. Water whooshed into the thing, then out the bottom with a rush of noise and pressure that left it as clean as it had been before she'd used it. She stared at the thing for a long moment, her hand pressed to her thundering heart.

And then she smiled, because she *had* a heart. A healthy, living, beating heart. And it was good. Surely she had experienced this kind of marvel before, while lurking inside Tempest's body. She simply hadn't paid attention.

Now she did. These bowls were called toilets, she knew that. And they were to be "flushed" after use. Apparently some of them flushed themselves. People today must be unbelievably lazy.

Finished with the nastiness of elimination, Beta washed her hands, enjoying the convenience and the feel of hot and cold running water, and the smell of the soap, which was nothing like any she'd smelled before. She even enjoyed seeing her reflection in the looking glass, after the shock of looking up to see a stranger's face. It wasn't a bad face. Attractive, in fact. She ran her hands through her auburn hair and over the trim figure. It was a good body.

But weak. She wondered why.

Finally she returned to the grocery store's aisles, and wandered up and down them, searching the shelves for something she could eat. Most of the items looked inadequate: cans and boxes with pretty pictures on them that didn't seem to match their size, shape or weight. Surely the large round can marked "Crisco" could not possibly contain the golden brown fried chicken depicted on its label. It didn't shake as if it had fried chicken inside.

Disappointed, she returned the heavy can to the shelf with a sigh. If only she were already a vampire, she thought sadly. She could just bite some stupid mortal and be done with it.

Like Tempest. She would *love* to drain the life out of that evil, husband-stealing wench. And she *would*.

For now, though, food.

She found some promising items behind a glass case in a section marked "Deli," and she eyed them. There were dishes of many sorts. Some salads, and piles of thinly sliced meats.

"May I help you?"

She looked up at the woman behind the counter. She wore a white hat and apron, and she smiled.

"I'm hungry," Elisabeta told her.

The woman's smile seemed to freeze, and her eyebrows rose a little. "We have sand-wiches. They're pretty good. I have one myself most days, for lunch. Roast beef is my favorite. But the turkey's great, too, with provolone cheese and all the fixin's."

Elisabeta didn't know what "fixin's" were, but since they came highly recommended, she didn't suppose they could be bad. "Beef. I'd like that."

"Sandwich, sub or wrap?" the woman asked.

Beta frowned. "What's the difference?"

The woman tilted her head to one side. "Are you okay, hon?"

"Yes. I'm just . . . not from around here."

"You're foreign aren't you? I thought I caught a slight accent, but honestly, your English is almost perfect. Where you from, hon?"

"Romania," she answered, thinking it was really none of the woman's business, but deciding the salesperson was friendly, so she would try to be, as well.

"Romania! Imagine that. Well, don't you worry any. I'll help you out." She proceeded to explain the differences between sand-witches, subs and wraps; then she made a sand-witch for her, wrapped it in white paper, put it into a little basket, then added a bottle of something called "Coke" that looked like a very dark ale of some sort, and a shiny, small package of some kind of chipped potatoes. Then she led Beta to the front of the store, where another woman took her items from the basket and punched buttons on a machine.

Cash register, whispered the knowledge inside her mind.

The woman at the machine took her money. She gave Beta some coins in return and put her sand-witch into a plastic bag.

She didn't need the bag, Beta thought. She was going to eat the thing right away. People today were not only lazy but terribly wasteful.

She left the store, painfully aware that she still had to walk all the way back to the house where Vlad was staying. Fervently, she hoped the other woman would be long gone by the time she returned. She needed to apologize to Vlad for hurting him the way she had. She needed to explain that he had made her angry, and that she had only re-acted in response to that anger. He really shouldn't do that anymore — make her angry. And he needed to transform her into a vampire right away.

Brooke's body had seemed strong and fit when she had first entered it. Why, then, did it get so tired and so sore from a simple walk?

Elisabeta unwrapped the sand-witch and ate it on the way. It was good. And eating was good, as well. The taste of the food on her tongue. The act of chewing. She almost choked several times before she mastered the rhythm of chewing and swallowing the food. But aside from that, eating was a pleasant experience. Only now did she realize how much she had missed it.

When she finished the sand-witch, she tossed the bag and white wrapper onto the roadside, and carried the package of chipped potatoes in one hand and the "Coke" in the other. She stopped long enough to open them both. The potatoes were terribly salty, but she enjoyed the crunch and flavor of them very much.

They made her thirsty, so she took her first large drink from the bottle, after a mighty struggle to remove its stubborn lid.

She drank, and then she choked. The fluid burst from her mouth, and shot from her nostrils. It was *strong!* And it *tickled!*

She caught her breath, wiped her face, swallowed hard. The inside of her mouth still tasted of the remnants of sweetness from the drink. Drawing a breath, she stared at the bottle and tried again, taking only a tiny sip this time.

Taken slowly, it wasn't so bad. She'd only been surprised. She supposed it took getting used to, and determined that it tasted better than the sour dark ale she'd mistaken it for. Each sip, though, made her belch. Disgusting. Why were the bubbles necessary at all? Surely the sweetness of the beverage would be as good without them.

When she finally made it back to the house where Vlad was staying, it was very, very late, or perhaps even very early — dawn might be near. She tried the door but found it locked tight, and a surge of anger rose up inside her, heating her face. How *dare* he lock her out? Didn't he know better than to make her angry again? Why on earth would Vlad push her to this extent?

She was tired and sore and thirsty, even though she'd drained the bottle of "Coke." Her legs hurt and her back ached. She felt heavy, and her head throbbed. She wanted a warm bed and Vlad's strong body wrapped around hers. But as it was, she settled for a comfortable patch of deep, dry grass off to the left of the house's front door, near a large maple tree. She curled up there to rest for a while. She would figure out what else to do later on. When daylight came, she thought, she would be able to find a way to get into the house. When the sun rose. She would be able to see then.

And he would be unable to stop her.

12

Stormy stayed with Vlad, wrapped in his arms and wondering where the hell this insanity could lead. Okay, maybe he still desired her to some extent, even though Elisabeta no longer lived in her body. But he felt no more than that. And in all likelihood, that desire had only been spurred by the blood lust. She knew his kind, knew sexual heat and hunger for blood were one and the same to them. Beyond that, there was the bond he'd created when he'd taken her blood before. He would feel that pull, just as she did, though maybe not to the same degree.

She was in love with him, after all.

As she lay there holding him, she searched her mind for more memories of the past they had shared. And she was surprised when she found them there, though she probably shouldn't be. Had he released her from the blocks he'd created in her mind deliberately? Or were they falling away on their own? Did he want her to remember, for some reason? Why had he wanted to make her forget in the first place?

It didn't matter. What did matter was that the memories were there, waiting for her to seek them out, retrieve them, relive them. And she needed them, needed to fill in the gaps in her past and to know what had really happened between them so long ago.

After Rhiannon and Roland had taken their leave from Vlad's castle, Tempest showered, put on a fresh nightgown and headed for the bed, to find Vlad already there, lying on his side facing her, his head propped up by one hand. He was undressed — from the waist up, at least. The rest of him was under the covers. But his shoulders and chest were unclothed, and the sight of him turned a switch in her that had no business being there. And the way he looked at her, his eyes moving up and down her and glowing with heat, didn't help matters a bit.

She didn't know why the hell she'd stayed. Being here wasn't helping her — if anything, it was only making matters worse. Elisabeta was stronger here, in her homeland. Taking over seemed to be getting easier for her here. Stormy felt almost sick, weak and achy, and she knew it was the constant fight for control that was to blame.

Rhiannon thought exorcism was the answer. And of all the vampires Stormy had ever known, none of them was more experienced or knowledgeable about matters of spirit and the occult than she. So why hadn't Stormy jumped at the chance to get out of here and let her try?

She thought she knew the reason. And she didn't like it, but she wasn't the type to hide behind self-delusion. Straight-up truth served her much better. And the truth was that she thought she might be falling in love. With Dracula. Which, to her mind, pretty much confirmed that her little red caboose was pretty close to chugging around the bend. She was freaking nuts. What kind of sense did it make for an ordinary mortal chick to fall in love with any vampire, much less Dracula himself?

Damn.

"Are you afraid to come to bed, Tempest?"

She shook free of her thoughts, realized she'd been standing there with her eyes glued to his powerful chest for a couple of minutes now, and forced herself to meet his steady gaze instead. "Should I be?"

"Given where you ended up last time you slept, yes, I would think you might be."

"Oh. That." She shrugged and tried not to shiver at the memory of waking up on a cliff, so close to the edge. "Not much that can be done about it."

"There is, actually." He nodded toward the door. "I've locked it. And the windows. You won't be able to sleepwalk any farther than the confines of this room."

"Yeah? And suppose I decide I want to get out?"

"Why would you want that?"

She shrugged. "The castle could catch fire, I suppose."

"Then break a window."

"Lovely." She moved closer, and he flipped the covers back. The nightgown she wore was like all the others she'd found in the drawers. Flimsy and sheer, black this time rather than white, and shorter. She started to wonder if she should have just worn one of her T-shirts to bed.

She got into the bed, lay down on her back, not touching him, tugged the covers over her and stared at the ceiling. Vlad sat up long enough turn off the bedside lamp, then returned to his former position, on his side. It wasn't fair. The room was black as pitch now, and she couldn't see a thing, but he could. She knew all too well that he could.

"You were wrong before," he said. Something trailed over her face, down her cheek, then. She thought it was the backs of his fingers.

"About what?" She managed not to stammer, but the words emerged a little breathy.

"About me wanting her and not you."

"Was I?"

"Yes." Those fingers trailed over her jawline and then down her neck. "I was surrounded by memories of the past, Tempest. I misspoke when I said her name. It didn't mean anything."

"I doubt that very much." He was lying. He had to lie, to keep her here long enough for him to get what he wanted. His precious Elisabeta, in full control of Stormy's body.

"I only wish there was more time before dawn, so that I could prove it to you." His hand drifted across her chest, along her collarbone. Then his palm rested there. "As it is, though, we only have twenty minutes, give or take."

She shrugged. "Don't assume we'd be doing anything else, if we had longer. I do get a vote in that, you know."

"You wouldn't refuse me."

"That sure of yourself, are you?"

"I know when a woman wants me, Tempest."

She shrugged. "What I want and what's good for me are two different things, Vlad. In fact, in this case, I think they're polar op-

267

posites."

He said nothing, but his palm moved very slightly, a caress so light she could only barely detect it.

"Twenty minutes, huh? I suppose we could talk."

"Of course."

She nodded, rolled onto her side to face him, but kept enough space between them that he wouldn't get distracted from the subject. "Tell me about you and Rhiannon."

He was silent.

"You said you were her sire."

"How is this information going to help you remember your past life with me, Tempest?"

She shrugged. "It's not. I'm curious, is all."

He was quiet for so long that she thought he wouldn't reply at all. But then he did. "She was one of The Chosen. You know how powerfully vampires feel the instinct to protect and watch over them."

"Yes."

"And do you also know that for each vampire there is one of The Chosen with whom that bond is even stronger?"

She nodded in the darkness, knowing he could see it. "She was that one for you?"

"Yes. I sensed her need while traveling near Egypt and went there in response to it. She was the daughter of Pharaoh, but he'd wanted a son and considered her a curse from the gods, punishment for some crime, imagined or real. He'd sent her to be raised and trained by the priestesses at the Temple of Isis. She was never to be allowed to leave there, even when she fell ill. She was a virtual prisoner to them."

"The Chosen always die young, if they're not transformed," she muttered. "She must have been younger than most when the symptoms kicked in."

"Yes. At any rate, I went there, and I took her away. Not without effort. Both of us were nearly killed when another organization intervened on behalf of the priestesses. Still, we escaped with our lives. I told her what I was, what she could become, and she accepted the offer."

She wished to God she could see his face in the darkness, because she was sure there was more to the story. "I've seen the bond between vampires and their special Chosen ones. It's pretty intense."

"Yes."

"Even if they don't get involved sexually —"

"Are you asking, Tempest?"

She licked her lips, then lowered her eyes, because she could feel his probing them. "No. I only meant — you must have been close. Powerfully connected. It's a special and potent bond."

"It is."

"And yet you were willing to ruin it tonight. Because of Elisabeta."

He said nothing. And that told her as much as a full admission would have.

She licked her lips, focused on his face again, barely able to make out more than the shapes and lines of it in the darkness. She was quiet for a moment, as she lay there working up the nerve to ask the question that was burning in her mind. Minutes ticked past. Finally she drew a breath, closed her eyes and blurted it. "Are you going to make love to me when the sun goes down tonight?"

She lay there, eyes still closed, awaiting his answer. But it didn't come, and finally she rolled onto her side and touched him. "Vlad?"

Nothing. She frowned and slid out of the bed, hurrying to the nearest window, which was heavily draped, and shaded besides. Going to the side farthest from the bed, she carefully lifted the drapes and saw the first rays of morning sunlight, cool, dim and gray, slowly lighting the sky beyond the thick old glass.

Sighing, she arranged the drape back in place again and returned to the bed. He was at rest, then. Probably hadn't even heard her question. And she wondered what answer she'd wanted to hear that time. Because she honestly didn't know.

Hell, maybe she did know. She wanted him. Burned for him, and was growing increasingly frustrated with having to wait and wonder.

Maybe she should stop waiting and wondering. Maybe she should just give in to what she knew they both wanted, get it over with and see what happened.

Maybe it was time she stopped trying to be smart and logical, and just tried listening to the demands and hungers of her own body.

Yeah. It was time.

By the time the sun set and she hadn't slept a wink, she was ready. Her time with Vlad was coming to a close. This would be their last night together, assuming he kept his word and let her go. She wanted him. She could get through life without him, if she just had this one time with him to cling to, to remember.

He raised his head from the pillows and turned it her way. She lay on her back, the covers over her all the way to her shoulders, which were visible. His eyes moved over them, then over her neck, which seemed to tempt him. Swallowing hard and cursing herself for her own nervousness, she forced herself to lie still when he lifted the sheet and comforter as one and peered underneath.

She was naked. For him. And he knew that now, if he hadn't already sensed it.

271

He peeled the covers away, folding them back. She rolled onto her side, curling up a little in response to the chill in the room. He couldn't seem to take his eyes from her; they moved over the curve of her hip, the length of her thigh.

He put his hand on her shoulder and stroked a slow path down her upper arm, then slipped to her waist, and she shivered at his touch. Then he moved it lower, to cup her hip, slide his palm gently over her thigh.

He left his hand there, where it kneaded and caressed, but drew his gaze back to her breasts and finally to her face, staring into her eyes.

"Surprise," she whispered, her voice hoarse. She couldn't have spoken aloud had she wanted to.

He pushed with his hand until she rolled onto her back again, and his body moved with hers, his chest pressing her to the mattress as he finally took her mouth. She opened to his kiss, welcomed it and responded in kind. Their mouths locked, taking and releasing, suckling and freeing, over and over; a mimicry of the mating their bodies would be indulging in soon.

Soon.

He clasped her hip to hold her to him as he shifted his lower body over her, nestled himself between her legs. He moved against her there, rubbing her with his erection as he fed from her mouth. Then he slid one hand there, as well, and caressed her folds, felt the moisture, the dampness, there.

"Tempest," he whispered.

"Yeah. Tempest. Not Elisabeta. Remember that, Vlad. You're making love to me, not her."

His fingers moved inside her, and she sucked in a sharp breath. "I know who you are," he told her.

"It's been killing me to wait, to want you so badly, Vlad," she whispered. "Torture. Pure torture."

He delved more deeply with his fingers, kissed her again, then moved lower to take a breast in his mouth and tease its peak until it went tight and hard. She arched her back to him and shivered with pleasure.

"Take me," she told him. "Do it now, Vlad."

"I want it to be good for you."

"I don't think that's going to be a problem." She moved her hips, rocking herself over his fingers, rubbing against them.

"I promise you, it won't be."

He taunted her breast again, then replaced his mouth with his hand and slid lower, until he could press his head between her legs and taste her there. He licked deep, and her entire body shuddered. Her hands closed on the back of his head, clasping his hair and holding him. He took that as consent to ravage her, not that he required it at that point. She thought he was beyond holding back, and he lapped and suckled and invaded her mind with his own. She felt him there, feeling every sensation he caused in her. He knew when she was on the brink of orgasm, and that was when he stopped, drew away, gave her a moment to come back down.

She growled in frustration and need.

"I want you to come with me inside you," he told her, and it sounded more like a command than a request. "I want you to know release only when I possess you, body, blood and soul."

She was panting, shaking.

He moved up her body and lowered himself again, and this time he slid into her. She tensed a little, unused to his size and shape. He was big and thick, and he filled her, stretched her. But he didn't change his pace. He pressed on, deeper and deeper still, and then he took her knees in his hands and lifted them, pressed them wide, and slid into her even farther than before.

She whimpered, close to asking for mercy. But if she felt full, it was a good fullness. If she felt stretched, then it was what he wanted, and that made her want it, too. And if she felt pain, it was the blissfully delicious pain that couldn't be distinguished from the most intense pleasure imaginable.

He withdrew then, slowly, and entered her again. A little faster this time. And again, still faster. His pace increased, but slowly, teasingly, and the force with which he drove into her increased, as well.

She moved her hips to accept him, to mesh with the rhythm he'd begun. She wanted more, but he wanted her to want. To crave. So he held back, damn him.

Her hands slid around him, gripped his backside and tugged him into her. And when he still didn't give her enough, she dug her nails into his flesh and flashed her eyes open, staring up into his. "Harder, Vlad. Faster."

It was almost a growl.

His control seemed to shatter. He drove into her, hard and fast.

She wrapped her legs around his waist, linked her ankles at the small of his back and snapped her hips up to meet his with every thrust. How she stood the force he was using she didn't know, but she did, and silently asked for more. He slid his hands beneath her backside, tipped her hips up so he could penetrate even more deeply, then held her to him to take every thrust, every inch, every ounce.

And just as she neared the precipice, he drove even harder and bent his head to her neck. He bit down, sinking his fangs through her jugular, shocking her, and sucking the lifeblood from her body as he plundered and took.

She shrieked his name as she came, and he drove into her twice more, and shot his seed into her body as he drank from her throat.

They clasped each other that way as the spasms of an endless orgasm ripped though them both, bodies straining, his rod piercing her to depths no man had ever touched, his mouth drinking at her throat. Her back was arched, her arms and legs locked around him, and she trembled with the force of the spasms.

It was only as her grip on him began to weaken that he seemed to realize he was still feeding, still sucking the blood from her throat, still spilling semen into her body. She was fading, fading fast.

He stopped drinking, withdrew his teeth. Beneath him, her body relaxed into the mattress. Carefully, he withdrew from her body and lay beside her, sliding his arms around her and drawing her into his embrace. His hands stroked her hair. "I own you now," he whispered.

She didn't reply. She couldn't. But she

heard. As if from deep within a canyon, she heard. What did it mean? What had he done to her?

How long had that orgasm held him in its grip? How much of her blood had he taken? Was she dying? If felt as if she was.

He patted her cheek with his hand, softly, then with more force. "Tempest? Tempest, open your eyes. Look at me."

Her eyes did open. She felt them open, but she didn't open them. She was trapped inside, and suddenly she understood why. The climax, and maybe the blood loss, had weakened her grip. The other was in control now.

"Don't call me by that bitch's name," she whispered, her accent thick, her voice deeper than Tempest's had ever been. But Tempest, weak and trembling, trapped in her own body, heard it all.

"Elisabeta?" Vlad backed away slightly.

"Yes. It is me." She clasped his face between her palms, kissed his mouth. "Oh, Vlad, darling, do you still love me? Tell me you do."

"Of course I do," he whispered.

Inside, Stormy felt her heart break.

"Then find a way, Vlad. Find a way to let me stay. To let me have this body. You have to, Vlad. If you don't, I'll die."

He nodded. "I'm trying, Beta. I'm trying."

"You're the one who set this into motion, my

love," Elisabeta said, her tone harsh. "You with your sorcerers and magicians. They with their spells and charms. Do you know what it's been like for me? Trapped between the worlds all these years, with no way to come back and no way to move on?"

He gasped.

"You didn't know?"

"That wasn't how it was supposed to be, Beta. I vow to you, it was never my intent —"

"Your intent matters very little now. It is done. My suffering, being imprisoned as if buried alive, is done. So long as you follow through. You need to finish this, Vlad."

He met her eyes, shook his head slowly. "I don't know where to find the ring and the scroll with the rite. I'm not sure I can finish this without those items."

She closed her eyes. "Then I'll die."

"I won't let that happen, little one."

A tear rolling down her cheek, she sniffled and said, "Do you promise?"

"I do. I'll make this right, I swear. Somehow."

"Thank you, Vlad. Thank you." She kissed him.

"Now I want you to rest. Go to sleep. Let Tempest return to her body, and wait for my call."

"Yes. Yes, Vlad, I will."

"Good. Good."

She faded off to sleep, or something like it, and Stormy felt her own control slowly returning. But she'd learned something tonight. Learned it beyond doubt.

Elisabeta was the woman Vlad loved. And he would say anything, do anything, even if it cost Stormy's own life, to get her back.

Stormy had tears dampening her cheeks as the memory faded. She knew now what it meant, what he'd done to her, so long ago. By taking her blood, he'd created a bond between them — one that could not be broken. He'd known that. He'd done it deliberately, probably to keep her vulnerable to his power, his control, for as long as it took to steal her body for his precious dead wife.

No wonder she loved him so much.

Part of her argued that she'd loved him even before that night. But she refused to listen to that part. He was using her, he cared nothing for her. Except that she provided a home for Elisabeta.

She remained with him until the sun rose. She couldn't see the sun, of course. The windowless room gave no hint what was happening in the skies beyond it. But she felt the change in him. He went very still. No sounds emerged, not even a breath, and his always cool skin went even colder. There was a different feeling to him once the sun came up. She imagined this must be what lying with a dead man would be like.

He didn't love her. He never would. She needed to get the hell out of here, get some perspective. But she sat there instead, looking at him as he slept. She still wanted him, although with her, want wasn't even close to a strong enough term. She craved him. Hungered for him. Ached and pined and bled for him. And why the hell wouldn't she? Even beyond the bond he'd deliberately created, then empowered again and again, now, she thought, she would want him. He was the sexiest man she had ever seen. God, he had the body of a twenty-year-old. A ripped twenty-year-old. And he played hers the way Santana played the guitar. He made it sing. There was no one who could make her feel the way he could.

But he'd commanded that, hadn't he? That she would know release only with him. Was that why she'd never gotten off with anyone else, not in all this time? The bastard.

He would still be with the other woman, the Elisabeta-Brooke creature, if she hadn't stabbed him in the belly. Stormy ought to hate him. Why the hell couldn't she?

She relit the candle. Then, carefully, she pulled back the covers and removed the bandage she'd placed over his wound. She pulled at the gauze, wincing at how it tugged the tender, wounded area. But he was beyond feeling any pain. And even when she bit her lip and ripped the bandage away, no fresh blood welled in the seam of the wound she'd painstakingly stitched up.

She sat on the edge of the bed, holding a blanket to her chest to fend off the early-morning chill, and kept her gaze riveted to the injured flesh. As she watched, the skin along the edges of the wound changed. It paled and it blended, the cut edges melding into each other by slow degrees. She was ready with the tiny scissors and tweezers from her purse. The stitches would be rejected by his body within a few days, but it would be irritating and perhaps painful. And she was fool enough to want to spare him that. So she waited until the skin had begun to knit itself together, then snipped each thread and tugged it free. The minuscule holes those threads left behind closed almost as soon as she pulled the threads from them.

When she finished, the wound was almost impossible to detect. A tiny red line marked its former position, and within a few more moments, even that was gone.

Sighing deeply, Stormy lingered a moment longer. She ran her hands over the beautiful shape of his chest, feeling every ripple of muscle beneath his smooth skin. She touched his belly and shivered at the feel of his abs. She traced his shoulders.

He was incredibly built, and that was far from the norm. Vampires tended to be lean and wiry. Sometimes even skinny. She supposed that was because the Undead tended to keep the form they had at the moment of their transformation. Every vampire had the Belladonna Antigen as a mortal. And the antigen tended to make them weak and ill over time. Max's sister Morgan had been a shadow of herself from its effects. Had nearly died, in fact, before Dante had shared the dark gift with her. And so she would always be as she had been then. Painfully thin and slight, and though far stronger now, she would always be weak for a vampire.

Vlad must not have been feeling the effects of the antigen yet when the vampire Anthar had transformed him.

Yes, Anthar. Another memory in the long list of them. He'd told her of his true origins. He'd been the helper of a Sumerian by the name of Utnapishtim, a man whose name was still known today. His story had been the precursor to that of the biblical Noah. Utnapishtim, it was said, had survived the great flood sent by the gods and had been given the gift of immortality. He'd been a relative of Vlad's. And Vlad had been sent to live with him as his servant and companion.

One day, the great king Gilgamesh himself had come, begging the old man for the secret of immortality. Vlad had been sent from the room, so he'd never seen what transpired, but he knew Utnapishtim had granted the king's request, in direct disobedience of the dictates of the gods.

Later, another man had come, an evil man, named Anthar. He was seeking Gilgamesh, and his intentions were dark. He, too, had demanded the gift, but the old man had refused. Anthar forced him at the point of a blade, then beheaded him, leaving him dead on the floor, and took young Vlad captive, to be his slave.

Vlad had been held by the dark vampire for years, all the while working to grow stronger, so he could one day escape. By the time Anthar had decided he needed his slave to be like him, a vampire, in order to better serve his needs, and changed him over, Vlad was a powerful young man in the peak of health.

And so, by the time of his change, he'd looked . . . the way he looked now. Like a centerfold. A powerful, muscular, beautiful young man.

She lowered her head and pressed her lips to those rippling abs. God, she wanted to kiss every inch of him. But no. She had work to do. And she needed distance and perspective. She needed to find a way to be free of him, of the hold he had on her, the bond he'd made, the love that possessed her. Getting to her feet, Stormy tucked the covers back over him.

Her hand rose to press against her throat where Vlad had left his mark on her. She felt it clearly — two swollen, tender places. Tiny wounds. And her body heated all over again as she remembered the sensations he'd aroused.

She needed to remain aware of what he really wanted from her. She needed to make it very clear to her desire-glazed brain. She mustn't forget. He felt passion for her, a burning, nearly insatiable desire. And yes, drinking from her again might have intensified it even more, on his side as well as her own.

But he didn't love her. He loved Elisabeta. He was willing to trade Stormy's life for hers. She mustn't forget that.

Carefully she unlocked the door, then turned the lock again before she pulled it closed. She did the same with the cellar door at the top of the stairs, and then exited the house through the front door, making sure it was locked, as well. She needed to get back to Athena House and formulate a plan to capture Elisabeta so Rhiannon could perform the ritual on her.

Vlad wasn't going to like it. In fact, he would probably never forgive her for it.

Elisabeta was still half-asleep in the grass when a sound brought her fully awake. Her first thought was that it was Vlad, coming out to get her, to apologize for his behavior, to bring her into the house and tell her how much he loved her.

But as she came fully awake, she realized it couldn't be Vlad. The sun had already cleared the horizon, and it beamed brightly down on her — so brightly that she had to shield her eyes to see who was coming out of the house.

And then she saw, and her anger burst into a full blown rage.

It was *her!* Tempest. She had spent the night with Elisabeta's husband. Dammit, she had known all along! He was infatuated with her. And too confused to realize that he'd only ever been drawn to her in the first place because she, Elisabeta, had been there, inside her.

"I am going to have to kill her," she said softly. "It's the only way."

She rose from the grass as the woman walked away from the house and along the side of the road. Elisabeta started to walk after her, her hands clenched, her rage burning. But before the second angry step, her head was spinning, her knees trembling.

She pressed a hand to her forehead, closed her eyes and braced her hand on a tree to keep from falling. What was this?

She stood there for a moment, holding her head, and waited for the dizziness to abate. When it did, she tested her footing and found her legs once again solid. Even so, she wasn't at her best. Perhaps it was the shock of adjusting to this new body. Or perhaps Brooke had some physical imperfection or illness that hadn't been apparent to Elisabeta until now.

Damn this body. She'd wanted a strong and healthy form, not this.

No matter. What needed to be done, needed to be done. Tempest was coming between Elisabeta and Vlad. That was the only reason he had refused to transform her.

Beta had no choice but to remove Tempest from the equation. Vlad could not be distracted when she needed him to be focused only on her.

She was in no condition, however, to murder the woman with her hands alone. She remembered, with a flash of pain, the way Tempest had spun and kicked and hit her before. She was not experienced at physical combat. She would need an aid. A weapon.

She looked around and came upon a perfect one — a rock larger than a grapefruit, smooth and round. She picked it up and then hurried in the direction Tempest had gone. She must be heading back to Athena House. The road curved, looping around a stand of red pine forest. While Elisabeta was unfamiliar with the place, Brooke knew it well. And by now Beta had mastered the skill of probing Brooke's mind, mining it for information.

She veered off the road and into the pine forest, traveling through it unerringly. Its carpet of browning needles and fragrant pungence were soothing to her senses, and the pine cones that littered the ground only tripped her up once. After that she watched for them. She emerged on the far side of the woods, and the road was there, only a few feet from the edge of the trees. So she backed up a little, sheltered by the scented branches, and she waited.

Within a few minutes, Tempest came along the road. There was purpose in her step, a troubled, pensive look about her face. Was the contemplating the hopelessness of her future without Vlad? For she had to know his heart belonged to another. Was she in love with him?

Beta waited until Tempest had passed by her hiding place, so she wouldn't see movement from the corner of her eye and be warned. The attack had to be completely unexpected. A blow from the blue.

When Tempest had gone past her, Beta crept out of the trees, moving quickly and quietly up the grassy incline to the road. She raised the rock over her head, clasping it in both hands so she could bring it down *hard,* and she ran at Tempest's back.

Tempest spun around at the last possible moment and ducked to the side. The rock hit her shoulder instead of her skull, but it must have hurt her all the same. She grunted in pain and toppled over sideways, landing on the ground with a solid impact that must have hurt nearly as much as the blow had done.

Furious, Elisabeta lifted the rock again

but even as she brought the rock down, Tempest swung her legs in a powerful arc that took Beta's feet right out from under her.

She went down hard, slamming her own head into the very rock she'd intended to use to crush Tempest's.

And then it was dark.

13

Stormy got to her feet, one hand on her shoulder, which felt as if it had been hit by a freaking freight train. "What the hell is the *matter* with you, you freaking maniac?"

There was no reply from the woman on the ground, and Stormy moved closer, cautious, but not too worried. "Damn sneak attack. That's not a very dignified way to fight, Elisabeta."

Still nothing. And, Stormy noted suddenly, a trickle of red marked the miniature boulder on the ground beside the fallen woman.

"Hell, you brained yourself with that thing, didn't you?"

She used her foot to turn Brooke's body — and it *was* Brooke's body, not Elisabeta's — over. Beta was unconscious. There was a little blood coming from a gash in her left temple, and Stormy figured there would be a goose egg damn near the size of that stupid rock later on.

Sighing, wanting to haul off and kick the bitch for the throbbing pain in her shoulder, she instead reached down and yanked the ruby ring from the other woman's limp finger. Then she searched her pockets and found the scroll. "I imagine we'll need these," she said. "And you never deserved them to begin with." She dropped the ring and scroll into her backpack, took out her cell phone, dialed Athena House and waited.

At sundown, Stormy was sitting watch over the unconscious woman in Brooke's bed at Athena House. She was sitting watch because it was her turn. She, Lupe and Melina had been taking shifts with the injured woman all day long. They couldn't do the ritual without Rhiannon. But if Beta's soul wasn't set free soon, Stormy would die with her. It was only now that the patient opened her eyes.

Stormy tensed in the chair beside the bed, then frowned. Because her eyes were pretty. And they were blue. *Brooke's* eyes, not Elisabeta's. Those eyes met Stormy's, and they were wet with unshed tears. And then Brooke said something so softly that Stormy couldn't hear her.

Her heart ached for the woman, despite the fact that she had brought all of this on herself with her foolish actions. She closed a hand around Brooke's and leaned closer. "I didn't hear."

"I didn't think . . . it would be . . . like this," Brooke whispered.

"I know. I know what you're going through, believe me. We're going to try everything we can to get her out of you, Brooke. I promise."

Brooke closed her eyes. "She . . . she wants . . ."

"What, Brooke? What does she want?"

"She wants you dead."

Stormy knew that already, but hearing it still sent a chill down her spine. Not, however, the same chill that came a split second later when Brooke's hand closed more tightly around Stormy's, and her other hand clamped to the back of Stormy's head and drew her face down even closer.

"And I will *see* you dead, too. I promise you that. Vlad is mine."

Her eyes, blazing into Stormy's, were black now, like glittering pieces of polished coal. Stormy jerked free of her. "Not having much success at that so far, are you, Elisabeta? Tried to brain me with a rock and wound up hurting yourself instead. And

292

now you're here, and trust me on this one — you aren't going anywhere."

"He will save me. He loves me."

"Yeah, right, and you love him, too, don't you? That's why you tried to kill him last night."

"I did *not!*"

"No? Sinking a blade into his belly was what, then? Kind of like a little love bite?"

"He is *vampir.* He is immortal."

"There is no such thing as immortal, Beta. Everything that lives can die. Vamps just die a little harder than the rest of us." Stormy wrenched herself free of the clasping hands, twisted her own hand around and gripped Brooke's wrist hard. "If you hurt him again, I'll kill you. Do you understand me? I'll *kill* you, and damn the consequences."

Beta blinked, winced in pain and stared up at Stormy with a suddenly wide-eyed and child like expression. Utterly innocent and afraid. "You . . . you would really kill me?"

"Don't even doubt it. I should have picked up that rock and crushed your skull today. The only reason I didn't was because —"

"Because Melina came and stopped you," Beta said in a frightened little girl voice. And now there were tears rolling down her cheeks. "You're hurting my wrist."

Belatedly, the alarm bells sounded in Stormy's mind. That wasn't what had happened at all. She'd called Melina, asked her to bring a car to help her get Elisabeta back to the mansion. Why would the woman try to accuse her of something when they were alone in the room?

An instant later, she knew why, she heard Vlad's voice coming from behind her. "Let her go, Tempest."

She was already in the process of doing just that, and she rose from her chair and turned to face him. He held her eyes for a moment, then shifted them to the other women, when Beta spoke again.

"Thank goodness you've come, Vlad. Thank God."

Great. He'd been standing there long enough to hear what sounded like a threat, and maybe even a confession of attempted murder.

"She tried to kill me!" the bitch in the bed sobbed. "I tried to speak to her on the road this morning when she left you, Vlad, and she attacked me. She *hurt* me." The little phony lifted a trembling hand to the white bandages Melina had plastered to her head, her crocodile tears flowing like rivers.

Stormy let her head fall forward until her chin nearly touched her chest and expelled all her breath. Vlad was moving past her, making a beeline for the actress in the bed, and then he bent over her to peel up one corner of the bandage and peer underneath.

Straightening, then, he fixed his eyes on Stormy's. "Tempest? Is this true?"

She opened her mouth to supply a full blown denial and a long winded explanation, then stopped herself. She tipped her head to one side. "Why should I bother? You're going to believe the word of this psycho bitch from hell, even after she drove a knife into your gut and left you to die. Even after I gave my own blood to save your life. So why should I bother?"

"Tempest —"

She held up a hand, palm facing him, and smiled a bitter smile at the irony of the situation. "Fuck this. And fuck you, Vlad." Then she turned and left the room, slamming the door behind her. Let him care for his pathetic little murderess. Elisabeta would destroy him in the end, and it would be no less than he deserved.

She met Rhiannon partway down the hall but didn't even acknowledge her, just kept walking.

"Wait!" Rhiannon said.

Stormy didn't wait, so Rhiannon changed direction and caught up with her. "Stormy,

295

where are you going?"

"To pack. I'm done with this. I got her here, all right? And I got the damn ring and the scroll." She turned, tugged the things out of her pocket and pressed them into Rhiannon's hand. "You can do your thing, exorcise her, send her to hell for all I care. And you can deal with Vlad, because he's not going to let her go without a fight, I guarantee you that. There's no longer any reason for me to be here. It's not my problem anymore. If I wake up tomorrow morning, I'll know it worked. And if I don't, well, then I guess I don't. I'm sure as hell not going to spend what might be the last several hours of my life watching him fawn over that bloodthirsty lunatic."

"Stormy, don't do this."

Stormy stopped walking. She was outside her own bedroom door. She forced herself to lift her gaze and meet Rhiannon's eyes, even though that meant revealing the unshed tears in her own. "Thanks for trying to help me. I owe you one."

"You can thank me when it's over, if I'm successful."

"I hope I get that chance, Rhiannon." She blinked her eyes dry and turned away. "This is getting disgustingly sappy. Go on, go to Brooke's room before Vlad has the chance to take his pathetic excuse for a bride out of here."

"She is pathetic, isn't she?"

"She's bloodthirsty, selfish, violent and insane. But worse than any of that, she's a whiner." She glanced at Rhiannon and saw a small smile appear on her lips.

"That was my first impression, as well. It hasn't changed. Goodbye, Stormy."

Then she turned and hurried back up the hall to Brooke's room.

Vlad sat beside Beta. The sight of her, lying in the bed, her tears, her pleas and the painful wound beneath the bandages, got to him. He wanted so much to heal her, to help her and make her well again. It killed him to see her suffering this way.

Rhiannon stepped into the room, took a seat on the opposite side of the bed. "Hello, Vlad. I'm surprised the Athena woman let you in."

He met her eyes, noting how stiff and guarded Beta had become the moment Rhiannon entered the room. "The one they call Lupe tried to forbid me from entering."

"Oh? Is she still alive?"

He noticed Rhiannon's smile, the touch of humor in her voice, and felt an answering smile tug at his own lips, in spite of his pain. "Of course." He rose to his feet, and went to her, wrapped his arms around her, half expecting her reaction to be cold. But it wasn't. Rhiannon hugged him in return. Whatever had happened between them, their bond was strong. Had always been. Would always be.

"It's been a long time," he told her.

"Too long. And I fear this embrace of yours will not last, Vlad. It's likely we'll end this thing on opposing sides."

"I wish that wasn't the case," he told her, stepping back to look into her eyes. "Regardless of what I say to you later, Rhiannon, even if I'm forced to destroy you, know that I love you."

"As I love you. I'll love you even when I'm killing you, Vlad."

He nodded. "Understood."

Rhiannon glanced at Beta. "Melina says the head wound isn't serious."

"Do not trust them, Vlad!" Elisabeta pleaded. "They are lying. They want me to die."

Rhiannon gave her a dismissive look, then focused on Vlad again. "She's right. We *do* want her to die. But we don't want Tempest to die, and we have no right to just execute Brooke, though her so-called sisters will likely do that in any event."

"You cannot save Brooke," Beta hissed. "This is *my* body now."

Rhiannon sighed and rolled her eyes. "Do you mind if we speak in the hallway, Vlad? This is growing tiresome, and my patience with this body thief is wearing thin."

He nodded and rose. Beta grabbed for his hand. "Vlad, no! Don't leave me!"

"You'll be fine," he promised her, patting her hand even as he pried loose her grip. "Beta, you've been here for the entire day. If anyone truly wanted to harm you, they would have done so by now. And you know now that I'm here, I won't let anyone hurt you. Don't you?"

She met his eyes, searched them, and finally nodded.

"Just rest. I'll keep you safe."

He went to the door, stepped into the hallway and pulled the door closed behind him.

"Did Stormy tell you what happened?" Rhiannon asked.

"No, but Beta did."

"Oh, did she." Sarcasm dripped from her words. "And what fiction did that little liar spin?"

He scowled at her. "Said she tried to speak to Tempest on the road, and that Tempest attacked her, would have killed her, if

Melina hadn't arrived in time to prevent it."

Rhiannon just gazed at him, her eyes calling him an idiot. "And you believed that?"

"Tempest has felt attacked by Beta for sixteen years. Still, that doesn't justify —"

"Oh, for pity's sake, Vlad. You could put it together yourself if you were thinking clearly. I got the entire story from Melina. Stormy stayed with you in the house until sunrise. She watched over you until the knife wound your devoted little wife gave you had healed completely. And then she left. She was walking back here when Elisabeta ambushed her. Attacked her with a large rock. She'd have caved Stormy's skull in if Stormy hadn't glimpsed her shadow and spun around. The blow missed her head, thank the gods. Her shoulder took the brunt of it."

He didn't alter his expression in the least. "How bad is it?"

"She refused to let me see, though Lupe tells me it looks as if someone dumped blue and purple ink over her shoulder. She doesn't think anything is broken, however."

He nodded thoughtfully. "So Tempest was defending herself when she hit Elisabeta with the rock?"

Rhiannon frowned. "She didn't hit Elisabeta at all. Just kicked the madwoman's feet out from under her when she came at her again. Beta fell and hit her head on the rock with which she'd intended to crush Stormy's skull."

He closed his eyes. The other two women were coming along the hallway now, and they joined them there, outside the bedroom door.

"At least they're both all right," he said, glancing at the door, feeling with his senses.

"They're not all right," Melina said softly. "Brooke is in danger of dying, and Elisabeta . . . she's sick. It's not the head wound, it's . . . it's something else."

Vlad sighed, lowering his head. "Yes. I'm afraid I know what it is."

"As do I," Rhiannon said. "I can feel it from here. It's the antigen. Belladonna. It's killing her."

Melina frowned. "That can't be. Brooke wasn't one of The Chosen."

"No," Vlad said. "But Beta was."

"So she what?" Melina asked. "Brought it with her? Into another body? Is that even possible?"

Vlad started to speak, then narrowed his eyes and glanced at Rhiannon. "Why are we discussing this with them?"

"Believe me, I wouldn't be if I felt there were any other way. However misguided, though, I've come to believe these two are, at their cores, decent. Though I'm more certain of Lupe than Melina."

Melina gasped.

"I don't like it. You know this group can't be trusted."

She shrugged. "What could they do to us, Vlad? We could snap them like twigs before they could blink."

"Hey, hey, hold up a sec," Lupe interrupted. "Just what is your problem with the Sisterhood of Athena?"

Rhiannon faced her. "If you really want to know, look it up. You keep scrupulous records. Cross reference Egypt and my original name, Rianikki, daughter of Pharoah, priestess of Isis — a group once tightly allied with your own." She shrugged. "When you have time. For now, let it go, and let us focus on the matter at hand. How did Beta bring the antigen into a body that did not formerly possess it?"

"I don't know how it happened, or why, but it has," Vlad said. "I'm not sure it even matters how or why. The antigen is different in her, altered somehow."

Rhiannon nodded. "It's taken up residence in a body never meant to house it," she said. "According to what I've read in the ancient texts the recipients of the antigen have a common ancestor. It's said to be you, Vlad. But I suspect it goes back further."

"To Utnapishtim," Vlad said softly. "The first immortal. I was his servant, but also a distant relation."

"I'm not sure it has to be a blood descendant, though," Rhiannon went on.

"What other sort of descendant could there be?" Melina asked.

Rhiannon met her eyes. "A future incarnation of the same soul," she said. "There is a master soul for each of us. Think of it as your higher self. It spins off parts of itself to come into each lifetime. When we die, we return to meld with that higher self, to share with it all of the wisdom and experience gained from our mortal lifetime. It grows wiser and stronger and more enlightened, and spins off another part to live another life."

"And what happens, Rhiannon, if that melding fails to come about?" Vlad asked.

Rhiannon shrugged. "I suspect each future incarnation is somehow less than complete, for it is missing a part of its spiritual ancestry that would make it whole."

He frowned deeply. "What do you suppose that means for our kind, Rhiannon? We never . . . meld."

"I have my theories," she whispered. "But I think it's a conclusion one needs to reach on one's own."

He lowered his head, shaking it slowly. "What are we going to do to help Elisabeta?"

"I think you already know that answer to that, Vlad." Rhiannon put both her hands on his shoulders. "We have to exorcise her. We must free her soul from the influence of that ring, so she can move on to the other side and meld with her higher self the way she was meant to do."

"It does seem to be the only way," Melina whispered.

"It *is* the only way," Lupe agreed. "Especially since she's going to die anyway."

"And if she does, she'll take Brooke with her," Melina said quickly.

Vlad remained stoic. "We could transform her."

"We'd still be condemning Brooke to death," Rhiannon said. "If Beta stays in her body, Brooke will die. And while I'm not certain she can escape that fate either way, Vlad, it is not our place to take her life."

"She asked for this. She invited Elisabeta in." He closed his eyes to keep his feelings hidden.

"Honestly, Vlad, you know perfectly well

Beta is insane. You cannot tell me you would consider giving a lunatic the power of the Undead and turning her loose on the world of man. She would be a rogue. And a dangerous one. We would end up having to destroy her anyway."

She sighed, and when he said nothing, she went on. "And there's one more thing to consider. Unless Beta is set free, all of her spiritual descendants will die. That's the way your magicians worded the spell. And you know what that means, Vlad. Stormy, the only true innocent in all of this, will die. Tonight, Vlad. Midnight tonight."

He opened his eyes, parted his lips to speak, then closed them, rethinking his words. "Then I have to find a way to save Beta before then."

"Vlad? What . . . what the hell is wrong with you?"

Rhiannon stared at him as if she'd never seen him before. And he couldn't speak to her, not even mentally, not without risk. "I wish to speak with Tempest now," he said instead. "Where is she?"

Lupe, who'd been mostly silent until then, looked at him with worry in her eyes. "Um, I thought you knew. She left."

He blinked, stunned. "Left?"

"She said this was no longer her problem,

305

Vlad," Rhiannon said. "She was angry, furious — with you, I imagine."

Lupe added, "I saw her in her room, packing her stuff."

Vlad turned and ran down the hall to Tempest's room. He flung open the door, but it was empty. Then he opened the closet, the bathroom, but all were vacant, and every sign of her presence was missing — except the scent of her. That still lingered.

He went down the stairs and through the mansion to the front door, only to see that Tempest's car was gone. Only a trail of dust remained. She must have only just departed.

"Vlad!" Rhiannon shouted.

He returned to Brooke's bedroom door, which stood open. The others — Rhiannon, Melina and Lupe — were standing just inside.

He said, "You were right, Lupe. Tempest is gone."

"Yes, well, that might present a serious problem," Rhiannon said, and stepping aside, she gave him a view of the empty bed. "Because so is Elisabeta." She wrung her hands, closed her eyes.

"She was listening at the door only moments ago!" Vlad exploded.

Rhiannon lifted her brows and met his eyes. "Is *that* it? Is that why you —"

"Not now, Rhiannon." He closed his eyes. "We have to find them. And we don't have much time."

14

Elisabeta had dragged herself from the bed and across the room. She'd leaned close to the door to listen to what they were saying on the other side. And so she knew it was good that she had failed in her attempt to kill the feisty little blonde who was trying to steal her husband, because according to Rhiannon, Beta needed her.

She needed the woman's body. They'd still been talking outside her door when Elisabeta made her escape. The moment Rhiannon had stated that the only solution was to exorcise her, kill her, she had fled.

This body, the one she had taken from the foolish Brooke, was weakening, and at last she understood why. It was this Belladonna Antigen, yes. But it was more than just that. The body was wrong for her. A poor fit. She couldn't last in this home. She belonged in Tempest's body. It was the only way.

But how? Tempest had taken the ring and the scroll from her.

First, she knew, she had to get out of this place, before those fiends could send her to her death. Even if Vlad intended to protect her, as he'd promised, he was outnumbered. And the vampiress Rhiannon was, Beta sensed, a powerful foe. Escaping in her weakened state would have been more difficult had she not been able to plumb the depths of Brooke's memory for the solution. She knew this place. *She* knew everything about it — more than just how to get out. She knew where the weapons were kept.

And she would need weapons if she hoped to defeat Tempest. She took a change of clothing from the dresser and rapidly put the new outfit on. Then she grabbed a bag from Brooke's closet, one that contained all the items Beta would need to perform the ritual.

Her borrowed body was weak but not helpless. Not yet. Beta knew now that it was going to get a lot worse, and she might not have much time. She went to the window, and it opened easily. Then she climbed out and made her way down, finding every chink and bump in the stone outer walls, just as Brooke had done many times before.

Brooke. Elisabeta almost felt sorry for the

woman. She understood, oh, so well, Brooke's hunger for immortality. It was what had driven her to risk her life by inviting Beta in. It was the same hunger that had driven Elisabeta herself all these long years. To live, to be immortal, to have limitless power and endless life. It was a dream, the one she craved beyond all others. Just as Brooke had.

She found another window, but it was locked. So she dropped the remaining distance to the ground, where a jarring landing subdued her, but only for a moment. She shook it off and hurried behind the massive house to the sunroom in the back, praying that door would be unlocked.

It was, and finally she was back inside the house. She crept through it, into the main parlor, listening. But there was no one. They were all still busy plotting her destruction upstairs. Bastards.

She made her way to the weapons room, quickly punching the code into the panel to unlock the door. Once inside, she armed herself, taking a sleek silver weapon Brooke thought of as a handgun, a supply of the "bullets" it would fire, and a deadly looking but small knife with a sheath that clipped onto the waistband of the jeans she wore, since that bitch Tempest had divested her of the blade she'd had before. She clipped the sheath in back, so that it hung down inside the jeans, rather than on the outside where it would be visible.

Would it be enough?

It would have to be — they would discover her missing soon.

She hurried to the front door and outside, then ducked behind a hedge when a shiny black car pulled swiftly up to a spot directly in front of the main entrance. Staying low, Elisabeta peered over the bush to watch. The car's trunk popped open, and a woman got out and hurried toward the front steps.

It was her. Tempest.

Beta's fingers itched to draw the handgun, even as she probed Brooke's stores of knowledge to learn how to use it. But she restrained herself. She needed Tempest alive.

She noticed, then, the small suitcase and duffle bag resting on the bottom step. Tempest was leaving? No. Beta couldn't lose her. What if she couldn't find her again in time?

Making a hasty decision, Beta leapt the hedge and ran to the car while Tempest's back was to it. The trunk would never do; she would be seen. Instead, Beta moved to the far side of the vehicle and got into the roomy back seat. She crouched on the floor and hoped the whore wouldn't look there before leaving.

Silently, she huddled there, not moving, barely breathing, as she waited.

She felt the car move when Tempest slung her bags into the trunk, and then the thud when she slammed the lid closed. Elisabeta tensed as the woman walked by the car, but she never looked inside. She just opened the driver's door and got in. And then they were in motion.

Elisabeta had no idea what to do next. Wait, she supposed, until they were in some secluded place. Tempest had the ring and the scroll. Surely if the ritual had worked once, it would work again. All she had to do was subdue the twit long enough to put the ring onto her finger and perform the rite the way it was meant to be performed. Her soul would be transferred into Tempest's body — this time, though, Tempest's would be evicted. She would be gone.

Beta would be strong again, and whole. And Vlad would be hers.

Carefully she settled into a more comfortable position on the cramped floor of the vehicle, leaned her head on the back of the front seat and closed her eyes.

■ ■ ■ ■

As she drove, Stormy tried to put Vlad out of her mind, but she couldn't. The more she tried not to think of him, the more he invaded her soul. Memories of their past together, the one she'd forgotten for so long, those few forbidden days with him in Romania, lay waiting for her to find. So rather than dwell on her unrequited and hopeless love, not to mention her probably impending death, she let them come.

"You're not well, are you?" Vlad asked as they drove along winding tracks through the Romanian countryside.

"I'm fine. It's probably jet-lag catching up with me." She knew it wasn't that, though. It was Elisabeta. The woman's presence was stronger here, and the constant struggle for control of her own body was wearing Stormy down.

"You're pale," Vlad said. More worried, Stormy thought, about Elisabeta than about her.

"So are you." She sent him a sideways look, but he only scowled in response to her lame attempt at humor.

"Are you sure you're up to this excursion?"

"If not now, when?" she asked. Then she

shrugged. "Keep driving, Vlad. Take me to Castle Dracula."

"I'm afraid this is as far as we can go by car." He pulled to a stop and got out. She got out, too, and looked in the same direction he was.

They stood at the foot of a peak, and the path up it was so steep, it was nearly vertical. At the top, shrouded in mist and darkness, she could barely make out a shape that might be a castle.

She sighed, unsure she had the strength to make the climb. But then Vlad turned to her. "Come to me, Tempest. Put your arms around my neck."

She frowned, told herself this wasn't the time or place — and complied anyway. Anytime she could put her arms around him was the right time. And she didn't think she had the will to refuse him, anyway. She slipped her arms around his neck. He quickly scooped her off her feet and whispered, "Hold on."

There was a rush of speed and motion too sudden and rapid to absorb, much less follow. Seconds later, he was lowering her to her feet again. He kept his hands on her waist, and it was a good thing, because her knees didn't want to hold her weight. They started to buckle as soon as she tried to stand, and her earlier dizziness was magnified a hundred times.

She let him hold her while she pressed her hands to either side of her head and tried to blink her vision into focus. "What the hell was that?"

"I didn't think you were up to hiking the distance. And really, there was no need. We're here."

Frowning, she searched his face briefly, then turned to follow his gaze. The castle wasn't a castle at all. It was a crumbling pile of ruins, ancient stone blocks piled atop one another to form walls, with little or no mortar left in between. A path wound amid them, and someone had put a modern railing along parts of it, to protect unwary tourists, she supposed, from what would be a deadly fall. "This is it? I thought Castle Dracula was big and white and fancy."

"That's Bran Castle. I was rarely there, but the tourists seem to like it. This . . . this was where I lived. Poenari Castle. There's . . . very little left to explore, I'm afraid."

"Is it safe?"

"Come." He took her hand — not because he cared, she reminded herself, but just to keep her from falling, and that only for Beta's sake — and led her closer. They moved past the walls toward the tallest section, a rounded portion. The top of it was long gone, and it was higher on either side, lower in the middle, where more stones had fallen away, so that its top formed a crescent. He led her all through the place, pointing out what used to be the keep, the courtyards and so on. But nothing was even vaguely familiar to her.

Finally she sighed and touched his shoulder. "Vlad, where is the tower? The place where she died?"

He stopped walking, stopped speaking, lowered his head.

"Is it going to be too hard for you? Seeing that spot again? Because I could go alone."

"No. It's fine. Come."

He took her hand again and led her along a twisting path through the crumbling stones, finally stopping to point at a cluster of other ruins, though they were in far better shape than the first one. "Do you see the tower down there?" he asked, pointing.

"Yes. Is that . . . ?"

"No. That's where the legends say she died. They say she pitched herself from that tower as the Turks approached, in order to prevent herself being captured. But as you know, that's not precisely the way it happened."

"I suppose it makes her rather a heroic figure, to remember it that way."

"I suppose." He turned and looked at a narrow circle of stones, barely four feet high.

"This was the actual tower. My chambers were near the top. I liked to be able to see all the way down the mountain as soon as I rose and before I slept."

He lifted his gaze, and she did, too, trying to picture the place before it had fallen to ruin. But what she saw in her mind's eye could have been more imagination than past life memory.

She moved to the far side of the circular base, where it came within a few yards of a steep drop. She went to step closer to the edge, but Vlad gripped her shoulders. "Careful. The ground is no longer stable here."

Holding her, he moved a little nearer the edge, then stopped. Stormy stared down, such a very long way down, into a sea of mist. The rocky slope dropped straight out of sight beneath the glittering stars. And then, as if on cue, a wind came, and the mists below swirled and then dissipated, so she could see all the way to the bottom, where a narrow stream wound over jagged rocks and boulders far below.

She felt it, then: the powerful sensation of her body falling, plummeting. The sense of weightlessness, of flying. The deathly silence of her descent. Her hair was tugged tight by the force of the air through which she fell. The wind whistled past her ears and stung her face. Heartache pounded inside her chest, so large it felt she would split open and bleed. She felt the crushing impact, pain beyond human endurance exploding in every part of her, and then it vanished and there was nothing but blessed relief. Release. Her breath rushed out of her. Her final breath. And she smiled as she died. *Finally,* she thought. *Peace. An end to this endless grief. Finally. Let me go.*

"Tempest!"

She blinked slowly and found herself lying on the ground, her upper body cradled in Vlad's arms as he smacked her cheeks and shook her shoulders.

"Tempest, talk to me. For the love of the gods . . ."

"Okay," she managed. "I'm . . . okay."

"Far from it, I think." He held her closer, folding her to his chest as he knelt there, stroking her hair. For that brief moment she could almost have let herself believe he really cared. Almost.

"What happened just now? What happened to you?"

She rested against him, closing her eyes, even though she knew this wasn't real, this show of affection. "I think it was her. Elisabeta. I felt what she felt as she plummeted to her death, Vlad. And it wasn't horrible. I mean, there was pain when she hit the rocks. But it was very brief, and it was nothing compared to the pain she was feeling beforehand. The emotional pain. God, it was killing her. But it left her, Vlad. As she died, there was this incredible feeling of relief — of release. She didn't want to hurt anymore."

He'd been rocking her in his arms, but he stopped then. "And yet, she did, didn't she?"

Stormy swallowed hard, lifted her head from his chest and tipped her chin up to stare into his eyes. "I think she still is. Vlad, the woman I feel in these memories or episodes of possession or whatever they are — she's sweet. She's innocent and naive, and very weak and needy. And in a lot of pain, almost all the time. But sweet. But the one who comes in now, to take over the way she does, she's none of those things. She's cruel and angry and violent. I'm not sure she's the same woman at all."

"Or perhaps she is. Perhaps this is what she has become, what my actions caused her to become." He lowered his head. "Perhaps Rhiannon was right. The ritual I had the sorcerers perform was a mistake."

"I think that might be true."

"God, what have I done to her?" He tipped his head back to stare up at the stars.

Stormy sat up, brushing her hair back from her face. "Maybe Rhiannon was right about that, too? Maybe we need to find a way to exorcise her? To set her free?"

His head came down, and his eyes locked onto hers, sparking with anger. "Kill her, you mean?"

"Vlad, she's not alive. Not really."

"Oh, she's very much alive. I see her in you. Even now, I see her. She's trying to come through, trying to speak to me through you, isn't she, Tempest?"

She set her jaw, stiffened her spine. "She has been, ever since we . . . I'm not sure how much longer I can keep on fighting her. It's . . . exhausting."

He averted his eyes quickly. "You, too, are suffering because of what I did."

She lowered her head then. "Guilt isn't going to solve this, Vlad."

"No. I'm not ready to give her up. Not yet, Tempest."

She lifted her head, met his eyes again. "I can't go on like this," she told him. "Not for much longer, Vlad. At least when I'm not with you, she stays . . . dormant. Asleep. But here . . ."

He sighed, impatient, angry perhaps and frustrated. He still expected her to suddenly remember and become the woman he longed for. All *she* wanted to do was figure out how to get rid of her.

And maybe convince him to love her, instead.

She swallowed hard. "Would you . . . take me to her grave?"

"Are you certain you're strong enough?"

"No. But I want to try. I feel as if I have to."

"Don't, not for my sake, Tempest."

"I'm not. It's for her sake, Vlad. Part of me . . . loves her as much as you do. I mean, the woman she was. Not the presence that haunts me now, but that girl. That innocent, grieving, heartbroken child who is, maybe, somehow, a part of me. I have to help her if I can."

"You're a generous woman."

She let her eyes go hard. "I want to help her by setting her free. Not by bringing her back."

His features hardened, but he got to his feet and held out a hand. She took it and let him draw her upright. "The night is aging."

"Yeah," she said, and she slid her arms around his neck. "So let's do this the fast way, all right?"

He nodded. She tightened her grip, and they whirled into the night.

Stormy resurfaced from her memories. She had recovered nearly all of them now, she sensed. She knew when she had fallen in love with him, and why he'd held her heart captive for so very long. Always it had been about Elisabeta. Never her. He'd never

321

loved her.

He never would.

"There is no reason to believe anything dire has happened to either of them," Rhiannon said for the tenth time.

But that was exactly what Vlad believed, and he was kicking himself for his part in it. By the gods, if anything happened to prevent him doing what must be done in time . . .

Melina was on the telephone yet again, dialing Tempest's cell phone number. She met his eyes and shook her head. "I got her voice mail again. She must have the phone turned off, Vlad. If she doesn't want to hear from us, she's not going to pick up the messages I keep leaving."

Lowering his head, Vlad resumed his pacing. "This is my doing. All of it."

Rhiannon stepped into his path, blocking his progress. "Stop this. You can find her, Vlad. You, more than any of us, can find her."

He stared into Rhiannon's eyes, frowning. "I don't know. My bond with Elisabeta isn't as powerful as —"

"Not Beta, Vlad. For the love of the gods, would you stop focusing on her for one second? Are you that obsessed? It's Stormy. I'm talking about Stormy. Do you think I can't smell her on you?" Rhiannon snapped, looking as if she would like to knock him over the head with something heavy. "You drank from her, Vlad. And more than once. Her scent and her essence are still alive in you. The bond created by that act is a powerful one. You, more than any of us here, can sense her."

"You think I haven't tried?" He tipped his head back and pushed his hands through his hair in frustration.

"I think," Rhiannon said, "that you are trying too hard."

"I'm going after them," he said. "Tempest is likely going home, to her mansion in Easton. I'll go there and —"

"Not just yet." Rhiannon glanced at Melina and Lupe. "Does either of you have any skill at scrying?"

"I do," Lupe said.

"Then get a map, and a pendulum, and try to narrow the search. For both of them." Then she turned to Vlad. "Come with me, we have work to do."

He didn't want to go with Rhiannon. He wanted to be out hunting for the women. But Rhiannon was a wise woman. It wouldn't be smart to ignore the help she offered, though why she offered it, he couldn't fathom. He'd all but destroyed her trust in him. He went where she led him, into a room he'd never seen before — a room with sculptures and candles everywhere. It resembled a spiritual temple. There were huge satin pillows strewn about the floor, and she nodded at one, so he sat.

Then she closed the door behind them. She stood in the room's center and turned in a slow circle, waving her hand before her as she did. One by one, the candles came to life, flames leaping onto their wicks in obedience to her gesture and her will. He was impressed, in spite of himself.

"You're going to need to relax," she told him.

"Far easier said than done, Rhiannon."

"Lie back on the pillows, Vlad."

He did, pulling more of the cushions around behind him to make a bed of sorts.

"Listen only to my voice," Rhiannon said, and her tone had become deep and low, soft and, at the same time, commanding. "Thoughts will come. Just move them away and return your attention to my voice. Gently, steer your focus to my words. Only to my words."

"I'll try."

"You'll do it. Keep your eyes open. Choose a candle you see easily and focus on its flame. See the way it dances, the way its fire

324

waxes and wanes like the tides. Like the moon."

He focused on a nearby candle flame.

"See how the wax heats and melts. Do you see it, Vlad?"

"I see it." He watched beads of wax roll slowly down the sides of the candle, pooling at the bottom.

"Feel your body heating and melting just as the wax does. Your feet are warming, melting. Feel the flame relaxing them into liquid."

He felt her words, her will, flowing into him. And he felt his feet grow warm until it seemed they were melting into the floor.

"And now your calves. Feel them pooling, like warm wax. Dripping, liquefying. And your knees, your thighs, warming, heating, melting."

He thought about the women as his body obeyed, wondered what was happening between them right now.

"My words, Vlad. Listen to my voice. See the candle. Feel it heating you. Your groin and your hips. Your pelvis and your belly. Warming, melting, pooling."

She continued, and the thoughts that kept drawing him away seemed to come more slowly and to take longer to return each time he pushed them away.

When she had convinced him that his entire body was a puddle of hot wax on the pillows, she said, "Let your focus go soft. Let the candle flame split into two flames and become blurry. Relax your vision. See now, with your inner eye. See her. See Tempest. Taste her blood again. Feel it coursing through your body. She is inside you, Vlad. She's a part of you. You are bound. See through her eyes. See her."

His vision blurred, and in a moment his eyes fell closed.

"Where is she, Vlad?"

"She's . . . in her car. Belladonna, she calls it. She loves the thing." A smile tugged at his lips. "She's driving."

"Yes. Good. Don't strain, Vlad. Just let the images flow into you. Flowing like that warm, melting wax. Filling you. Warming you. What else do you see?"

He stopped trying and relaxed. Rhiannon's voice made resistance futile, even if he'd wanted to try. "She's . . . crying."

"That's all right. Don't let those tears distract you. They flow, warm and liquid, like the wax. They flow for you. They show you her heart. They are the waters of true emotion, and they are cleansing and healing to a woman's soul."

"She loves me," he whispered, feeling the

emotion that filled her heart to bursting.

"Yes. And she wants you to know where she is. She wants you to come to her, Vlad. Listen to her thoughts now. Move gently into her mind and listen. Open to her. Let those thoughts roll like the melting wax. Let them seep into you. Let them. . . ."

Her voice faded, replaced by the voice of Tempest's heart, of her thoughts.

He doesn't love me . . . never loved me. He loves her. I was just a means to get her back all along. He was using me. I've wasted my life, loving him, longing for him, waiting and hoping, when all the time he never . . .

Have to stop thinking about him. God, why can't I get him out of my mind? Have to go home. No, no, not home. Don't want to face Maxie and Lou, not now. Don't want to tell them what a fool I've been. Don't want to be around anyone, no one. Not now, not yet. I need to be alone. I need to get past this.

I wonder if he'll let Rhiannon exorcise Elisabeta from Brooke's body? He won't. I know he won't. I wish Rhiannon could exorcise him from my heart, though. Maybe she can. Maybe I should ask her. Then again, maybe it won't matter. I'll be dead anyway, if Rhiannon can't send Beta to the other side.

She looked through the windshield of the car, seeing darkness, a road and a sign.

"Seaside, 80 km." And she thought of the sea, the coast, a cozy inn where she could rest and try to heal. *Far enough away from him? Maybe. Maybe far enough. It's only another hour. I'll go there. I love the ocean. If I'm going to die tonight, it can be right there, on the shore, with the waves rolling in around my feet. A good place to die.*

"Seaside," he said aloud, though even to his own ears, his voice sounded a bit hoarse. "A town called Seaside. She's going there."

"Good, Vlad," Rhiannon said softly. "Very good. Now I want you to pull yourself out of her body, out of her mind. I want you to see what's around her, in the car. Is there anyone else there with her?"

"I am with her."

"Yes, but besides you."

He gently withdrew from Tempest's mind, the voice of her thoughts fading away, until he was in the car, in the passenger seat. He felt something, a presence, a familiar one, and he frowned, guiding his attention toward it. And then he saw —

The door to the room burst open, jarring Vlad back into his own body, into the room, into reality, where he landed with as much impact as if he'd fallen from a tall building. The trance state shattered on impact, and he sat up so fast it made him dizzy. He had

328

to press a hand to his head. Rhiannon's hands closed on his shoulders as she snapped, "Lupe, what are you thinking, barging in here during —"

Vlad growled an interruption. "When I can stand upright, you bungling mortal, I'll —"

"I've got her!" Lupe blurted almost at the same time. Then she looked at Vlad as his threat sunk in, and her face went tight with fear. "I'm sorry, I didn't mean —"

He held up a hand to shut her up.

"Ground yourself, Vlad. Here, hold this." Rhiannon handed him a large quartz crystal the size of his fist, and he took it and held it between his palms, trying to get his bearings again.

"We know where Tempest is going, Lupe," Rhiannon explained. "To a town called Seaside."

"I got the same thing. But not just for her," Lupe said, a little breathlessly. "I got the same results when I scried for Elisabeta. I think she's following her or —"

"She's not following her," Vlad said softly. Gripping the edge of a table, he got to his feet, still a bit shaky. "She's *with* her."

"With her?" Rhiannon searched his face.

"She's hiding in the back of Tempest's car."

A gasp came from the doorway, and they turned to see Melina standing there. Her fists clasped, she said, "The weapons room door was open, so I went in to check. There's a handgun missing."

Tempest pulled over and patted Belladonna's dashboard the way she would pat the neck of a sweaty horse, one that had just carried her away from trouble. "Thanks for taking me the hell out of there. You've been a pal. I'm gonna miss you."

She cut the engine, slid one arm through one of the straps of her backpack purse, and pulled it onto her shoulder as she got out of the car. Then she stood for a moment, looking down at the spot that had beckoned her. A rocky shoreline, choppy sea beyond, shallow waves rolling up and breaking over the stones and boulders. It appealed to her, this rough-faced beach. Not all smooth and sandy, but rugged and forbidding, harsh beneath the star speckled velvet black of the sky.

Stormy hitched her bag up higher onto her shoulder, walked down the little incline to the shore and stood for a moment, staring out at the sea. And even as she tried to find a positive spin to put on her heartache, warm tears welled in her eyes and rolled slowly down her cheeks.

"It's not entirely bad," she told herself. "At least I got rid of *her*."

She took a moment, then, to feel the lightness in her soul. No more was there that sense of something foreign, lurking and waiting to take over. Hating her from within.

It felt good. It was a huge relief.

And yet, there was another weight in her, this one crushing heavily down on her heart. She loved him. She loved him even now. And it was stupid — pathetic, really — to love a man who didn't love her back. She knew it. And yet there was nothing she could do about it. Pretty sad to think that she, the independent and notoriously feisty Stormy Jones, was going to die loving a man who cared nothing for her.

"Pathetic," she muttered, and bent to pick up a small stone, then straightened and hurled it out into the waves.

"Yes. Terribly pathetic."

Stormy spun around at the voice coming from right behind her, knowing before she saw her, who it was. Elisabeta, in Brooke's body, holding a handgun and pointing it right at her chest. The wind blew in from the sea, tossing Brooke's normally sleek hair into a wild mass of auburn tangles as Elisabeta's black eyes glinted from her face.

Stormy stiffened, stifling the words that flew to her lips, realizing she was face to face with an armed lunatic who wanted her dead. Better to try to diffuse the situation.

"I left because I want no more to do with him, Beta," she said. "He's all yours. I won't be back."

"Sadly, that's not quite good enough."

Frowning, Stormy tried to size up her situation. She had no weapon. There was a cell phone in her bag, but Beta could squeeze that trigger before she would be able to take it out, much less dial 911. There was no one around. No one in sight. She tried to remember the last place she'd passed where there might have been people or even lights, and knew it had been a while.

"What do you want from me, then?" she asked.

"Not so much. Just your body."

Stormy went stiff. Could the bitch know, somehow, what was ailing her? Her face was drawn and pale, her eyes slightly sunken. Dark circles were beginning to form underneath them. "What's wrong with the one you've got?"

"It's dying," she said. "So I need yours."

"Sorry, but I'm using it right now." She could have kicked herself for letting the words out, heavy with sarcasm and impatience. She schooled herself to calm. "Maybe . . . there's some way I can help you, Elisabeta. Maybe —"

"Oh, there is. I need your body before midnight, or we'll both die. In order to do that, I must have my ring back. And the scroll. Give them to me."

She would need the ring and the scroll to perform the rite again. And this time, Stormy realized, she wanted to perform it on *her*. "I'm sorry. I can't —"

"Give them to me or I'll kill you!"

Stormy swallowed, held up a hand as if to calm the woman. "If you kill me, you'll never have my body."

"If you don't give them to me, I'll die anyway," Beta said. "Now give them to me."

Stormy waited a beat, trying to decide the best answer to give, and finally decided not to push her luck. "I don't have them."

"You're lying!"

"No, I'm not. When I left, I washed my hands of this entire case. I wanted no more to do with you or with Vlad — *or* with that cursed ring. I'm telling you, Beta, I don't have them."

Beta closed her eyes, but popped them wide open again before Stormy could even think about going for the gun. "Who does?"

Stormy almost smiled. Almost. Because of

333

all the lies she could think of, the truth was still the best option. "Rhiannon," she said. "Good luck getting them from her."

Beta was silent for a long moment, her eyes seeming to search inwardly. It was almost as if she were listening to something, or someone, and then she focused again, blinking and frowning. "You have a . . . *Cele-phone? Yes?*"

"A cell phone? Yes, I have one. It's in my bag here."

"Take it out."

Stormy started to take the bag from her shoulder, and Elisabeta wiggled the gun. "Slowly."

"All right. All right. Easy with that thing. If you shoot me by accident, we'll both be screwed." They were both screwed anyway, Stormy thought. Clearly Beta had escaped before Rhiannon could exorcise her from Brooke's body. And time was ticking away. Slowly and carefully, Stormy slid the cell phone from its holder on the side of the backpack. "It's right here, okay?"

"Call her."

"Who? Rhiannon?"

Beta nodded, her gun hand starting to tremble. She was getting tired.

"Okay. Just . . . it's turned off. I have to turn it on." She flipped open the phone, and as soon as it powered up, the message signal sounded. No time now, though, for retrieving her voice mail. Instead, she located the number for Athena House in her phonebook and hit the call button.

It rang. And rang. And rang some more. She licked her lips, held the phone out so Beta could listen if she wanted. "No one's there," she said.

"Does she not have a . . . cell phone she carries with her. Like yours?"

"Yeah. You want me to try that number?"

Beta nodded, so Stormy placed the call. Rhiannon didn't pick up, though. Vlad did.

"Tempest?" he asked. And God, he sounded as if he really hoped it was her. Yeah, he probably did. He still needed her to save his lunatic bride.

"Yeah, it's me."

"Are you all right? Where are you?"

And now he sounded worried. *Really* worried. "I'm here with Beta. She has a gun on me."

"Give it to me!" Beta commanded.

"Hold on. Your wife wants to talk to you." Stormy held out the cell phone.

Beta snatched it from her, keeping the gun aimed, one handed now, and her eyes focused on Stormy. "Get the ring and the scroll from Rhiannon and bring them to me.

If you want to save me, Vlad, do this for me. If you don't, Tempest and I will both be dead soon. And you know that's the truth. And if you come, Vlad, and you are not alone, I will shoot her, just to be sure you don't try to save the wrong woman."

Without waiting for a reply, she handed the phone back to Stormy. "Tell him where we are, so he can come to us."

Stormy nodded as she pressed the phone to her own ear again. "We're on a deserted stretch of beach off the Seaside exit. Take a right, about two miles down. You'll see my car along the roadside." She met Elisabeta's eyes and said, "She's going to try to take my body. If it were me, I'd let the bitch die, but I don't suppose you feel the same."

Beta snatched the phone from her hand and hurled it into the sea. "I should kill you right now."

"Go for it. I've got nothing pressing."

She swung. It came out of the blue; Stormy hadn't expected it. The gun hit her right in the side of the head, behind her left eye. There was a brief explosion of pain, and then the ground was rushing up to meet her as she went down for the count.

Her last thought was that her words to Vlad had been wasted and she'd taken the blow for nothing. There was no way he would let his precious Elisabeta die. He would probably bring the ring and the scroll and assist in Stormy's execution.

15

"She said to come alone. And that is *precisely* what I intend to do." Vlad hovered near the mansion's front door, addressing Rhiannon, while the other two mortal women stood a short distance behind her. They looked nervous, as if they expected a vampiric battle to break out at any moment and wished to avoid being caught in the crossfire. "And frankly, I'm growing weary of repeating myself. Give me the ring, Rhiannon. And the scroll."

He held out a hand, palm up, and looked into her eyes.

She held them in one hand but didn't offer them to him. He hoped to the gods she wasn't going to force him to take them from her.

"There is strength in numbers, Vlad. And she's not one of us. She'll never know if I'm lurking in the shadows nearby, ready to back you up, if needed."

"And since when does Dracula require backing up?" he asked. "Rhiannon, she's a mortal. A sick one, at that."

She pursed her full lips and stared at him, her eyes speaking volumes. "She's your wife," she said.

The words penetrated. The meaning clarified in his mind. "You don't trust me."

She averted her eyes. "I'm going with you. That's all and that's final. If you want to prevent it, Vlad, you'll have to kill me, and I don't think you're willing to do that." She shrugged and met his eyes again, hers less serious this time. "Moreover, I don't think you could best me even if you were willing to try."

"Don't bet your life on it."

Rhiannon locked her gaze on his. "I never thought it would come to this. The two of us on opposing sides. I'm going to Stormy, Vlad. And I'm going now." She moved toward the door, but she would have to pass him to get to it.

Vlad threw his will at her, hitting her squarely in the chest with a surge of energy that stopped her in her tracks and made her suck in a quick, sharp breath.

She glared at him. "You dare . . ."

"Give me the ring and the scroll, Rhiannon."

She flung out an arm in a powerful arc, sending a bolt of energy that knocked him backward until he hit the wall, hard. A nearby painting crashed to the floor.

He righted himself, shook off the pain and hurled his powerful will at her much harder than he had before. Rhiannon flew into the air as if hit in the gut by a wrecking ball, landed hard, on her back and struggled to suck in a breath of air.

Vlad lunged at her then, straddled her, and searched her until he found the items he needed in a deep pocket of her gown. He took them from her, paused only to gaze at her face, to touch her cheek as she blinked to clear her vision. "I'm sorry, Rhiannon. You left me no choice."

Then he turned from her and raced from the room, out through the front door and into the night. Regret gnawed at his soul. But he hadn't harmed her. Not truly. Hurt her, yes, but she would suffer no lasting effects. In fact, she would likely be strong enough to follow on his heels within the hour. So he'd best hurry.

He whirled, right there on the steps of Athena House. Spun like a top, gaining momentum and speed, and exerted his will to alter his form. As a giant raven, he flexed his wings, beat them once, twice, three times, as he pushed off with his legs and took to the starry sky. As he made his way to her, Vlad remembered the way their time together had ended in the past. He let the memories flow through him, hoping they would stiffen his resolve to do what he knew must be done.

He had been losing hope of ever finding a way to solve the riddle that had become his life. He stood beside Tempest at the site that had been his bride's grave, and he watched her stare at the ground that bore no marker, no memory. All had been lost to the ravages of time. Grasses and trees grew. The stream still bubbled and laughed its way past. The stars still shone down on her resting place.

Rest. That was a bitter joke, wasn't it? There had been no rest for his beloved. No peace, not in all this time. Why hadn't he had the strength to let her go?

Why couldn't he find it still?

Tempest looked ill. She was pale and trembling at intervals. She rubbed her arms with her hands as if she were cold, and he put an arm around her to warm her. "You haven't eaten all night," he said. "Perhaps we should go —"

She whirled on him, her hands fisting and rising, her eyes blazing into his. Black, black

341

as coal. "Do not think to leave me here, Vlad! Do not dare think it!"

He recoiled, taken unaware by the sudden change in her. But he knew she was not Tempest any longer. He was staring into the eyes of his beloved, of his Elisabeta.

He lifted an unsteady hand, touched her face. "I wouldn't leave you."

"You have!" she accused. But she didn't pull away from his touch. Rather, she covered his hand on her cheek with her own, leaned into it, closed her eyes. "You've abandoned me to this existence, trapped, unable to return, unable to move on. I want to return, Vlad. I want to be with you. I will never give up."

Tears sprang into his eyes, though he fought them. "You shouldn't have taken your own life, Beta. You should have waited for me. Gods, if only you had waited."

"I have waited. All these centuries, I've waited. And now I've found you again. Don't let her come between us, Vlad. Don't let her take me away from you."

"I —" He searched her face, unable to speak, because it was as if she knew exactly what he'd been thinking.

"She wants to, you know. She wants to force me back into that infernal netherworld that's neither life nor death. That limbo. That prison between the worlds. I cannot go back there,

Vlad. I will not."

"I won't let that happen, Beta. Not if I can prevent it."

"She wants you for herself," she whispered.

He lowered his head.

"I'll never let her have you."

Vlad's head rose again at the venom in her tone. At the hatred in her voice. She did not sound like the Elisabeta he had known.

"I'll kill her first, Vlad. I vow to you I will."

"Beta, don't think that way. It's not —" He broke off there, because she had whirled away from him and taken off running through the forest.

Vlad took off after her. "Wait! Beta, dammit, wait!" He poured on a burst of speed, even as the horrible scene unfolded before his eyes. Beta had flung herself — no, she had flung Tempest — into the stream at its deepest point, and she lay face down in the water. Her arms flailed as if she were trying to get up, as if something were holding her down. She was drowning!

Vlad gripped her around her waist and chest, and hauled her, dripping, out of the water. Then, turning, he took her to the grassy bank and laid her down on her back. He pressed his ear to her chest to listen to her breaths and heard none. But then, suddenly, her head came up and she began choking, water spewing from her nose and mouth.

"Thank the gods," he muttered, and rolled her onto her side, to help her eliminate the icy water from her lungs.

Leaning over, weak, and shaking now from head to toe, she gagged and spat and gasped, until, finally, she managed to empty the water from her lungs. As she sucked in breath after breath of air, he took off his coat and wrapped it around her shoulders.

"Tempest?" he asked.

She lifted her head, eyes tired and unfocused. "What . . . happened?"

"I . . . I don't know."

A twig snapped behind him, and Vlad whirled to see Rhiannon standing there, Roland at her side. She looked furious. "You know exactly what happened, Vlad. Elisabeta just attempted to murder Tempest. You saw it. You know it's the truth."

He closed his eyes, lowered his head.

Rhiannon moved closer, knelt beside Tempest. "Has this happened before, Stormy?"

Still shaking, she tugged the coat closer around her shoulders and nodded, the movement jerky. "Yes. I think so. I mean, I wasn't sure until now, but —"

Her words were cut off by another round of coughing.

"We have to get her back to the castle," Roland said. "She needs to get warm and dry. Mortal bodies can't tolerate this sort of trauma easily."

Nodding, Vlad got to his feet, reached to gather Tempest into his arms, but Roland stopped him with a hand to his shoulder. "Let me, my friend. I'll get her there quickly, bundle her by the fire and care for her until you arrive."

"But why?" he asked, searching the man's face.

It was Rhiannon who answered him. "I think you know why. You know what must be done, Vlad. There are things we'll need, for the rite of exorcism."

Vlad gasped, and his gaze shot from Rhiannon's to Tempest as Roland gathered her weakened, battered body into his arms. She was not doing well. She couldn't take much more of this attack — and he knew now that she was indeed under attack. Without the ring and the scroll, he couldn't hope to help her find union and harmony with the soul he believed to be her former self, a part of her own. But she couldn't go on like this, either. Not and survive.

His tears spilling over, he no longer tried to control them as he whispered, "So be it, then."

By the time Rhiannon and Vlad arrived back

at the castle, Tempest was warm and dry, as Roland had promised she would be. She'd changed clothes, and now wore a nightgown and a heavy velvet robe, and had a blanket wrapped around her shoulders besides. She was sipping hot soup from a large mug, and sitting with her legs curled beneath her in front of a roaring fire. Her hair was beginning to dry, its tendrils springing into their natural curls around her face. She looked exhausted, drained, as she stared into the fire.

Rhiannon had explained that she and Roland, knowing full well Vlad's folly could only lead to disaster, had decided to stay on another day, another night, in case they were needed. Rhiannon had deliberately tuned into Tempest's mind, and had picked up on her distress and located her easily.

Just as well.

His quest was at an end. And yet a spark of hope remained. He had to say goodbye to his goal of almost six hundred years. He had to say goodbye to Elisabeta. But perhaps something of a chance would remain for himself and Tempest. He didn't know. He didn't know if her feelings for him were her own or a part of the possession of her body by his long dead wife. In fact, he wasn't even certain his own feelings were truly for her or for the woman she had been in another time, another place.

And even if it turned out they did still care for one another, there was the inevitable end they both must face. She was mortal. She was not one of The Chosen. She would die. He would live on.

But one thing was certain. She couldn't go on this way.

"Are we ready to do this?" Rhiannon asked.

Vlad looked at Tempest. "Are you certain she can withstand it?"

"It shouldn't be too trying, Vlad. It's only a ritual."

He nodded. Tempest turned to face him. "I'm ready," she said, her voice soft. "I'm sorry, Vlad. I'm sorry I wasn't strong enough to give her a chance."

He moved closer, touched her hand. "Perhaps this was the way it was meant to be, Tempest. She needs to be at peace. We can give her that, if nothing more."

She nodded, then looked to Rhiannon. "What should I do?"

"Just lie down. Relax." She nodded toward the chaise that stood a few feet from the fire, and Tempest rose unsteadily. Roland gripped one arm, Vlad the other, and they helped her to the chaise. She slid the blanket from her shoulders as she lay down and pulled it over her instead.

"Very good." Rhiannon slid a pack from her

shoulder, and opened it began taking items from it one by one. Weeds she'd gathered from the forest. A handful of dirt from Elisabeta's grave, a stone from the stream where her body had landed, a vial of water she'd provided herself, and salt and candles, black ones. A bell. She gathered candles from around the castle and brought them to place with the rest of her items.

She pulled a small table closer and began laying the items out one by one. Then she carried the black candles to the extreme directions of the room. One on the mantle by the fire in the south, another on a table in the west, where she poured the water into a bowl. A third rested in a spot she cleared on the bookshelf in the north, the fourth beside a dish of herbs in the east.

She stared at the candles, and one by one they burst into flames at the sheer power of her will. Then she touched one burning wick to the herbs, until they began to blaze. After a moment the died flames out and left the herbs to smoulder in a silver dish. The spiraling smoke they emitted was pungent and strong.

"You two sit on either side of her. If Elisabeta realizes what we're doing, there's a chance she could come through and try to prevent us from completing the ritual, or if that fails, to try again to harm her. You'll need to hold her to prevent that."

Vlad looked down at Tempest, the way her eyes widened at Rhiannon's words, and he stroked her forehead. "I won't let that happen. I promise you."

When she nodded, he turned to Rhiannon. "Proceed."

Rhiannon stood still for a long moment, as if gathering her thoughts, but Vlad thought she was doing something far deeper than that. She was connecting to some force within her, or perhaps beyond herself. When she opened her eyes again, she looked different, more powerful than she ever had — and that was saying a lot.

She moved as if floating, lifting a hand and tracing the shape of a circle around the room, encompassing all of them as she muttered words in what he thought was Egyptian. And Vlad swore he could see an ether forming a sphere around them. Thin, barely visible, it wavered and danced, and he had the odd sensation of being contained within a bubble of power.

Then she moved to the westernmost part of the circle and moved her arms as if parting a curtain. And he glimpsed a darkness there, a dark portal within the bubble's wall.

Finally she moved to Tempest and began her work. She chanted over her body, and used her fingers to sprinkle it with water from the bowl. Then she returned the bowl to its place and came back to take up the incense, and again using her hands, she wafted the smoke over Tempest, from her head to her feet.

She continued chanting haunting, mesmerizing words in a melodic, hypnotic tone. Deep and rich and commanding yet gentle.

Tempest's eyes fell closed. Her breathing grew shallow, and she began to turn her head to the left and right.

Vlad held her shoulders, wanting to speak to her, to comfort her, but Rhiannon caught that urge and then his eyes, and told him without speaking to remain silent. She kept chanting.

She put the smouldering herbs back in their spot and took up the bell, ringing it over Tempest, over her head, her chest, her belly, her hips, her knees, her feet. And now her chanting took on a more urgent tone. It was louder, more commanding.

Tempest twisted her head harder. Her breaths came short and sharp and fast, and she started to move her body, twisting and writhing from side to side.

Rhiannon slipped into English. "Leave this body, Elisabeta. Go, through the western gate and on to your reward, to rest. To peace. Go,

Elisabeta. Release this woman and go!"

Tempest's eyes opened wide and blue. She shrieked as if in agony, and her body lifted from the chaise as her back arched nearly double.

Roland and Vlad gripped her, and to his amazement, it took all their strength to press her down again.

"Go," Rhiannon commanded. "You do not belong to this plane! Go, Elisabeta!"

Tempest's entire body began to spasm, as if she were having a seizure of some sort. The men struggled to hold her, and Vlad shot a panicked look at Rhiannon. "I don't think she's breathing. She's not breathing, Rhiannon!"

Her face turned red, and then her lips turned blue, and the rest of her skin tone followed.

"It's killing her, my love," Roland said. "This isn't going to work. Elisabeta will not leave her alive."

Rhiannon hesitated only a moment as the spasming continued. But then she ran to Tempest and gripped her shoulders. "It's ended," she said. "It's over. Breathe again, child. Breathe."

Immediately Tempest's body relaxed and stopped shaking. But it was a long, long moment before she sucked in a breath so powerful Vlad wondered that it didn't burst her lungs.

Rhiannon sagged in relief. "See to her. I

must attend the circle."

"Did it work?" Vlad asked. "Is Beta gone?"

Rhiannon met his eyes and shook her head sadly. "Her grip on our little mortal is more powerful than I could have imagined, Vlad. If I'd forced her out, she would have taken Tempest's soul with her. I'm sorry."

Vlad sighed. He wasn't certain if it was in disappointment or relief. Perhaps both. He gathered Tempest into his arms, carried her to the chair nearest the fire and sat there, holding her in his lap, her body resting against his chest. He held her and pondered what on earth he could do now that the exorcism had failed.

Rhiannon had taken away the sphere of energy, extinguished the candles and poured the smoking herbs into the fireplace. She turned to him then, her face grim as she moved closer, her hands going to his shoulders. "We cannot exorcise the trespassing soul from her body. But we can minimize its strength and power over her. That power, Vlad, is at its peak when she is near you. You know that. You've seen it." She closed her eyes, and Vlad thought he glimpsed a tear on those thick lashes before she spoke again. "You have to let her go, love. For her sake, you have to let her go."

Vlad stared down at the beautiful woman in

his arms. Her eyes were closed, her breathing deep and regular at last. He stroked her hair away from her face. "It won't be forever, Tempest. Only until I can locate the ring and the scroll. Only until then. I promise you." He bent to press a kiss on her lips, committing their softness to memory. "It will be easier for her if I can make her forget," he said. "Give me just a few more moments with her. I'll erase her memory, and then you can take her away."

"Rhiannon?"

Melina and Lupe knelt on either side of her as Rhiannon regained her senses and struggled to sit up.

"Are you all right?" Melina asked.

"Of course I'm all right." She gathered the shreds of her dignity and pushed her hands against the floor in an effort to rise. To her utter humiliation, the two mortals helped her, gripping her arms and tugging until she was upright again. As soon as she had her footing, Rhiannon shook their hands away. "I don't desire your help."

"I don't blame you," Lupe said. Melina shot her a look, but the younger woman ignored it. "I looked in the archives, as you suggested, Rhiannon. I know that members of our order assisted the priestesses who tried to hold you against your will, so long ago."

"What they tried, mortal, was to kill me. Had Vlad not taken me from that place, not transformed me when he did, I would have died. And that was precisely what they wanted. They nearly killed both of us in trying to prevent my escape."

Lupe lowered her head. "It was wrong, what they did. I'm sorry."

Rhiannon lifted her brows.

"Rhiannon," Melina said. "You have to know those women were not acting in accordance with the laws of the Sisterhood. They took it upon themselves to align with the priestesses of Isis to act against you in exchange for the reams of wisdom those priestesses promised them in return."

"Of course. And I suppose the Sisterhood punished them for it. Or were they given some sort of medal, instead?"

Melina glanced at Lupe and said nothing. Lupe frowned and returned her gaze to Rhiannon's. "I couldn't find any mention of what action was taken against them, if any," she said.

"We don't keep written records of that sort of thing," Melina said.

"What sort of thing?" Lupe asked.

Melina licked her lips. "They were executed. Hanged, both of them, for betraying the laws of the order." She met Rhiannon's eyes. "Read my mind if you don't believe that's the truth, Rhiannon. I'm not proud of what they did, and I'm not proud of what was done to them as a result. But I suppose you have a right to know. You *can* trust us."

She was skeptical. "An order is only as trustworthy as its members, Melina. And this order seems to me to be lousy with traitors. Take Brooke, for example."

"Three, in all these centuries," Melina countered.

"Three that I know of. I have no doubt there have been more. You don't exactly choose wisely when you recruit these women."

"I've made mistakes, that's true. I'm only human."

"Precisely."

Lupe licked her lips nervously. "We're wasting time. We need to go after him if we want to have any hope of saving Stormy."

"We?" Rhiannon cocked one brow as she speared the woman with her eyes.

Melina stepped closer, clearing her throat nervously. "We . . . need to go along, Rhiannon. And I'm afraid I can't take no for an answer. If Brooke survives, she'll need us there. We need to bring her home."

355

Rhiannon rolled her eyes. "Where she'll no doubt be tried, convicted and executed for betraying the order."

"Don't pretend to understand our ways, Rhiannon. You're making assumptions. If there's a way I can save her, I will. But she has to face the repercussions of her actions."

Lupe came up to stand beside Melina. "I don't want to tell you guys your business, but it seems to me we also need a plan."

She had a point, Rhiannon thought, though she hated to admit it. With a deep sigh, she said, "If you mortals are coming along, I suppose we'd best travel by car. I have copied the rite we'll need to exorcise Beta from Brooke's body, to set her free of the power of the ring. It's right —" She dipped a hand into her pocket, but it came up empty. She frowned.

"I have the copy you gave me," Melina said.

Rhiannon swallowed hard. "There's one thing I must tell you, and on this I am adamant," she said. "We do not intervene until we are certain of Vlad's intentions."

"We already know his intentions," Melina said. "He's going to help Elisabeta take Stormy's body. He's going to kill her, Rhiannon."

"Perhaps," Rhiannon said. But deep down,

she hoped she was wrong. Vlad had made the right decision once before. She had to believe he would do so again, despite the fact that his obsession for Elisabeta seemed only to have worsened over the past sixteen years. For his sake, she had to give him the chance to do the right thing.

And then she was going to kick his ass for what he'd done to her tonight.

"We do not intervene," Rhiannon said again, "until I am certain. If either of you tries to step in before I give the word, I promise you, you will not see the sunrise. Is that understood?"

The woman looked at each other, fear wide in their eyes. "Understood," Melina said softly.

As she lay there, drifting in and out of consciousness, Stormy was flooded with memories, the missing pieces of her time with Vlad, sixteen years ago. The memories Vlad had erased from her mind for so long.

He'd tried to save her. He'd tried to let Rhiannon exorcise Elisabeta from her body. He'd been forced to choose between them . . . and he'd chosen her.

The knowledge made her heart sing, gave her a surge of strength, enough to bring her back from the stupor into which Elisabeta's blow had plunged her. But the moment she did so, her joy faded and her doubts returned. Just because he had chosen her in the past, that didn't mean he would make the same choice again. He'd shown no hint of his feelings for her since their reunion. He'd given her no reason to believe he would act against his bride to save her.

Would he?

Stormy forced her questions to the back of her mind and tried to take stock of her current situation. She found herself paralyzed. Panic at being unable to move her limbs hit her like a blast of ice water in the face, and she came fully awake, eyes flying wide as the instinctive need to move surged through her. She strained and pulled.

Something hit her, a hard, stinging smack across her face.

She went still, blinking through the surge of hot tears that sprang into her eyes and tried to focus.

Brooke — no, not Brooke, Elisabeta — stood before her, silhouetted by the moon against darkness, the pounding sea at her back. There was something different about the beach. And slowly as her mind cleared, Stormy became aware of several things all at once. First, she wasn't paralyzed at all, but bound by lengths of rope that had been in the trunk of her own car. They held her immobile. She lay on her back, her arms outspread and staked to the ground on either side of her. She felt the ropes chafing her skin. Her ankles were bound together, and staked, as well. And she had been moved. She was no longer on that gorgeous stretch of rocky shore where she had stopped to work through her feelings and her pain and, perhaps, to die.

No, this spot was different. There were trees and brush around, and the ground was just as rocky here, but amid the rocks was soil, not sand. The waves crashed to the shore beyond Elisabeta, but that shore was farther away than it had been before.

Finally she drew her gaze back to the woman who stood before her. And the cold breath of panic crept into her veins as it fully hit her — she was bound. Completely vulnerable to the whims of this insane, unnatural being. A being who wanted nothing more than to see her dead.

Hell.

Elisabeta seemed satisfied that Stormy had stopped her struggling, and she turned and resumed what she had been doing. What she had been doing, it turned out, was placing candles on the ground. And as Stormy slid her gaze back along those she had already set out, she saw that they would form a complete circle around her staked body. A circle in which she lay not in the center, but toward one side. There was room for another to lie within the ring beside her, and she had no doubt Elisabeta intended to be that other.

At four equally spaced points around the circle, censers were at the ready, heaped high with herbs that would burn to surround her in clouds of fragrance and power; herbs that would help Beta in her purposes. No herb had the power to eject a soul from its body. But the right ones would grease the wheels, so to speak. And though Stormy had no idea where the insane woman had located the candles and herbs, she had little doubt that Beta knew what she was doing.

She had to get the hell out of this. She resumed tugging at the ropes that held her. Elisabeta paused with the lighted match in her hand, poised at the wick of one of the candles, and sent her a scowl. "Stop it. It's no use, anyway. You're only wasting your energy."

Stormy stopped but not because of what Beta had said. She stopped because of the way the other woman looked there in the light of that tiny flame. Her eyes were even more deeply sunken than before, and rested atop giant, dark brown half moons. Her face was gaunt and pale in the flickering match-light, and her skin seemed papery and loose. Dry to the point of peeling, and hanging from the bones of her face as if it were no longer attached.

"My God, how long have we been here?"

Beta shrugged. "A couple of hours. Why?"

Clearly Beta didn't know about the drastic and rapid changes in her appearance. But as Stormy watched her, she could tell the woman didn't feel a hell of a lot better than she looked. She walked in tiny, weak steps, feet barely leaving the ground, back bent, head low. She was out of breath, it seemed. She had aged fifty years in the space of a few hours.

"Where did you get the candles?"

"They were in Brooke's bag. She saved them from last time."

"And the herbs?"

"The same. I only wish Brooke had memorized the rite itself, but she didn't." She shrugged. "It doesn't matter, I suppose. I need to wait for the ring."

"I see. And, uh, what are you doing now?" Stormy asked.

"Lighting the candles." Her voice was hoarse.

"Well, yeah, I can see that. But could you

361

elaborate?"

"For the ritual," Beta said. "Vlad is coming. He's bringing the ring and the scroll."

Stormy would have liked to think he wouldn't go through with it. That he would arrive like some kind of a dark knight in onyx armor and save her from the madwoman. But the madwoman was his wife. The love of his life. That was fact. Anything else she might come up with was guesswork. Hell, he'd never told Stormy how he felt about her. Not even in the past. Maybe if Beta had never been squatting inside her body, he never would have felt a damn thing to begin with.

And yet he tried to save me from her, all those years ago. Maybe he would again.

No, she couldn't count on him to get her out of this mess. She had to save herself.

She tugged, pulling her right arm, but not jerking it as she had before. Best to keep her efforts hidden. She exerted steady pressure and hoped to feel the stake in the ground give a little.

It didn't.

Perhaps sensing something, Beta turned to study her. "What are you doing?" She had lit half the candles by now.

"I can see why you moved us to a different spot," Stormy said. "The wind isn't even touching the flames, is it?"

"No. We're sheltered here by the trees and those bigger boulders over there," she replied, nodding toward the giant rocks that flanked their spot. So dark, the boulders. They blended into the night; Stormy hadn't seen them there behind the trees before.

Elisabeta resumed lighting the candles.

"You don't look so good," Stormy said. Making conversation, hoping to mask her movements by keeping Beta distracted. She'd had no luck with the stake at her left arm and so was tugging surreptitiously on the right one now. One at a time, she thought, would let her exert more strength on a single goal. But so far this stake wasn't moving any more than the first one had.

"It doesn't matter. I'll be out of this body soon enough."

"Yeah, it looks like any minute now."

She felt the glare Beta shot her and stopped tugging on the right stake. No progress at all. Okay, maybe the one at her feet. She tugged hard, bending her knees upward a minuscule amount.

"Ahh, he's coming," Beta said, straightening from the final candle and turning slowly. Her form was bowed, as if she were very old or very tired. The change in her from only a few hours earlier was astounding.

Stormy twisted her head to look in the direction the other woman was staring, and she saw a giant raven, as large as an eagle, easily, land heavily on the ground nearby. And then it opened its wings and seemed to stand straighter, stretch higher, and right before her eyes it changed until it became a man, all dressed in black.

Dracula.

Smiling, an expression that was downright frightening to behold, Beta called out, "Here, Vlad. I'm here."

Stormy closed her eyes and tugged harder against the ropes holding her ankles. They burned, scraping her skin. It didn't matter. She had to get away. Dracula had arrived. To kill her or to save her? There was no way to know. She kept her eyes trained on his approach and struggled against her bonds, no longer trying to be quiet or still.

And then he stepped into the light cast by all those dancing candles. His eyes sought her out, found her, but gave nothing away. No sign of affection. No hidden, reassuring smile. Nothing. He just looked at her, his eyes skimming her face, then the stakes that held her arms and her ankles. She stopped straining to pull free while his attention was on her.

Then he looked at Elisabeta, and this time

his face *did* change. He couldn't hide his shock and horror at the way she looked.

"By the gods, Beta —"

"I know," she said. "I know how I look. I'm dying, Vlad."

He nodded, moved closer, and lifted a hand to touch her hideous face. Damn him.

Stormy tried not to see the tenderness in his eyes, but she saw it anyway. He was here, and his mission might very well be to take her life.

And yet she loved him.

God, she was sick. Hopeless. Possibly helpless. And love him or not, she wouldn't hesitate to slit his throat and let him bleed if it meant the difference between her own living and dying. Not for a second. Maybe she wasn't totally hopeless after all.

She tugged harder. And the stake at her feet moved just a little.

Vlad couldn't believe the change in Beta. Though he supposed, logically, the changes were happening in Brooke's body, not in Beta at all. Just to the body she happened to be occupying at the moment. She looked weak. And in pain. She was suffering, and it hurt him to see it.

Tempest, on the other hand, seemed fine. Her eyes flashed the same fire as always, and though there was a swollen, purplish lump on one side of her head, she was well. Strong. Whole. Frightened, though. And angry, too.

He'd felt her eyes searching his, probing, as if for some sign of his intent. She didn't trust him, then. No. Why would she?

"Did you bring the ring and the scroll?" Beta asked.

"Yes."

"Give them to me."

He glanced at Tempest. Her eyes pleaded with him, but he tore his gaze away, and took the ring and the scroll from his pocket.

Elisabeta snatched the scroll from his hand, unrolled it and bent to set it on the ground, using small rocks at the top and bottom to keep it from rolling up again. She positioned it between two candles, so she could see to read it; then, as her eyes raced over the lines, she spoke to him without looking up. "Put the ring on her, Vlad."

He looked at Tempest again.

She stared back at him, her eyes holding his powerfully as she shook her head slowly left, then right, then left again.

He hadn't moved. Beta swung her head toward him. "Do it, Vlad. We haven't much time. I . . . am weakening, even now." Then she moved to the first pot of herbs and touched one of the candles to the pile until it caught and blazed. She let it burn a moment, then bent close and blew it out. Smoke wafted then, thick and fragrant. And Beta moved on to the next pot, and the next.

Vlad forced himself to step past the ring of blazing candles. To kneel beside Tempest, between her outstretched arm and her legs. He held the ring in his fingers, and he moved it toward her hand.

She bent her wrist, flinching from his touch. "Don't do this, Vlad."

He looked at her, and saw the mistrust and hurt in her eyes. "I'm doing what I have to do." The smoke from the herbs was increasing, growing thick, swirling around them.

"Look, I get that you love her and not me, okay? I totally get that. You want to be with her, and you'll do whatever it takes to be with her."

"Stop it, Tempest."

"No, I won't stop it. This is my *life*. I don't blame you for wanting to be with the woman you love, Vlad, but it's not fair that I should have to surrender my life to make it happen."

He hesitated, the ring near the tip of her finger. He had to put it on her, but his hand was shaking.

From beyond him, Beta said, "And is it fair that I should have to die? Was it fair to keep me trapped between life and death for the past five hundred years?" She paused to draw a breath, exhausted, it seemed, just by the act of speaking. "One of us has to die, Tempest."

"One of us already did, Elisabeta. One of us *chose* to die, by her own hand. You made that decision. Be woman enough to deal with the consequences."

"Enough," Vlad said. But his voice was choked and shaky, even to his own ears. "It's enough. There's no point in arguing. The decision is made. What must be done, must be done." He clasped Tempest's wrist in his hand to hold it still.

She clamped her hand into a tight fist. "No! I won't let you do it."

"Open your hand, Tempest."

"No!"

Gods, he hated this. If emotional pain could kill, this would surely be the end of him. He stared into her eyes through the smoke that made his own water, and for one brief moment he let his heart show through. "Please, Tempest. Open your hand."

She held his eyes, tears pooling in her own. "Vlad?"

Trust me, just this one more time.

He didn't know if their bond was powerful enough to allow her to hear his thoughts. But he thought it must be, when slowly, her fist unclenched, her fingers unbending slowly. "Damn you for this, Vlad," she whispered. "Damn you. I love you."

"I'm sorry." He slid the ring onto her finger, then turned away, unable to meet her eyes for even a moment longer.

Elisabeta took his hand in hers and tugged him to the spot at the top of the circle of candles. "Here. You can read from the scroll here. Follow each instruction precisely."

Nodding, he knelt and bent to look at the words on the scroll, then turned to observe what Elisabeta was doing.

She was lying down, taking a position beside Tempest.

"Begin," she said.

"Don't do this to me, Vlad," Tempest begged.

Vlad ignored her, though it wasn't easy. Not when there were tears sliding from the corners of her eyes and down her face. "Beta, this ritual isn't going to work."

"Of course it will. Just begin, for the love of the gods. We haven't much time."

She lay there, eyes closed. He slid a look toward Tempest but didn't dare let his eyes linger on her. "No. It's worded in a way

369

designed to release you from the bonds of the ring, into the body of the one who wears it. But you've already been released from the bonds of the ring into Brooke's body."

"We have to try, Vlad."

"I didn't come unprepared," he said. "I was afraid of exactly this problem, in fact. But I located another ritual, this one designed to do specifically what we need it to do."

Beta opened her eyes but didn't look at him. "And what is it that we need it to do?"

"Free your spirit from Brooke's body." He said it slowly. "Once we do that, *then* we can proceed with the original rite, the one to take you into Tempest's body."

Beta drew a deep and stammering breath. "I . . . see. And where did you get this ritual?" She tried to sit up, struggled, and Vlad quickly went to her side, gripped her shoulders and helped her.

"I stole it from the files of the Sisterhood of Athena. No one knows I have it." It was a lie. He'd stolen it not from the Sisterhood's files but from Rhiannon's pocket.

Once sitting upright, Beta leaned forward, bending over herself, hugging her waist. "Thank you, Vlad. I just . . . I'm not sure I —"

And before he knew what she had intended — the very instant the alarm in his mind began to warn him, in fact — he heard the explosion and felt the red-heat impale him. The gun barrel stabbed into his chest at the same moment she pulled the trigger, sending the bullet straight through him. The pain was blinding, and he sank to his knees to the sounds of Tempest's screams, blood gushing from his body.

Beta tore the ritual from his hand and moved toward the candlelight to read it. "I knew it," she rasped. "I knew it was a trick. This ritual would exorcise me! You . . . you were going to kill me!"

"No. Beta, no," Vlad said through clenched teeth. "I was going to free you."

"You were going to save me," Stormy whispered. "You . . . you chose me."

He met her eyes, though his vision was beginning to blur. "I made that choice long ago, Tempest. I love you. All this time, I have loved you."

"Bastard!" Beta shouted.

She crumpled the ritual Rhiannon had copied down for him, then held it to the flame of a candle until it caught and burned. Then she bent over the original sheet, the one with the ancient rite that would condemn Tempest to death, and she began to read the words. "Powers of the ancients and of the Underworld Gods, open the gates between life and death. Open the gates and take this one, this Tempest Jones. For her body belongs to me — Elisabeta Dracula."

Vlad lifted his head, knew he was growing weaker by the second. "It won't work, Beta. It won't work, not this way."

She paused to send him a hate filled glare. "How do I know you are not lying to me yet again, *print, ul meu?*"

"I swear it. I swear it on . . . on her life."

"Her life? Yes. She matters that much to you, doesn't she? That the most meaningful vow you can imagine is to swear on her life. It does not matter, Vlad. Her life is about to end."

"It won't work, I tell you. You'll both die if you go through with this."

"I am dead either way," she said. "Better I die trying to save myself than to simply give up. Better she die with me than I should die alone. She will never have you, Vlad."

"I have him now, Elisabeta," Stormy told her. "I've had him for sixteen years. Only I didn't know. I'm sorry I didn't trust you, Vlad."

"I gave you no reason to trust me. And yet you did, in spite of everything, when you let me put that ring on your finger."

"Shut up, both of you! You're making me

sick!" Beta turned and moved to where Tempest lay, bending to clasp her ankles in a brutal grasp. *"Sînge la sînge! Minte la minte! Corp la suflet! Al t u la al meu!"* She shouted the words, and then she shouted them again and again.

Around her hands at Tempest's ankles, a silvery mist seemed to take shape.

"It is working," Beta whispered.

"No!" Vlad cried. "Stop this, Beta! I beg of you, stop it now!"

"Soul to soul. Mind to mind. Body to body. Yours to mine," she chanted. "Tempest, out! Elisabeta, in! By the powers of the Underworld, I will it so. Tempest, out! Go! Cross the veil! Do it now!"

The mist around Tempest's body began to spread up her legs, over her torso. It was like a thin shadow of Tempest, rising from her form as she lay there, wide eyed, thrashing and fighting to hold on. And now there was a similar shroud around Elisabeta.

"Hang on, Tempest!" Vlad cried. "Beta, don't do this! I beg of you!"

"Out, out, out!" Beta cried, her head tipping back now, her voice growing softer, her eyes taking on a glow not unlike that of a hungry vampire about to feed. "Guardians of the Underworld, take her now!"

Vlad used his remaining strength to rush at her, hitting her body and knocking her over onto her side. Her hands were wrenched free of Tempest's ankles, her chanting silenced. But as he lay there, struggling with the blinding, crippling pain, she wrestled free of him, got to her feet and, drawing the gun once more, pointed it at him.

Vlad felt hope desert him, and then it returned in a rush as he sensed Rhiannon's presence. She had followed him. Just as he had known she would. He turned his gaze toward where he sensed his dearest friend stood, just beyond the shadows. He felt her there, felt her waiting. He found her mind with his, nodded once. "Do what must be done."

And she spoke. "Now, Melina."

There was no sound other than Elisabeta's sudden shriek as her body jerked backward, away from Tempest. Stumbling, she landed on her side on the ground, gazing, stunned, at the dart that was embedded in her chest. She lifted trembling hands, grasped it and tore it free with a whimper of pain; then she tossed it angrily aside.

Melina stepped out of the shadows, a weapon in her hand. A gun made to shoot tranquilizer darts. Lupe stood beside with a gun of her own. A real one. It was Rhiannon who rushed forward, bending over Vlad, pressing a large piece of cloth to the wound in his chest.

"Don't waste time with me. It's Tempest you should be attending," he cried. He stared at Stormy even as the mist that had been rising seemed to settle into her body once more. "Please, Rhiannon. Is she all right?"

Reluctantly, Rhiannon left him to crouch over Tempest, touching her, sensing her. She stroked a hand over her brow, then rose with a nod and returned to Vlad's side. "She'll survive. I'm not so certain about you." She lifted her eyes and looked at Melina, who was kneeling now beside Elisabeta. "What about her?"

Leaning close, Melina spoke softly. "Brooke? Brooke, are you there?"

A clawed hand shot upward and raked Melina's face. She rocked backward. Lupe jerked her weapon into position and fired a shot at Brooke's body, but the bullet only hit the ground beside her, spitting sand and soil with its impact. Beta jerked at the sound, then went still.

"Are you trying to kill her?" Melina shouted. She whirled on Lupe, snatching the weapon from her hands.

"Elisabeta is still inside her," Rhiannon said.

"It doesn't matter. We have the rite we need now, Rhiannon," Melina said softly. "The one you wrote for us. We know how to set Elisabeta free."

Vlad closed his eyes, moaned.

"What is it, Vlad?"

"I took the rite. I tried to use it myself, but Beta caught on. She burned it."

"No matter," Rhiannon said. "I knew it went missing — and hoped to the gods my guess that you had taken it was correct." She glanced at Melina. "You'll find another copy of the rite in the library desk at the manse. Use it."

"We will," Melina said. "Tonight. There's still plenty of time to get Brooke back to Athena House and perform the ritual. We'll take care of it. I promise you that." She got to her feet, and brushed herself off, then moved closer to Vlad, while Lupe removed handcuffs and shackles from a bag, and snapped them around Elisabeta's wrists and ankles.

Melina knelt beside him. "If you don't make it, I promise you, your love will be awaiting you on the other side. I'll see to it."

Vlad shook his head, glancing toward

Tempest, who lay still, barely conscious now, her eyes unfocused and wet. "No," he said. "The one I love is here."

Melina nodded and turned to Rhiannon.

"Take her and be done with it," Rhiannon said. "I've work to do here."

"I hope . . . I hope we're okay now. You and me," Melina said to her.

"My issue has been with your organization, not with you, Melina. And that remains the case." She thinned her lips. "However, I will concede that the Sisterhood of Athena has a few . . . worthy members." Quickly Rhiannon gathered Brooke's ravaged body up into her arms. "I'll take her to the car for you." She shot a look back at Vlad. "Don't move. And for the sake of the gods, don't bleed out."

Vlad wished he could promise not to. Instead, he waited until she was out of sight and then dragged himself toward where Tempest lay. He pulled himself alongside her and then lay still, his head close to hers, one hand in her hair. He used what strength remained in him to free her hand from the rope that held it.

"Vlad?" she whispered. Her newly freed hand came up to cup his cheek.

"It's you, Tempest," he told her. "Not her. It's been you all along. I'm sorry it took me so long to tell you. But if I had revealed my heart, she would have known. I had to make her trust me in order to save you."

"Vlad, you're bleeding again." She turned to the side, rapidly freeing her other hand; then she sat up, untied her ankles and cradled his head in her lap.

"Please, just listen to me," he said. "There may not be much time. You were right all along. I barely knew Elisabeta. We met at a time of crisis, when neither of us had anything to live for. We clung to each other. But I didn't know her. You — I know you, Tempest. I knew you sixteen years ago. You are the woman I love. There can be no other. Nor has there ever been. Not really. Perhaps the reason I was drawn to Elisabeta so long ago was because she was foreshadowing of her spiritual descendant. Of you, Tempest. Only you."

"Vlad, we have to help you. You're . . . you're . . ."

"No, love. There's nothing you can do. Just tell me, please. Tell me you believe me this time. I came here to save you, not to hurt you."

"I believe you. And I love you, too, Vlad. I have all along. I've loved you for sixteen years."

He felt as if a weight had been lifted from

378

his soul, and he smiled. "Thank you, Tempest." And then his eyes fell closed.

16

Rhiannon dropped to her knees beside Vlad, who lay still in Stormy's lap. She touched his face, and tears rained from her eyes. "My sire," she whispered. "My beloved friend, my preternatural father. Gods, how I hate to see you go."

"No!" Stormy shrieked the word, clutching Vlad's shoulders, shaking him. "He can't die. You can't just let him die. Rhiannon, we have to *do something!*"

"I . . . it's too late."

"No. No, it's not. Give him blood. Give him mine, and then we'll patch the wound and keep him alive until dawn comes and —"

"I'm sorry," Rhiannon said softly. A sob seemed to catch in her throat, and she averted her face. "You've no idea how sorry."

"Step aside, Rhiannon."

Stormy gasped at the deep voice that came

from the darkness. She'd heard no one approach, but then, she'd been entirely focused on Vlad. The man who stood there was dark, and exuded a palpable aura of strength and power. Stormy had seen him only once before, but she knew him. He was Damien — the once great king, Gilgamesh. He was the oldest, most powerful of them all. The only vampire alive older than Vlad himself. The first.

"Damien," Rhiannon whispered, rising to her feet. "How did you know?"

Stormy stared at the man. He looked stricken and went immediately to Vlad's side, kneeling there and clasping his hand. "Though it's been years since I've seen him, Iskur is my brother, in a way. Our connection is powerful."

"Iskur?" Stormy whispered.

"That was his name, before he adopted his new identity. It's the name of —"

"The Sumerian Stormy God," Stormy filled in. Tears filled her eyes to brimming as she gazed at Damien. "Can you help him, Damien?"

"I don't know. If I can't, there's no one who can." Damien rolled back his shirt sleeve, unfolded the pocketknife he carried and swiftly drew the blade across his wrist. Even as the blood pulsed from the wound, he moved lower.

"What are you doing? Aren't you going to . . . ?"

"He's too far gone to drink, Stormy," Damien muttered. "I only hope my blood is powerful enough to reach him this way."

He held his wrist, wounded side down, over the wound in Vlad's belly. Stormy scrambled over the ground to tear the shirt away, giving him better access. But that gave her a horrifying glimpse of the bullet wound, and she had to close her eyes. It was too much. Too much.

"By the gods," Rhiannon whispered. "Stormy, look. Open your eyes and look."

Forcing herself to obey, Stormy opened her eyes and focused on Vlad again.

"Oh, God, what's happening?" There was mist, or steam of some kind, hissing and rising from the bullet wound as the blood trickled down into it. She'd never seen anything like this. Never even heard of anything like it. "What's happening, Damien?" she whispered.

"I'm unsure. I've never done this before, but it's the very method by which Utnapishtim gave me the gift of immortality. He was no vampire. His immortality was bestowed by the gods. He had no fangs, could walk about by daylight, exist on meat and vegetables. When he agreed to make me immortal, he sliced me open, right across the chest, then slit his own wrist and poured his blood into the wound." Damien's gaze was riveted to Vlad's face.

"And created a whole new race."

"I only hope . . ." He lowered his head, then lifted it again and shook it as if trying to shake away sleep.

"Enough, Damien," Rhiannon whispered. "You're weakening."

"Just a bit more," he said.

"You've given all you can," she told him, clutching his shoulder. "It will either work or it won't. Bleeding yourself dry won't make the difference."

He sank back onto his heels, head falling forward, a lock of his hair slipping over his eyes. Rhiannon gripped his arm, rapidly twisting a length of fabric around it and yanking the knot so tight that Stormy thought she would break his wrist. She realized a second later that the cloth had been torn from the hem of Rhiannon's own gown.

Vlad's wound was still hissing, steam still emanating from it, but dissipating now, until it finally vanished altogether. She stared at Vlad, watching his face, praying, hoping, *willing* him to live.

And then he moaned and blinked his

eyes open.

He was alive!

Vlad lay there, blinking and unfocused, clearly confused. Stormy leaned over him, barely able to believe what she had just witnessed. "Vlad?"

He stared at her. "I didn't expect to be seeing you again, my love."

He lifted a hand, cupped her cheek, and she fell against him, sobbing in relief and holding him. "You're alive. God, Vlad, I thought I'd lost you."

"So did I." His arms came around her, and he held her close. "Perhaps . . . there's a chance for us after all, Tempest."

"There is," she whispered. "There has to be."

Then Vlad's gaze shifted to Damien's and widened. "My king," he whispered.

"Your brother and friend," Damien corrected. "I'm glad you have survived, Iskur."

"Survived?" Vlad's gaze turned inward for a moment. "I feel . . . empowered beyond reason. Something new is burning through my veins." He blinked as he took stock and sat up to stare at Damien. "You gave me your blood."

"And it did the job," Rhiannon said, reaching down to clasp Vlad's hand and draw him to his feet. "I suppose now that you have the blood of the first running in your veins, you really will be able to best me in a fight."

"I already bested you with my own, don't forget."

"Don't fool yourself, Vlad. I let you win that little battle."

He crooked a brow.

"You two fought?" Stormy asked.

"He demanded the ring and the scroll," Rhiannon said. "I wasn't sure whether he intended to use them to save you or to kill you."

"And you fought him? For my sake?"

"Briefly," Rhiannon said. "But don't get a swollen head, little mortal. In the end I decided to risk your life by trusting in my friend." She smiled very slightly and turned to Vlad. "I'm very glad you didn't let me down."

"I'm very glad you didn't fight too hard. I would have hated to have to hurt you."

"You'd have hated more what I would have done to you, had I truly had the will."

They held gazes for a moment, then Vlad shifted his to Stormy again. His eyes met hers and stayed.

Damien cleared his throat. "We should take our leave, Rhiannon. These two have things they need to . . . discuss."

Rhiannon nodded, reached up to hug Vlad, kissed his cheek, then released him. "There's a boat docked a mile back that way," she told him. "We'll take shelter there before sunrise." She looked at the sky. "You have several hours."

"Is it midnight yet?" Stormy asked. She'd let herself forget for a little while how limited her own time might be.

"Eleven-thirty," Damien told her. "Why?"

"We should leave them," Rhiannon said. "I'll explain on the way."

She sent Stormy a look of sympathy, encouragement and hope. Clearly she realized that if Melina and Lupe failed to free Elisabeta's soul from Brooke's body, Stormy might have only thirty minutes left to live. Then Rhiannon hooked her arm through Damien's and raced away, vanishing in a blur of darkness.

"Did you mean what you said?" Stormy asked Vlad. "That you feel more powerful then ever? You're really all right?"

His smile was slow and full of all sorts of promises. He cupped her face in his hands and kissed her mouth tenderly, but deeply and long. "Shall I show you?"

"Yes. Yes, Vlad. And hurry. Because if Melina and Lupe —"

"Shhh. They're not going to fail. We couldn't have triumphed over all of this only to lose everything now."

His fingertips brushed over her cheek, then her neck, and her tummy tightened in pure sexual need. She vowed not to think about what might happen when midnight came. She wouldn't ruin what might be her last time with Vlad by letting herself be distracted. If she had to die, she would die in his arms. And die happy.

He loved her.

He closed his arms around her, bending her backward and kissing her as if he would devour her whole.

"Vlad," she whispered. He was kissing her neck now.

"Don't tell me to stop."

"If you stop I'll stake you." She smiled up at him. "I was just wondering if we could relocate."

He lifted his head, his eyes glowing with passion and hunger. "Where do you want to be, Tempest?"

"The beach. The shore. In the sand. Not here, where — ugly things happened."

He nodded, and before she could stop him, he scooped her off her feet and began striding away from the trees and boulders toward the beach. "No more delays, Tem-

pest. You're about to be ravaged by a vampire."

"By *the* vampire. Dracula himself. And
not for the first time," she said, gasping as
he bent his head to nuzzle her breasts right
through the fabric of her blouse.

"Nor the last," he promised.

He carried her down onto the beach, but
they didn't get very far. Just beyond an
outcropping of rock that gave them a little
privacy from the vantage point of the road.

Vlad lowered her to the grassy, stony
ground, laying her there on her back. Then
he darted away from her, into the surf,
where the washed the remnants of Damien's
blood from his belly. It took him only a moment. He was back at her side a heartbeat
later, sinking to his knees in the sand beside
where she lay.

"I love you," he told her.

"You'd have been stupid not to," she told
him with a teasing smile.

"The stupidest vampire in history." Then
he pushed her blouse up and attacked her
breasts as if he couldn't wait for them. It
was almost too much, too fast, the suckling
and biting. She moved to push at his head,
but he kept on, and she didn't want him to
stop. Not really. So he didn't. He pushed
her jeans down and impatiently removed

his own.

She couldn't get enough of running her hands and then her lips over his chest. Oh, God, and his belly. Washboard abs she couldn't stop touching. It amazed her to see no wound where the bullet had torn through him. Only a small pink scar remained. "You're the most beautiful man I've ever seen," she whispered.

"Then no wonder I chose the most beautiful woman. I've waited for you, Tempest. Centuries, I've waited."

Vlad pushed her knees up and outward as he lowered himself between them, and he slid into her so naturally she knew he belonged inside her, so deeply he felt like a part of her.

He brought her to screaming climax twice there on the beach before he let himself achieve release. And afterward he lay beside her, cradling her in his arms as if she were the most precious, most cherished, thing he'd ever held.

Stormy lay there in bliss. But it was still bittersweet. She knew they were both thinking about her mortality, though neither of them had spoken of it. Not yet. It wasn't yet midnight. Only a few ticks of the clock remained. But even if she didn't die tonight, there was still a dark future looming ahead of them, and she thought it was time, now, to bring it up.

"Vlad?"

"Hmm?"

"You know . . . even if Lupe and Melina are successful tonight, this can't last. I don't have the antigen. I can't become what you are. There is a formula that could extend my life . . . but there's no way to be sure it would work on me, or that I could even get hold of it."

He was quiet for a moment, and she felt his arms tighten a little, as if in response to the thought of ever letting her go. "I'll love you for your entire life. And even after that."

She let her head rest on his powerful chest, felt his fingers trailing in her hair. "I'll grow old, but you'll stay young."

"Not young, Tempest. The body doesn't age, but everything else does. I'm already old inside, though my body remains the age it was when I was changed over."

"And how old is that?"

He smiled at her. "Twenty."

Stormy closed her eyes fast and tight. "My God, I'm thirty-six. I'm robbing the cradle."

"I've been alive for thousands of years, Tempest. I'm the one robbing the cradle."

"Oh, I know that. But . . . physically, I mean, I'll age. And that's important, too."

"Not to me. I've spent the last few centuries believing myself in love with a dead woman, one who had no body at all, don't forget."

"I'll get wrinkles," she whispered.

"And I'll love you."

"My hair will go gray."

"And still I'll love you."

"My body will get flabby and saggy and —"

"And I'll love you all the more," he told her, kissing the top of her head.

She drew a deep breath, lifting her head a little so she could see into his eyes. "I'll die, Vlad."

He held her gaze steadily, intently. "Then maybe I'll know it's time for me to move on, as well."

"Vlad!"

He cupped her cheeks. "I don't want to talk about this now, Tempest. Not now. There will be time enough for all that later. Now, I just want to be with you. To experience the joy you've brought into my life. By the gods, do you have any idea how long it's been since I've felt this way?"

"What . . . way?"

"Happy, Tempest. Truly happy." He looked skyward and shook his head. "It's heaven. I'm in paradise because of you."

He kept on speaking, but Stormy stopped listening, because there was a sudden buzzing in her ears. In her head.

Frowning, she sat up and pulled her shirt on. It was long enough to cover her, so she didn't bother with the jeans, just got to her feet and looked around.

Vlad rose, his expression puzzled. He searched her face, spoke her name, but she could barely hear him because of the buzzing.

And then her vision started to close in, darkness surrounding her from all sides.

"What . . . ?" she muttered, unsure if she said the word out loud, losing the rest of her question before she spoke it.

She saw a woman — and she recognized her. Elisabeta, looking the way she had in the portrait. It startled Stormy terribly at first. My God, had she come back to finish what she'd tried to begin?

But no, she didn't look menacing, or cruel. There was something frail about her, and fear in her eyes. And it hit Stormy all over again how much the young woman's face resembled her own. They could have been sisters. Maybe they were, in a way.

"Beta?" Stormy whispered.

"They're making me go!" Beta cried. "I don't want to go!"

The pain in her voice gripped Stormy's heart and twisted, and in that moment she realized this Beta she was seeing wasn't physical. She was opaque, nearly transparent. Melina and Lupe must be performing the rite.

Stormy felt her throat tighten, her eyes well in empathy. "It's what we all do when we die, Beta," she told the frightened girl — for she was that, once again. Just a girl. Afraid and confused. "It's what we're supposed to do. Look, look behind you."

Beta turned slowly and saw what Stormy did. Beyond her, resting on the water, was a glowing, golden light. It had a texture to it like liquid gold, and it pulsed and called to her. There was something incredibly beautiful about it, something magnetic. It drew Stormy. She moved closer, involuntarily, and yet she wasn't afraid.

"It's beautiful," Beta whispered.

"Yes."

Beta paused, swallowed hard; then she closed her hand around Stormy's. "Will you walk with me?"

Stormy nodded and found she wanted to move closer to the glow. And as they drew near, something became visible within the light: a woman. She might have been a goddess or an angel, or the blessed virgin. But she felt much more personal than any of those. And she looked . . .

"She looks like us," Stormy whispered, glancing at her companion.

Beta had tears streaming down her cheeks. The woman seemed to be speaking to her, but Stormy couldn't hear. The golden woman's expression was incredible; serene and loving and transcendent.

"I know," Beta said to her in reply. "I know I was supposed to come sooner. But I was trapped. And then I was afraid."

The woman lifted a hand, holding it out to Elisabeta.

Beta turned to Stormy and blinked back her tears. "I understand now," she said softly.

"I don't. Who is she, Beta?"

"She's . . . she's us. She's you and me and all the women we've ever been. She's all of us. Everyone we ever were or will be. She's . . . our higher self."

Stormy looked at the beautiful woman standing within the golden light with her arms reaching out, and she heard herself whisper, "I love her."

As she watched, Elisabeta pulled free of her hand and moved forward. And then the woman opened her arms and embraced her, and it seemed that Elisabeta was absorbed into the light.

Stormy was awestruck, and then she moved closer, too, reaching out her hands.

The woman met her eyes. "Not you, Tempest. Not yet. Not for a long, long time. But at least now you will be complete. The parts of you that were missing, shall now be restored."

She held out her hands, and a beam of that golden light surged from her palms and hit Stormy square in the chest. It was like being hammered by heat and light. It knocked her backward as surely as a speeding train would have done. And then the light faded, and she was alone in the dark, yet unafraid. And she felt . . . wonderful.

Vlad carried Tempest aboard the yacht in a state of panic. "Rhiannon! Damien! Help her!" he shouted.

Rhiannon raced forward, meeting him at the hatch that led below, Damien close behind her. "What happened?" Rhiannon demanded. She took his arm and tugged him through the hatch, down the stairs and into one of the cabins. She led him to a small sofa, where he laid Tempest down and bent over her. He stroked her hair, her face.

"I don't know," Vlad said quickly. "She was fine — and then she just suddenly started walking toward the sea. She was . . . talking to someone — Elisabeta, I think. She kept saying her name. And then she just flew backward, landing on her back on the ground." He pressed his hands to his head. "Gods, is it past midnight? Did those Athena women fail to set Beta free? Is she dying now?" He closed his eyes. "It can't be. Gods, I can't lose her now."

Rhiannon bent closer, touching Stormy, seeking, Vlad knew, for signs of life in her. She was alive, he knew that. But when Rhiannon stood rigid and wide eyed and whispered "By the gods!" he was frightened, even more than he had been.

"What, Rhiannon? What is it? By the gods, tell me I haven't waited all this time for her only to lose her again so soon."

"Lose her?" Rhiannon blinked her long lashes several times. "Don't you feel it? Vlad, don't you smell it on her?"

Damien moved closer and whispered, "The antigen. Belladonna."

Rhiannon met his eyes and nodded, then shifted her focus to Vlad.

And he felt it. He sensed it the way a vampire could always sense one of The Chosen. That energy was coming from *her* — from Tempest.

He lifted his eyes to those of the vampiress

he'd made. "But . . . how can it be?"

Even as he asked the question, Tempest blinked her eyes open and whispered his name, drawing his gaze back to her. She smiled at him. "She's all right," Tempest said. "Elisabeta is all right."

He could only frown at her, searching her face.

"Melina and Lupe must have done the ritual. They must have freed her. I saw her, Vlad. I walked with her. God, it was so beautiful. There was this woman, all clothed in golden light. Or maybe she *was* the light. And Beta went into her arms and they just . . . they sort of melded."

Vlad sank onto the sofa to gather her gently into his arms. "I'm glad if Beta has found peace. But, Tempest, are *you* all right?"

Her smile grew brighter. "I'm wonderful. Better than ever. That woman, she . . . gave me something. She filled me with . . . something."

Rhiannon put a hand on Vlad's shoulder, repeating slowly what she had told him before. "When we die, our souls merge with our collective soul, our higher self. That being is our source. All that we are melds and combines to generate the next soul and the next, and the one after that. Stormy has been missing a part of herself. The part that was Elisabeta. The part that had never melded with her source. She has that part now."

"And that part includes . . . ?" he asked.

"The Belladonna Antigen," Rhiannon whispered.

Stormy shifted her gaze from Vlad's — though it seemed to take a great effort — to Rhiannon's. "What?"

"You're one of The Chosen now, Stormy," Rhiannon told her. "You can become one of us, if and when you choose it."

She shot her eyes back to Vlad's. "Is it true?"

He nodded. "I don't pretend to understand it the way a priestess of Isis does," he said. "But yes — you have the antigen now. And it's not weakened or diluted or different in you the way it was in Brooke's body. Perhaps because it was meant to be in you as it was never meant to be there."

"Then . . ." She blinked and searched his eyes. "Then we can be together? Forever?"

"If you want it, Tempest."

She slid her arms around his neck and hugged him close. "I do. You know I do."

Rhiannon smiled slowly. "Oh, may the gods have mercy on us all."

Stormy shot her a questioning look.

"Well, do you blame me? As a mortal you're almost unbearably full of yourself and . . . *feisty.* I detest feisty."

"You *exemplify* it," Damien said with a chuckle.

"No, I exemplify arrogance," she said. "And with good reason. It's not the same thing."

"I stand corrected."

"She'll drive us all mad," she said, turning as she and Damien walked to the cabin door. But she glanced back, caught Stormy's eye and winked.

Stormy took it as a "welcome to the family" sort of gesture.

Vlad walked her to the upper deck, where the full moon hung very low in the sky. It would set before too long, and the sun would rise. Vlad removed all her clothing, and all his own, and then he brought her legs around his waist and entered her. And while she moved over him, he sank his teeth into her throat and drank her very essence into him. He drank until she trembled, until she weakened, until she sank so completely into his arms that it was if they were one. And then he jabbed a blade into his own neck, gently, just piercing the jugular with the tip, and he brought her face to him there.

She didn't move until the blood touched her lips. And then she did. She parted her lips and tasted, and then she latched on and drank, and drank, and drank. He moved inside her as she did, and he bent his head to drink more of her.

They were locked that way, mouths to throats, bodies mated, straining and moving and striving. And he thought that by the time he released his seed into her that their blood had mingled several times over.

She went limp in his arms, and he picked her up, and carried her below into the cabin again. A bed and blankets waited. He lowered her into the bed and climbed in beside her.

"Listen!" she said suddenly. "Do you hear it?"

"What, my love?"

"The ocean! I can hear it. . . ."

"Well, we are in a boat," he said with a smile, though he knew exactly what she meant.

"Oh, it's different. I can hear . . . the fish swimming past. And I can smell it — not like before — I can taste it, but it's . . ."

He nodded. "I know. Your senses are heightened, all of them, a hundred times what they were before. And soon, perhaps, a thousand times. You'll be powerful, Tempest. As strong as Rhiannon. Perhaps stronger."

"Stronger than Rhiannon?"

He nodded. "Perhaps. In time. My blood is old. Only one vampire lives who's blood is older, and you've got his running in your veins, too, just as I do."

"Damien," she whispered.

"Gilgamesh," he confirmed.

She sighed and snuggled close to him. "I don't care how strong I am, Vlad."

"You're a terrible liar, Tempest."

She smiled and kissed his chest. "All right, I care. I'm going to love being powerful. And I'll taunt Rhiannon about that for the rest of our lives and enjoy every minute of it." She almost laughed at the notion. She liked the teasing, almost friendly relationship she seemed to have developed with the vampiress she'd once considered the haughtiest bitch of the bunch. "But more than that," she whispered, returning her attention to where it belonged, "more than anything else, Vlad, I'm going to love being with you."

"You'll be with me," he promised her. "Forever."

He kissed her deeply, and when he broke the kiss, she curled into his arms and knew she would still be there when they awoke. And she would be again and again, every sunset, for the rest of eternity.

ABOUT THE AUTHOR

Award-winning author **Maggie Shayne** has written more than forty novels and her books have been described as "brilliantly inventive." She loves to create edge-of-the-seat tension and impossible conflicts for her characters to overcome — elements that keep her readers eagerly turning pages. Maggie lives on a 200-acre farm in Otselic, New York.

We hope you have enjoyed this Large Print book. Other Thorndike, Wheeler, and Chivers Press Large Print books are available at your library or directly from the publishers.

For information about current and upcoming titles, please call or write, without obligation, to:

Publisher
Thorndike Press
295 Kennedy Memorial Drive
Waterville, ME 04901
Tel. (800) 223-1244

or visit our Web site at:

www.gale.com/thorndike
www.gale.com/wheeler

OR

Chivers Large Print
published by BBC Audiobooks Ltd
St James House, The Square
Lower Bristol Road
Bath BA2 3SB
England
Tel. +44(0) 800 136919
email: bbcaudiobooks@bbc.co.uk
www.bbcaudiobooks.co.uk

All our Large Print titles are designed for easy reading, and all our books are made to last.

303